Five-Alarm Kisses

Hot in Magnolia

Five-Alarm Kisses

Hot in Magnolia

Minette Lauren

Published Internationally by Minette Lauren
Magnolia, TX USA
minettelauren.com

Copyright © 2020 Minette Lauren

Exclusive cover © 2020 Fiona Jayde Media
Inside artwork © 2020 Tamara Cribley, The Deliberate Page

PRINT ISBN 978-1-7340968-5-9
EBOOK ISBN: 978-1-7340968-4-2

This is a work of fiction. Names, characters, places and incidents are either the prod-
uct of the author's imagination or are used fictitiously, and any resemblance to
any person or persons, living or dead, events or locales is entirely coincidental.

Acknowledgments

A special thanks to Joanna D'Angelo and Amy Sharp for their dedicated work in editing and polishing this book. I am really thankful for all of the shaping opinions and grammar knowledge, even if I don't always listen.

Cristina Donoso, you are an amazing friend. Thank you for your website design. The champagne is always on me.

A special thanks to authors Jacqueline Seewald and Belle Ami for proof reading and writing early reviews. And, another special thanks to Renee Pope and April Stevens for beta reading.

To Faye Kowalczuk for the best line ever and for all her love and inspiration.

I would like to thank my longtime friend, Joe Kuntz, for answering my firehouse questions and directing me to my local fire department. Thanks for the cocktail meatball recipe. I still serve them at every dinner party.

My deepest appreciation to the Travis County Fire Rescue in Jonestown, Texas. Captain Brittney Garner was nice enough to give me the full tour and answer all my fire rescue inquiries. I thoroughly enjoyed meeting this great group of dedicated firefighters that spends their time helping to educate and protect the community.

To my amazing husband who supports all the hours I write and edit. I couldn't have gotten this far without you.

To Firefighters everywhere. Thank you for putting your lives on the line and keeping our communities safe. It's a better world for your service.

Chapter 1

Raphe Nash squatted on the pavement and patted the lemon-colored basset hound. Lulu gave him a doe-eyed look of innocence. "Your momma says I'm supposed to ask the new librarian to the fireman's ball. See, I don't know if that's a good idea since she's probably not gonna be my type, and we'll probably not have anything to talk about, but let's face it, if I don't man up and take one for the Nash family team, my brother is gonna kick my ass."

Lulu stared at him with her big brown eyes and barked.

"Yeah, that's what I thought. But, since he's on his belated honeymoon with your momma, I can't argue with him. So—here goes nothing." Raphe pushed open the library door and waltzed in with Lulu trotting by his side. Her bluebonnet colored bikini bottoms had white polka dots and a cute ruffle around the top like a tutu. He didn't believe in dressing dogs in costumes, but after Lulu stained the comforter on his bed, he understood why his sister-in-law, Melvina, had left dog diapers.

Raphe strolled up to the information desk and said hello to a stern-faced, heavy-set woman with Coke-bottle eyeglasses sorting books on a trolley. "Um." Raphe stalled in asking his question, but finally asked, "Bonnie Bush?"

The grim woman looked up at him with narrowed eyes. "Whom should I say is calling?"

Relief poured over Raphe. At least this battle-axe wasn't Bonnie. "Raphe Nash. I'm Melvina Nash's brother in-law."

The information desk lady's terse harrumph followed her to the back of the library.

Raphe wanted to bolt. "Does she look pissed to you?" He murmured to a whining Lulu. As if agreeing, the hound flopped down. A moment later the librarian returned with a much younger and slimmer version of herself with matching horn-rimmed glasses.

Simultaneously, both women's jaws dropped, and the younger one covered her mouth to suppress a gasp. The older lady cried out in horror and pointed at the dog.

Raphe looked down just as Lulu was making a massive puddle around her not-so-absorbent diaper. "Dang, Lulu!" He stepped sideways to prevent the river from touching his new boots. Thank goodness the library had changed the real wood flooring to tile after the last roof leak. Raphe bent down and scooped Lulu up in mid-stream, carrying her out the front door as he threw an apology over his shoulder.

"No animals allowed in the library young man," the info desk lady shouted after him, "unless they are trained service dogs!"

Raphe set Lulu down on a patch of grass near the flagpole so she could finish her business. He straightened and glanced down at the dribble decorating his new shirt.

Pulling the wet material away from his chest, he frowned. "Great, just great."

Lulu let out a whine of apology, or maybe she just wanted that silly polka dot bottom taken off. Leaning down, he pulled the Velcro and tossed the outfit with its soaked pad in the nearest trash can. Melvina could fuss all she wanted later, but there was no way he was putting that soiled diaper in his new truck.

Raphe had moved to Magnolia six months ago. He was familiar with the small, bustling town since his big brother Riley married the cupcake queen, Melvina Banks, and settled there officially last year.

Raphe had never dreamed of moving away from Houston, but recent events made him reassess his life's purpose. Right now, that purpose was to find unsoiled clothes and maybe grab some grub at the Cupcake Diner and Dive. Even with the owners—Melvina and Riley—out of town, the coffee should still be good. Besides, Maria Salas, the new cook, had been trained by the best—the best being Melvina—so the pancakes were probably as heavenly as usual.

Raphe left his truck in the library's visitor parking area and decided to walk to the firehouse just down the road. He was new to town, but he wasn't new to fire stations. Raphe had been a firefighter all his adult years. And he'd recently started a new job at Magnolia's local firehouse.

As he approached the red brick building with tan and white trim, he was immediately greeted by Mona Calhoun, Melvina's best friend, who was scurrying out the front door while she pulled at the hem of her black mini skirt.

She whistled at him. "Hey, sexy. Are you and Lulu trollin' for trouble?"

"Naw, we already did that. Got kicked out of the library." He pointed at his shirt and down at Lulu, who was regarding them with a floppy-eared tilt of her head.

Mona chuckled. "I'm sure Manny has an extra t-shirt somewhere, though you may want to give him a minute to put his shirt back on before knocking on his office door."

Raphe took in Mona's rumpled chestnut-colored hair and smeared pink lipstick and grinned. Was that a pair of underwear hanging out of the side pocket of her purse? "Okay then. Will do." He glanced at the bay doors, noticing they were all open and the trucks were gone. "Where is everybody? Did half of Magnolia catch on fire?"

"Miss Kitty drill. I swear, that cat should be on the city payroll for giving those rookies a regular workout," Mona said as she opened her car door. Her skirt hiked up as she slipped into the sporty coupe.

Raphe cleared his throat and looked away. Mona was an attractive woman, but not his type and clearly hooked up with the chief, Manny Owens.

Revving the engine, she backed up too quickly and slammed the breaks. The window of the Lexus glided down. "Are you taking Bonnie Bush to the ball?" She called out loud enough for the whole town to hear.

Raphe shrugged his shoulders, trying not to grimace. "I tried to ask her, but that's when Lulu got us kicked out."

Mona laughed, throwing her head back as she pushed the gas. "Better luck next time."

Raphe shook his head, looking down at Lulu. "If there *is* a next time. Bonnie throwing us out of the library is a solid *no* if you ask me."

Lulu gave him a droopy-eyed look and whined.

"All right, Lulu girl, let's go find me a clean shirt."

He decided to put Lulu in the locker room where she would be safe until the men came back. Most of the station was tile, but Mona had hired a swanky interior designer to do up the chief's office and Raphe didn't want to take a chance of Lulu soiling any of the fancy furniture. Melvina said the dog was potty trained, but clearly Raphe hadn't figured out Lulu's signals.

Raphe grabbed a cup of coffee in the break room while Lulu checked out Jake's bed. Jake wasn't a typical firehouse dog—he was a rescue from one of the fires the men put out several years back. His blocky head said Labrador parents, but his red coloring was all Coon dog. There must have been something else in the mix, because of his shorter height. Unlike most larger breeds, Jake was only about fifty pounds. All the firehouse dogs before him had been purebred Dalmatians, but times were changing, and the community liked that Jake was a rescue amongst rescuers. No one knew his age, but Raphe supposed he was getting up in years now. The older dog still went on a few runs, like the Miss Kitty drill, but he usually moseyed around the station when the real calls came in.

Lulu scratched at the plaid pillow with its matching tartan blanket. After a few moments of doing a rendition of the moonwalk, she made a small huff and nuzzled her nose between her front paws.

Raphe grinned. "Lulu you are some kinda cute." Truth be told, he hadn't wanted to dog-sit. He'd missed two chances at a weekend getaway. Roxanne, one of the gals he was dating, had invited him to her Biloxi beach condo. Then, some of the guys from his old firehouse had flown to Vegas.

He could use a little R&R right now. He didn't want to admit to himself how the massive five-alarm fire a few months ago in Houston still haunted him, but then moving to Magnolia was an admission in and of itself.

His move to the small town had surprised everyone back in Houston, even though he'd come up with good reasons. He told his old firehouse that he needed to help his big brother, Riley, manage the ranch and he needed to be closer to home for his sister, Lexi, and her boys. But deep in his heart lay the truth.

He'd saved a woman and her three kids from their flame-engulfed high-rise apartment. When he went back inside to collect their new puppy, a huge metal beam gave way and pinned him to the floor. His men dragged him out just in time, before the top five floors of the building were completely ablaze. When he came to his senses thirty minutes later, he realized he'd come close to dying. He loved his job, especially saving lives, but as he thought about being trapped inside that fiery building, he admitted dead was dead. He couldn't get the *what if* out of his head. Afterward, Raphe worried his work anxiety might get the best of him and get someone killed.

Lulu whimpered and he drained the last of his coffee. "I'm goin', I'm goin'. You wait here and don't leave any presents for the boys. Jake will be back soon, so I need to get you outta here." He rose and made his way to find the chief. Plenty of time had passed since Mona had left. Manny surely had reorganized his office and his clothes by now. Raphe knocked on the door and waited for an invitation to enter.

"Come in," the chief bellowed.

"Hey, Chief."

The chief cleared his throat, looking a little caught out. "Hey there, Raphe."

Maybe Raphe hadn't given him quite enough time. That Mona was one sassy firecracker—perfect for mild-mannered Manny.

Chief Owens was respected by everyone in Magnolia, but he wasn't exactly a player. Mona had definitely added some much-needed sizzle to his life. Raphe didn't like barging in to ask for favors on his day off. He probably should have driven home. "Sorry to bother you, Chief, but I'm lookin' for a t-shirt." Raphe pointed to Lulu's dribble and the chief raised an eyebrow in question. "I'm watching Melvina and Riley's dog, Lulu, while they're on their honeymoon."

"I thought Eli was Melvina's backup. He takes those dogs everywhere." The chief stood and rifled through a large closet by his desk.

"Lulu's in heat and Humphrey's got it bad. Melvina means to fix the poor girl, but the timing's just been off. She's gonna do it when she gets back."

The chief nodded. "Timing is everything isn't it?"

Two years ago, Manny had his eye on Melvina, but she fell head over heels for Riley. A lot can change over time. Now, Manny was hot and heavy with Mona.

"This should do ya." The chief tossed a Hot Buns t-shirt to Raphe, who couldn't help but chuckle. He'd been in the Hot Buns Calendar Contest two years ago and had even graced the calendar. They dubbed him Five-Alarm for his fancy dance moves.

Melvina and Riley, both amazing cooks, had gone toe-to-toe in a bake-off to see who could bake the best dinner rolls in the county. Riley had won by a smidge, but then Melvina took home the best five-alarm chili prize. They were both equally good in the kitchen as far as Raphe was concerned, and he didn't care who won what, as long as they both still fed him when he went to the diner. His stomach rumbled at the thought. That's exactly where he needed to be.

"Thanks, Chief." He gave a small salute and turned to leave. He heard the rumble of the fire engines as the guys rolled into the station from their weekly Miss Kitty rescue. The loud ruckus of the returning men and the new recruits made Raphe smile. He jaw-jacked with a few of the men and then said his good-byes. Halfway across the parking lot he remembered Lulu and did an about-face, almost running to the break room.

"Lulu!" He called out, but he was greeted with only blank faces. "Have you seen Lulu, Melvina's basset hound?"

The men shook their heads, looking around the breakroom.

Raphe's pulse leapt. "Jake? Where's Jake!" He rushed into the locker room, but there weren't any canine shenanigans going on in there. "Lulu? Come here honey. I got a treat," he called out in desperation.

One of the new recruits snapped a towel at him. "Did you lose your girlfriend, Five-Alarm?"

Raphe pressed his lips together, biting back the words that threatened to tumble out. It may be bad timing, but the kid was just joking. He called out for Lulu as he searched every corner of the firehouse. He went full circle to the chief's office, but the chief wasn't there. However, Lulu and Jake were.

"Lord have mercy, Lulu." *Melvina's gonna kill me.*

Chapter 2

"Why me?" Raphe ran a hand through his tousled hair.

He ordered a coffee and deposited Lulu in Pop's office at the Cupcake Diner and Dive, deciding not to mention the firehouse incident to Melvina's dad. Sitting at the counter, he took a sip of his coffee and sighed. It was cold.

A waitress came to refill his cup with one hand on her hip. "What's wrong? You don't like?" Her accent gave away her Latin American heritage, but that was nothing new to the area and especially at the café. Melvina taught English as a second language at the library in her free time and two of her students worked at the café. This gal was new, and if he wasn't so depressed over how his day was going, he might have appreciated the fact that she was the best eye candy he'd ever seen in Magnolia.

He'd dated one of Melvina's waitresses before and it hadn't worked out. When they broke up, Melvina lost a waitress and he lost the right to date the diner's staff. It became a strict family rule. If Raphe dated an employee, he couldn't step foot in the diner. He was a single bachelor who hadn't a clue how to cook, and he knew which side his bread was buttered on. Besides, this was Texas. As far as Raphe was concerned, the state offered a smorgasbord of beautiful women. His eyes roamed over her dark hair, thick eyelashes, and body to-die-for. The beautiful lady was just another punch to his gut for the day.

Oh, man. Hands off for you, buddy.

He looked at his coffee. "Ah, it's cold." He lifted his cup to her.

The pretty waitress huffed. "Well, *cabron*, if you drink when I pour…" She filled a new cup and set it in front of him before she spun around on her pretty, petite sneakered feet. Raphe couldn't help but follow her curve-hugging jeans with his gaze as she sashayed away.

Lord help me. What did I promise Melvina? Surely Riley would take pity on me. That woman should be in the movies.

She reminded him of a young Salma Hayek. Raphe had a weakness for beautiful women and he certainly had dated his share, but lately, the revolving door routine was getting old. He'd turned Roxanne Remington down for the weekend and Gail Hartley the weekend before. He had no regrets, except for the Lulu fiasco at the fire station. He surely regretted that, and Melvina was going to be none too happy when she found out about it. How many days did a dog pregnancy last? Maybe he could move to Tahiti or somewhere before then. Maybe the hook-up hadn't taken. He was sure that not every mating session ended up with puppies. Maybe Jake was too old and was shooting blanks? Raphe could only hope, but it seemed rude to wish impotence on an old feller like Jake, not to mention bad karma for his own mojo.

The beautiful waitress bent over, searching under the counter between cups, lids and straws. Her derriere swayed as she reshuffled the arrangement. Raphe took a gulp of his coffee and yelped.

She swung around, staring at him in alarm.

Raphe choked a bit while grasping a napkin to wipe the spill from his t-shirt. "Damn."

"It's not *bueno*?"

Raphe tried not to look at her cleavage as she stretched both arms out on the counter, leaned toward him and gave him a challenging stare. He coughed a little and tried to look in her eyes. That was a mistake. They were sherry brown with glints of amber flashing in the center. The woman was blazing hot and had a fiery temper.

"The coffee was too hot." Too late, he realized he should have explained that he wasn't paying attention and scalded his tongue, but now the waitress was about to throw a tizzy.

"It's too cold. It's too hot. Okay, Goldilocks, you want some cream to cool it off so it can be *just* right?" She slowly enunciated her words as she slammed down a silver carafe—it tilted precariously on its side, wiggled and then settled into place.

Raphe's jaw dropped. Was this little spitfire mocking him? Raphe Nash, firefighter, community fundraiser helper, family supporter, hard worker, champion to all women, children and pets of any kind. "Look here, Miss ah...?"

"Salas." She put a hand on her hip that jutted out to one side. Her head was tilted at a challenging angle and she smiled as if she'd enjoy tearing his napkin into pieces.

"Okay, Miss Salas. I wasn't complaining about the coffee." He spoke slowly so she could understand. "I just drank it too fast. My mind was…" He touched a finger to his head and then let it go skyward. He decided then it was time to go home. The hole he'd been digging was getting too deep. He'd get some chips and beer from Wag-A-Bag and call it a day.

Standing up, he put a twenty on the counter and turned to leave. He heard the lady speaking in rapid Spanish through the cook's window. A few moments later he felt a hand on his shoulder as he reached the door. Maybe his luck was changing. Imagining the sexy waitress, he turned around with a wide grin. Maria, one of the café's cooks greeted him with a worried look.

"Mr. Nash, is everything ok? Please take back your money. Nina doesn't deserve it. She's a terrible waitress, but Roberta called in sick and I didn't know who else to call. Please don't complain to Melvina. She deserves to enjoy her honeymoon. I'll make Nina apologize. She'll do better. I promise." Maria's English was slow and carefully enunciated, but much better than when she'd first started at the café. The job had been a great help for her language-building and for her family.

Raphe assured Maria he wouldn't say anything to Melvina or Riley.

"Nina Salas." She didn't look like Maria past the long dark hair and tan complexion, but the last name was the same. "She's your sister?"

"Jose's cousin." The look Maria gave him said it all. She wasn't overly fond of her husband's cousin, and apparently, Nina wasn't fond of helping at the café.

He nodded with understanding, then squeezed Maria's shoulder. "Keep the tip Maria. Your secret's safe with me."

Chapter 3

"How's Lulu?" Melvina's voice was a bundle of excitement through the phone. He couldn't believe she called via video chat. Melvina often complained about Mona's desire to video chat and that no one over thirty should ever want to be seen on the phone or any other type of video screen that exposes their double chin.

He forced a grin. "Ah, she's great. Just great. Fabulous. We're havin' a good ol' time." He popped the top off his longneck and flopped down on the sofa next to Lulu, aiming the camera to include the lemon colored basset hound as she let out a big yawn.

"Aw, I miss them all to pieces. I just talked to Eli and he says Humphrey is in the dumps missing his girlfriend, but Lulu looks like she's doing great with you. You're not feeding her too many treats are you, Raphe? I don't want her to get overweight. Bassets have sensitive backs."

Raphe shook his head in denial. "No ma'am. It's strictly kibble for Lulu. One treat in the morning and one treat at night, just like you said."

She doesn't need to know the treats are sometimes pancakes from the diner or cold chicken from the station.

Raphe scratched Lulu behind her ears, wondering how long it would be before her pregnancy showed. He could put in a transfer to Dallas or maybe San Francisco. He had a buddy out there who kept hounding him to visit.

"Did you ask Bonnie to the Fireman's Ball?"

Raphe took another long swig of his beer. "We tried, but I don't think your new friend cared much for us coming to see her."

Melvina's forehead crinkled, pulling at the smile lines around her eyes. She was a pretty lady with a heart of gold. His brother Riley had chosen well and was a happy man, with a beautiful wife, living on their new ranch with lots of good food and soon—a litter of pups to keep them up all night.

"Oh, she's super nice, Raphe, and has a great sense of humor.... Wait a minute. *We?*"

"Yeah, I thought Lulu and I would stop by the library and meet her on my way to the diner, but then Lulu might have soiled the library floor and we might have gotten kicked out."

Melvina covered her mouth, but a chuckle escaped. Riley could be seen in the background reeling in his fishing line. Raphe nodded to Riley's toothy grin. "Catchin' anything worthwhile?"

"More than you apparently," Riley grinned.

Melvina gave Raphe a sobering look. "Are you going to ask her?"

"I'll try again tomorrow, but I'll be honest, Melvina, she's not really my type."

Melvina frowned. "I don't want you to ask her to marry you. It's just that she's new in town and could use a few friends is all."

Raphe heard that do-good conscience kicking in. Melvina had a big heart and she wanted something good for anyone who fell into her path. He wondered if she was teaching Nina English at the library like she had Maria, Jose and Maurice.

"I met Jose's cousin today when Lulu and I stopped by Pop's."

"It's been the Cupcake Diner and Dive for over a year now, Little Brother," Riley called over his shoulder as he cast his line again.

Melvina smiled. "That's okay, Raphe. A part of me will always think of it as Pop's, too."

"Is she attending your English classes at the library?" He tried not to sound obvious. He knew waitresses were off limits, and he didn't need the grief Melvina would give him over Darcey again.

"Nina? Was she at the diner?"

"Yeah, Maria said she was helping out because someone didn't show up." Damn, now he'd ratted out Maria. Hopefully, the cook wouldn't hold the slip against him. He was a bachelor and needed to eat. He was one of the few firefighters who didn't know how to cook and had no interest in learning. Hell, as long as Melvina and Riley were around, he wouldn't have to, but Maria was a close second.

"She speaks better English than most of Magnolia. Nina was born in Houston. She's here to help when Maria's baby comes in December."

That's just great. The hot waitress was poking fun at me. She thinks I'm a bigot or something.

Wait, didn't that make her a bigot for assuming he had stereotyped her? He shook his head.

A whoop sounded in the background. "Melvina get the net! I got a whopper of a granddaddy."

Melvina's face was aglow. Honeymoon life was obviously good for them. They'd chartered a boat in the Caribbean and were deep sea fishing for a few days near their exotic hotel.

"I gotta go, Raphe. Your brother just landed dinner."

The beer and potato chips filled him up for a time, but it was Raphe's night off and he wanted to stretch his legs for a few hours. Bubbles lounge was the hotspot in Magnolia with its trendy leather booths and fancy chandelier lighting. Manny and Mona visited the lounge frequently, as did Melvina and Riley. Raphe called his other brother Ran and left a message on his voice mail to meet him out at the bar, then he sent him a text for good measure. Maybe he could pawn the horn-rimmed glasses librarian off on Ran. He was playing with the Tomball Cats for the Fireman's Ball at the swank hotel in The Woodlands. As Raphe thought about it, he realized that Ran couldn't play in the band and be on a date at the same time, so he guessed the ball was back in his court. It was still early, so maybe he'd stop into the library on the way to Bubbles. He would pull the trigger and get it over with.

Hell, it's just one night. How bad can she be?

A few minutes later, he got out of his F-150 truck that cost him almost a year's worth of his fireman's salary. He patted the metallic pearl hood as he bolstered his nerve to try to make a better impression. He assumed it must be near closing time since there wasn't a soul anywhere. Even the information desk was deserted. He made a casual walk past the stacks and turned towards the men's room.

Might as well hit the head while I'm here.

He unzipped his jeans and started to relieve himself when a woman flew out of the stall in shock.

"What are you doing in here?"

Raphe quickly tucked himself back in his jeans and tried to pull up his zipper, catching part of his member in the process. He hissed with pain as he half doubled over, cursing a little louder than he'd intended.

The spitfire from the café looked at him with daggers. "Pervert!"

Raphe had had enough abuse. Pointing at the mint colored cake in the urinal he said, "Look, lady, last time I checked, they didn't put urinals on the walls in the ladies' room."

Her angry contours softened as she took in her surroundings. Pink rose to her cheeks, but she didn't miss a beat. "So, you admit you've been checking out the women's room. Shame on you." Spinning on her heel, she yanked open the door and stormed out.

Bent over, Raphe blew out a sigh, massaging his upper thighs, wondering how bad the damage was beneath his denim jeans. He breathed a few more times before straightening and going to the sink to wash his hands. When he exited the men's room, he spotted Nina near the checkout desk, where Bonnie Bush had her nose practically touching the computer screen.

Here goes nothin'.

Raphe approached the counter, glancing back over his shoulder to where Nina Salas sat browsing through books. He cleared his throat and kept his voice low. "Hi there Bonnie. I'm Melvina's brother in-law, Raphe. She asked me to come say hello, since you're new in town."

That didn't sound awkward at all.

"What? Speak up sir. I can't hear you. Do you need help finding a book?"

Raphe groaned inwardly as he bit the inside of his cheek.

She couldn't be serious. He glanced over his shoulder at Nina, who now perked up, her eyes gleaming with interest. He wasn't sure how much more his ego could take today. Maybe he should just play the book card and get out of there.

He raised his voice. "I'm Raphe, Melvina's brother in-law. She says you're new to Magnolia and I just wanted to introduce myself."

Bonnie squinted up at him through the half-inch-thick spectacles. Raphe thought she might be pretty if she wasn't wearing those birth control glasses like an iron-clad chastity belt. She smiled at him, showing perfect white teeth. "Why thank you for stopping by Mr. uh?"

"Nash, Raphe Nash, but you can call me Raphe. Magnolia's pretty casual." He gave her his winning, southern-gentleman smile.

"Nice to meet you Mr. Nash. If you'd like to check out any books, the library is closing in fifteen minutes."

Raphe pressed his lips together as he heard a chuckle come from somewhere behind him. No doubt, the feisty vixen from the bathroom was thoroughly enjoying his crash and burn. He knocked twice on the counter, startling Bonnie and gave a short wave as he turned on his heel and headed for the door. He loved his new sister in-law but enough was enough.

Raphe hit the front door with a little more force than he'd intended, and it bounced back, hitting him in the arm. More chuckles ensued. This time he thought he heard Bonnie's laughter join in, or maybe it was just his insecure imagination. He had nothing to feel insecure about. He'd scored countless hot dates in his lifetime. He had no reason to worry about what women who hung out at the library thought about his game.

Next destination, Bubbles. I need a stiff drink.

Chapter 4

Nina sat in an overstuffed club chair near the circulation desk. Her cheeks were flaming. How could she have missed the Men's sign on the door? She held a magazine open on her lap, and several romance novels sat on the table beside her to peruse for check out. She'd read the same paragraph in the *Debutants Abroad Magazine* three times but couldn't absorb the words in the article, "How to Reinvent Yourself."

Staying with her cousin Jose and his wife, who was expecting, wasn't exactly how Nina imagined her life at thirty-six. After losing her ex-fiancé, Derek, in the fire that incinerated their condo six months ago, she'd been emotionally lost and physically displaced. Nina had bounced around amongst friends' apartments for a while, until she felt like an imposition. Jose was the nearest family she had, living in the small suburb of Magnolia, which felt like the middle of nowhere. She often found herself huddled in the library to find a little peace and quiet.

Nina shook her head. If only life were like a romance novel, with a neat, tidy ending. Nope, it was messier. Especially when family was involved. Jose and Maria were the only family she had left in Texas, and she wasn't ready to pick up and move to California yet. The household with two kids and one on the way was full of energy, not to exclude the constant in and out of Maria's brother, Juan, and his wife, Esmeralda, who recently moved into the trailer next door. She felt bad for needing a place to stay and cramping their small quarters. What she wanted desperately was her own apartment, but that meant choosing a permanent home and she didn't know where that might be. For now, finding privacy sometimes meant hanging out at the library.

When Nina had waited on the tall, dark, and gorgeous stranger earlier, she hadn't known who he was. His too-perfect teeth, strong jawline, and sultry dark eyes reminded her of Derek. Her ex had been gorgeous, but a total player.

Nina tucked her feet under her in the comfy leather club chair and finally gave up on pretending to read, at least for this evening. That handsome guy in the diner was too much in her thoughts. Why? Maybe it was her guilt in finding the owner's brother attractive that needled her. Or maybe it was the couple who'd come in right before Mr. Tall-Dark-and-Handsome that had set her off and turned her into a shrew. The middle-aged couple were on their way to Houston to visit family and had stopped off at Pop's for lunch. They were nice enough, but they'd spoken to her using loud, precise words, like they'd expected her not to understand English.

Nina was proud of her Central American heritage, but she was Texas born and bred. Her natural born citizenship gave her the same rights as any other US citizen. Maybe what was really bothering her was that at thirty-six she was back to waiting tables and without any prospects of a life partner. She liked to think of herself as an independent woman, and she'd taken care of herself for far too long to say she needed a man to have happiness, but she did need a man to have children, or at the very least, his sperm. She wanted a family of her own one day and time was running out.

Nina had worked as a social worker for the city of Houston since her internship before she graduated. She liked to think she was a champion of children and families. Investigating complaints through the Department of Family and Protective Services for the state, she often found that she helped parents, too. They weren't all bad, but most of them needed direction and help as much as the children they were supposed to care for. When the five-alarm fire burned up the city's new high-rise, Nina had lost everything she owned, including her ex-fiancé. She was nearing a breakdown after that and couldn't face the daily heartache of the families in her caseload. She had enough to deal with and admittedly she wasn't coping so well.

Jumping on the handsome man at the café, who was just trying to enjoy a cup of coffee, and then terrorizing him for *her* being in the wrong restroom was admittedly out of character. Nina had always struggled with apologies, but Derek had made her feel like apologizing was an admission of idiocy. It was one of the many reasons she'd broken off the engagement just a night before the fire, along with the fact she'd just learned he was cheating on her with his partner's girlfriend.

Nina shook her head and picked up the stack of books she'd selected. *I've been Ms. Sarcasm all day and it doesn't sit right with me.*

She'd even laughed at Mr. Tall-Dark-and-Handsome as he made a play for the new librarian…She recalled his name was Raphe. Nina had given in to her snarky mood, and now she was having a hard time backtracking to civility. It's not that she cared what anyone in Magnolia thought, but Maria and Jose had opened their home to her. She was filling in today at the diner to be helpful, but a waitress position was open. Maria said the owners would hire her if she'd put forth a better effort. The work was physically hard but mindless. She didn't have to deal with caseloads of parents that were emotionally and economically at wit's end, she didn't have to go home crying after a particularly grueling investigation, and she didn't have to look up codes or log social histories into a statewide database. Nina needed a part-time job for now to keep her mind off the past, plus earn money for when she decided to put down roots. Until then, she'd have to catch her private time in the library.

Hopefully in the right restroom next time.

Standing up from the reading table, she smiled at Bonnie. "I think he was going to ask you out."

Bonnie scoffed, throwing a hand in the air to wave away the suggestion. "Get out of here." She rolled her eyes and stuck her tongue out sideways.

Nina smiled at the young librarian. Bonnie would be a knockout with a little lipstick and contacts. She wondered if the hot guy knew it. He sounded like he was on brother-in-law duty. His heart didn't seem fully into it. "Well, you might want to go easy on him next time. I think you crushed his ego."

Bonnie pulled off her glasses and rubbed her eyes. She was a natural beauty. "Oh, honey. Men like him aren't into gals like me. He spends his weekends out on the town trying to get women into bed. I spend mine reading in bed with Maxi."

Nina tried not to look shocked. Had she misread the prim and proper librarian?

Bonnie Bush likes bush?

"You have a partner?" Nina said carefully. It wasn't a big deal. Several of her friends were lesbian or gay, but she just hadn't gotten that vibe from Bonnie.

Bonnie chuckled. "Partner in crime. Maxine is my standard French poodle. She's a great bed partner, but constantly getting into the neighbor's garbage. I swear that prissy bitch has no class."

Both women giggled and Bonnie's caught on a snort, sending them into peals of laughter.

Nina liked this cool as a cucumber librarian. She was smart and surprisingly funny. Maybe it was her after-hours persona. Thinking of the time, she gathered her things and started toward the door. Halfway across the library, she turned to Bonnie.

"Hey, you know what? We both have something in common." Bonnie's head peeked up from the computer and she stood, coming around the circulation desk.

"What's that?"

"I heard Mr. Nash say you were new. I'm new in Magnolia too. You want to meet me at Bubbles for a drink?"

Bonnie smiled. "You're not hitting on me, are ya? Maxi will be jealous. Besides, I don't swing that way. Though I would be flattered. You're pretty hot." Bonnie winked, making a light purring sound.

Nina laughed again. Bonnie was an all-out hoot.

Chapter 5

The air conditioning in the lounge was on super freeze and Raphe noticed a display of button-hard nipples. He wasn't a leering jerk, but women who dressed in tops the size of a napkin wanted some appreciation, and he did appreciate their efforts to dress up the room tonight. He sipped a whiskey neat, savoring the slow burn as it made its way down his throat, past his chest to his stomach. He hoped it soothed the damaged goods from the bathroom incident. It had been a long time since he'd made that sort of rushed mistake.

With all the eye candy in the room, it irked him that he couldn't get the beautiful Nina out of his head. He found her curvy body and rich mahogany hair mesmerizing, but what really hooked him was her quick wit and sass. He didn't usually care for bitchy women. Along with his brother and the chief, he'd had his chance with Cecilia Lockwood, the former Blossoms president, but after one dinner at Braised, he'd had enough. Celia was a plastic kind of pretty with no heart. Raphe found it odd that she'd been a part of the ladies' league that donated so much time and money to charitable events. After she left the organization, the chief's gal, Mona, took over.

Celia was smoking hot, but bad goods as far as Raphe was concerned. He'd heard the ice queen of Magnolia moved to Dallas after her fall from grace, and she now worked for her daddy's accounting department of all things. After the IRS business she dumped on Melvina a couple years back, Raphe was surprised anyone would hire Celia to dally with their bottom line.

His bottom line was that he was sitting at the bar on a busy night, in a crowd of eye candy, nursing his pride in a glass of whiskey over a feisty little gal that didn't give a fig about him. On top of that, Melvina had set him on an errand that seemed impossible to achieve, and that stung.

Ladies love me. So why am I sittin' here alone?

Motivated to find a distraction, he stood and strolled across the bar to the woman who'd been making eyes at him since he'd walked in. Her friend had gone to the restroom, and it was the perfect time to say hello.

"Hello, pretty lady. Can I buy you a drink?"

She twisted her barstool toward him. Her crossed legs grazed his crotch and he tried not to flinch. After the zipper fiasco, he was skittish.

"Sure handsome. You can buy me anything you want."

Raphe grinned with pleasure. *I'm back!* He asked the waiter to bring the lady and her friend another cocktail and he ordered another whiskey. They made small talk and he was finally lost in a decent distraction. It felt good to lose himself for a while. After the fire that almost swallowed his life, he hated to admit his search for distractions happened often. He thought Lulu would cramp his ability to go out, but she seemed to be okay for a few hours on the couch watching the Food Network. She got to watch re-runs of Riley's celebrity chef show, and that seemed to make her happy. It just made Raphe hungry. Truth be told, Lulu was a great distraction. When Riley and Melvina got back, Raphe might calm Melvina down by adopting one of the puppies.

He was lost somewhere in the ladies' chatter as he thought of Lulu home alone. Raphe glanced at his watch. The woman brought his attention back when she crossed her legs and brought one up between his. He stepped back a little to make room, but she put a hand on his chest.

"So, what else do you wanna buy me?"

Raphe raised an eyebrow. She was awfully sexy but wore too much perfume and something told him that he wouldn't really enjoy a one-night stand tonight, though he could probably use the release. He batted it around in his head.

"Well, I can't afford the moon, but I can show you the stars." He grinned, thinking he might need to call a cab. He was feeling the three whiskeys he'd downed. The next round would be light beer.

"Why ask for the moon, when you have the star right in front of you."

Is she talking about Riley? Raphe was used to women asking about his celebrity chef brother. Maybe she was a fan of the Food Network. Texas was wild about cookin'. He didn't really care if she was into Riley or anyone else. It seemed they both had only one interest.

Nina walked into Bubbles and made her way to the bar to wait for Bonnie to arrive. She spotted Raphe right away and was going to approach him to apologize for her earlier behavior. Even though she was sleep deprived and moody, there was no reason to take out her frustration on others. She didn't know one thing about him except his brother and sister in-law owned the Cupcake Diner and Dive, and it seemed to her she'd better suck up if she wanted to save up enough to get her own place and thank Maria and Jose for putting her up.

She stood, intending to go to Raphe, but two ladies came back from the restroom and started to paw all over him. The one closest to him had her hands on his bicep and chest. Her head tilted back with laughter and then she leaned closer, as if she would kiss him right there at the bar. *What a letch.* First, he was drooling over her cleavage at the diner, then he walked into the same bathroom she was in, though admittedly, she'd been in the wrong bathroom. Afterward, he tried to pick up Bonnie and now he was practically undressing the blonde lady at the bar with his eyes. Something about the situation needled her. She mentally shook herself from the irritation. What did she care if he was a player? He might be the owner's brother and true, under different circumstances he would have made her drool, but what did she care if he picked up ten ladies and brought them all home? Hot irritation bloomed inside her, making her sit back down and order a glass of champagne to cool off.

"Looks like you found trouble." Bonnie sidled up beside Nina and waved to the bartender, pointing to Nina's empty glass and making a lasso move with her hand. The bartender arrived with two fresh glasses of bubbles for them both.

"Trouble?"

Bonnie dug in her small leather purse, but the bartender motioned to Raphe. "It's on Mr. Nash." He said it like they should know who he was. It irked Nina that she did. So, he did know she was there. With the blonde hanging all over him, she was surprised he could see anything except the bimbo's cleavage.

"Yeah, that kind of trouble is impossible to miss, and the way you're staring daggers at that woman, I'd say he's gonna be a lot of trouble for you." Bonnie clinked glasses as she let out a small sigh. She smiled at Nina. "Well, at least I know you're not hitting on me." She winked.

Nina sputtered. "You think—Oh, hell no. He's not my type, and obviously he's a womanizer."

Bonnie looked across the bar, studying Raphe with the two women. "It looks like she's the one putting the moves on him. He's not interested. But with a mug like that and a body of a Greek god…"

"Well, I don't care who he's interested in." Nina took a rather large sip of her champagne. A few drops escaped the corners of her mouth and she grabbed for a napkin.

Bonnie chuckled. "If you say so."

Nina tried to change the subject. "So, what brings you to Magnolia?"

"I have an aunt here who needs some help. She had a hip replacement and I'm helping out around the house until she feels better."

"Is the library temporary?"

"I don't know yet. I moved here from New Orleans. It's real different in Magnolia, but I kind of like the slower pace."

Nina's eyes widened. "Wow, that is a big change. Hurricanes and Mardi Gras? How can you give up all the excitement?"

"There's hurricanes here too. Remember Harvey? My aunt was scared to death when Houston flooded."

"Oh, I meant the cocktail, but I'm sure you won't miss the excitement of actual hurricanes. Magnolia is pretty far north of the city, and it didn't flood much during Harvey. I moved here from Houston and I sure miss the downtown life. The Galleria, brunch at Brenner's on the Bayou, running in Memorial Park." Nina sighed, not realizing just how much she missed her old life. But after her apartment building burned along with her ex and several other people, she just couldn't return to the memories, not now, not yet.

Bonnie smiled. "New Orleans has a lot of places I'll miss, but I've been there all my life and I think I'm ready to settle down."

"You mean kids, a family?" Nina was surprised. The way she blew Raphe off at the library didn't exactly spell interest in finding love.

"Sure. I love kids. It's half the reason I became a librarian. I love reading to children, helping them find books, and the looks on their little faces when they find a story they really like…" Bonnie tapped her chest, "it makes my heart flip." The look on her face was pure pleasure as she spoke about her job. "I just love books. It's part of the problem, though."

Nina's eyebrows lifted. "What do you mean?"

Bonnie frowned. "I spend so much of my time in the stacks that I've forgotten how to talk to anyone."

Nina looked at her new friend with amusement. "You're talking to me."

Bonnie tilted her head with a grin. "Why, you're easy to talk to. I hope I don't embarrass myself by saying I feel like I've known you a long time." She smiled at Nina who nodded in agreement.

"Yeah, I feel that way too, and I have to say, being new in town, I kinda need a friend."

They clinked glasses just as Raphe walked up to their seats at the bar. "Hello ladies. Fancy meeting you both here." He lifted his light beer and tapped glasses with them.

"Thanks for the drink," Bonnie said politely. The vibrant woman who'd been sitting next to Nina now shrank back into the lady librarian.

Raphe's smile seemed genuine. "Pleasure is all mine. Besides, I feel like I've bungled things up with both of you and wanted to try to see if I could start over again. Hi, I'm Raphe Nash. Nice to meet you both. Bonnie, Melvina tells me that you're a great addition to the library, and Nina, she tells me you're helping Maria through her pregnancy. That's really nice of you."

Nina let go of her earlier irritation. He was calling a truce and in truth, he hadn't done anything to make amends for. She shook his proffered hand. Bonnie gave him a timid handshake as well. She really was like a clam when it came to men.

"It's nice to meet you too Raphe. Sorry about earlier." Bonnie threw her a questioning look, but Nina ignored it. She would fill her in another day, and they would probably have a good laugh at her own expense.

I can't believe I actually went into the men's room and sat down for a time out, geez Louise!

He nodded, looking a bit piqued, and Nina smiled at him a little too long. He cleared his throat and tugged at his collar, then called the bartender for another round. She noticed he changed his beer for Perrier with lime. He didn't seem drunk, but she appreciated a man who knew his limits. Her ex-fiancé, Derek, never did. There were many occasions when she wondered how they would get home. Derek always insisted on driving, even if she hadn't imbibed. He was a wild card on those nights, and they always ended in an argument.

Blondie sashayed by and shoved something in Raphe's jeans pocket as she passed. Nina assumed it was her phone number or a note. She couldn't help but notice the vamp caught quite a few male gazes as she made her way to the ladies' room.

Raphe smiled sheepishly, pressing his lips together as he blew out a small breath. He shifted slightly, leaning his weight toward the bar. Nina was silent. She'd let him sweat it out.

Bonnie was more kind. "Mona pointed that lady out to me last week when we had an after-library meeting here."

Raphe looked relieved, "You know Mona?"

"Yeah, the Blossoms are planning a *Book Drive with a Guy* dance next month. It's sort of like a Sadie Hawkins dance. Us ladies are supposed to ask the guys to the party while simultaneously getting rid of all our old books. The money raised will go to the literacy program. It's growing faster than we can handle. Mona's planning a lot of events so we can build a new library to fit all the media equipment and extra classes."

Raphe smiled like he was remembering something funny. "That Mona is something else, but I haven't met anyone with a bigger heart, except Melvina of course."

"Yeah, I really like your sister in-law. I don't know what would happen to the library without her. But Mr. Nash, I think you should know—" Bonnie's eyes darted left then right. "That woman's a hooker."

Nina missed her mouth and rivulets of the sparkling beverage ran down her chin to her blouse. She was totally unprepared for the shy librarian's admission. "Really?" She couldn't help but ask.

Raphe, to his credit, smiled with ease. "Then it's a good thing I told her I had other plans tonight." He chuckled, then grabbed a napkin from the bartender and offered it to Nina. "Have you asked anyone to the dance?"

Nina took the napkin, carefully blotting her silk blouse and jeans. *Great, now he thinks I'm drooling over him.*

"No, I only just learned about it, like you." She didn't look up at him for fear he would see how flustered she'd become.

"Well if you ask me to yours, I might ask you to mine."

Nina's gaze lifted to Raphe's. Those dark-brown irises with flecks of green were inviting. His face was tan with a slight after-five shadow that glinted in the bar light. It framed his straight white teeth and infectious smile. He had a striking face with a strong jawline and sculpted chin. His wavy brown hair was streaked with highlights from all the time he no doubt spent outdoors.

She suddenly found herself wondering what he did for a living but felt it would be rude to ask. People didn't ask direct questions like that anymore. It was like saying, *how much do you earn?* It made her feel like she was a car salesman pre-qualifying a buyer, and he didn't look like the buying type. This man had one-night stand written all over him given the little love note in his back pocket. He was smooth, though, because he almost had her believing he was nice.

"Do those lines really work on women?" It sounded bitchy even to her own ears. Nina inwardly cringed. *Why am I doing it again?* It's like she couldn't control her behavior around this man. Maybe it was this place. She wasn't exactly in love with Magnolia. Unlike Bonnie, she couldn't see herself in a small town permanently. Maybe she should call her brother, Carlos, and take him up on his offer to pay for her to relocate to San Francisco.

Raphe looked taken aback. He held up his hands. "Uh, sorry. I didn't mean to sound cheesy. I actually have a ball to go to this weekend and I haven't asked anyone yet. It was a dumb question. Sorry." He motioned for the bartender and handed him a credit card. Directing his attention elsewhere, he asked the bartender to add twenty-five percent and close the tab. Turning back to Nina and Bonnie, he tipped his imaginary hat. "Ladies, it's been a pleasure, but I've got Lulu waiting for me at home. Y'all have a good night."

Nina fumed at her own behavior. He might be a player, but he'd been nice to buy their drinks and say hello. He'd been a perfect gentleman, but then again, he did say he had someone waiting for him. She watched the woman and her friend across the bar as they enjoyed another man's attention. Well, clearly, she wasn't the one he was meeting.

Curiosity got the best of Nina. "Is that woman really a hooker?"

Bonnie lifted her shoulders, "I don't know. I was just trying to clear a path for you to reel him in."

Nina's mouth dropped open. "Bonnie!"

"Oh hell, honey, all is fair in love and war. Besides, you were cock blocking him from the moment you sat at the bar. He didn't have eyes for a single other lady here."

Nina shook her head. "I think he's a player. He's just after one thing."

Bonnie gave her a smile. "Well, if I were you, I think I'd give it to him. I bet he's some kinda good in bed."

Nina gasped, then burst out laughing. She really liked Bonnie. It was obvious they were going to be fast friends.

They clinked glasses and finished their champagne. "I don't know about you, but I better call it a night. I'm helping my cousin's wife open in the morning and she's planning some serious training." Nina rolled her eyes, dreading her next shift.

Bonnie nodded. "Me too. I open the library at nine."

They made their way to the parking lot and spotted Raphe getting into a souped-up F150. It was probably an eighty-thousand-dollar truck with all the bells and whistles. Nina figured he must have some sort of money.

His clothes were designer and the single bracelet he wore was a work of art. Nina recognized the Greek jewelry designer, Konstantino. He was one of her favorites, too.

Yep, he's a player.

Raphe was talking to another good-looking guy on a motorcycle, who'd just pulled off his helmet.

Bonnie sucked in her breath, squeezing Nina's arm. "Pinch me! I think I've died and gone to heaven."

Nina giggled. "So, he's your type?" She motioned to the guy on the bike.

Bonnie fanned herself. "Quick, let's get out of here before I faint."

Nina laughed until she realized Bonnie was serious. The woman was flushed and perspiring.

"You probably had too much champagne." Nina walked Bonnie to her small Kia hatchback. "You sure you're okay to drive? I don't mind taking you home." She pointed to her own old jalopy. She needed a new car bad, but social workers didn't have the kind of bucks to buy fancy cars.

Bonnie waved her off. "I'm all right. Just need a cold shower." She winked.

Nina watched Bonnie drive off and then Raphe exited behind her. The cyclist strutted toward the bar entrance. He could have been Raphe's twin but with longer hair. There was something edgier about this guy and she could see why Bonnie found him attractive. He was hot.

Bonnie likes bad boys. Who would have guessed?

Chapter 6

Raphe rolled over and hit the snooze on his cellphone. Now if he could just slip back into the dream he'd been having at the exact place he'd left off. He lay there for what seemed like countless minutes, but the beautiful brunette had vanished with the cover of night. Now he lay sprawled in tangled bed sheets with a pulsing erection and a fast-beating heart. He groaned in frustration. He hadn't had a wet dream since high school and he didn't care for the idea of laundering his sheets before going into the firehouse today, but the dream he was having of Nina writhing beneath him in his bed was well worth the morning effort if he could have recalled the lucky lotto ticket back to slumber. No such luck.

He threw back the covers and sat up, swinging his legs to the side of the bed. He looked down at his state of alertness. "I guess it's just you, me, and the shower, buddy."

Lulu barked from the other side of the bed. Raphe tucked the sheet back around him, glancing back over his shoulder. He'd forgotten he had company. Lulu gave up her dog bed the first night she'd arrived at his apartment, settling into the other side of his king bed.

"Yeah, I hear ya'. I'll be out in a minute to take you out, okay?" Lulu answered him with another woof of acceptance and settled back onto her pillow. In his experience she liked to sleep in, so he didn't mind taking her out when she asked. Lulu was pretty low maintenance, except for the incident at the library and the fiasco with Jake at the firehouse. In his current condition, he couldn't really blame her. If Nina was within ten feet of him and willing, he'd have no choice. His body wanted release, but the hot-tempered vixen made it clear she wasn't interested. He needed to move on. Maybe he should call Roxanne and arrange a visit to her beach condo after Lulu went home.

He started his day with a vigorous cold shower, then walked Lulu around the small dog park at the apartment complex before climbing the steps back to his apartment for hot coffee. The new machine he'd bought from the fancy shop at the Galleria was the best purchase he'd ever made outside of his spiffy new truck. The pods cost as much as a coffee from the diner, but he didn't care. Some things were worth a little extra, and he deserved the pleasure of delicious simplicity in the morning.

Lulu happily crunched away on kibble laced with the meatballs Lexi had sent home with him last weekend. He hadn't gotten around to eating them and now they made Lulu happy, so nothing was wasted. He liked that part of having a dog around. She was great help cleaning up messes, like when he dumped spaghetti on the floor or couldn't finish his sub sandwich. There wasn't a speck of sauce left anywhere.

Raphe drained the last of his coffee, leaned down to pick up Lulu's bowl, and scratched her behind the ears. He grabbed his keys and Lulu's head snapped up. She trotted to his side.

"Sorry girl. Even I gotta go to work. If your condition was different, I'd take you, but after your behavior yesterday, young lady…" He shook his head and she looked at him with sorrowful eyes.

Putting down a pee-pee pad and securing Lulu behind the kitchen gate, Raphe left the apartment with only a small amount of guilt. She would be okay until lunch. If he was going to get a puppy, he'd have to get used to leaving it from time to time. He might have a nice nest egg tucked away from a few well-placed investments, but he still needed to work. His job as a fireman wasn't glamorous, but his grandfather had been a fireman and Raphe had spent a lot of time visiting the station when he was young. Firefighting was in his blood and he couldn't imagine doing anything else. He was lucky that his other grandfather, who owned an oil company, left all the kids a trust-fund for college and a bit of fun living. Raphe lived well. He didn't have monetary worries and he got to do what he loved. Life was good.

Sitting at a red light, he stared at the café. Most of the early breakfast crowd had come and gone. The parking lot was half empty. He wondered if Nina was working and he was half tempted to go in for another coffee before his shift. He shook off the urge. *You don't want her to think you're desperate, buddy.*

Besides, she's not interested. Maybe that's why he was so drawn to her—most of the women he liked all but fell at his feet.

The chief gave him a cool nod as he passed by the firehouse office. Raphe smiled sheepishly. Jake and Lulu had knocked over a ficus tree in their romp around his office and the soil went all over some Persian carpet that Mona had bought. The chief didn't mind the carpet getting soiled so much as having to clean up the mess. It took three other firemen to catch ahold of Jake while Raphe absconded with Lulu wiggling in his arms. At just under fifty pounds, it wasn't exactly a smooth exit. It reminded Raphe that he needed to sign up at the gym. The firehouse had a small weight bench area with kettlebells and an old treadmill, but it wasn't enough for Raphe's usual routine.

A few of the men chuckled as Raphe passed through the kitchen. He just smiled, kept walking, and put his gear on the truck. If it wasn't for Lulu being Melvina and Riley's dog, he'd probably chuckle himself, but he was dreading the wrath of his brother and sister-in-law. They wouldn't be thrilled to return from their honeymoon and learn they were having puppies, not to mention Humphrey had been outgunned by Jake.

Raphe finished checking through his structural gear and moved through the chores of his day. It was one of his last twelve-hour shifts for this rotation, and he'd worked things out with the chief to go home for lunch to take Lulu out for a short walk. Lexi and the boys would go to his apartment later in the afternoon and feed her.

Raphe looked forward to seeing what his sister would leave in the fridge. She wasn't a fancy chef like Riley, but her cooking was a mite better than Raphe's. Lexi always took pity on his bachelor status and brought food or sent it home with him when he visited. She said she and the boys would stay with Lulu and watch a movie until he rolled in around ten-thirty. He wondered if he should tell Lexi about Lulu and Jake. Then the boys could bring over Lulu's brother, Chef, for a reunion. Now that Jake had knocked her up, it didn't seem to matter, but the boys might get an early lesson in sex-ed, though he was sure they'd probably seen some of the livestock mate on the farm. Caught up in his own thoughts, the alarm startled him. Everyone jumped into action as the tone dropped, informing them it was an EMS call. The voice over the loudspeaker notified them it was a lift assist, not an emergency but urgent. Raphe jumped up, grabbing his kit and raced to the ambulance.

Matt, the engineer, called out, "Ready to go, Captain?"

Raphe's promotion to captain came after the incident that sent him running to Magnolia with his tail tucked between his legs. A certificate of honor was presented to him at a press release shortly after he was given the promotion to captain. The recognition had been nice, but he'd gotten caught out that night in the blaze. He'd been tired from a lack of sleep and too much partying the night before. He knew he did his job right, but could he have done it better? Saved more people, maybe avoided that beam that crashed down on top of him, nearly taking his life?

He was lucky to have walked away with two broken ribs and a few bruises. It was a tight situation and less experienced men would have succumbed to panic, but the men in his battalion used their notched PIGs to wedge just enough room for Raphe to slide out. He'd suffered from smoke inhalation and needed time to recover. The problem was his days off when he was left alone to think. Those thoughts filtered through his brain, causing him to feel anxious. He'd needed to get away from Houston and those massive high-rises that dotted the multiple skylines. He needed to be close to his family. Magnolia was just the place to hide out until he could mend his meandering thoughts and tamp down his needling anxiety.

Raphe grabbed the truck handle and hefted himself into the passenger seat. "We got a lift assist at three-thousand-ten North Maple, priority two, code two."

Raphe was surprised to be greeted at the front door of the home by the shy librarian. Bonnie waved for the crew to come in and they ran forward, following her to the bathroom where a much older woman lay wrapped in a towel.

"She was taking a shower, and she said she could do it alone, but after fifteen minutes I came back to check on her. It was then that I heard her call for help. My aunt doesn't weigh that much, but I was afraid to lift her because of her hip. She just had a replacement a few months ago."

Raphe asked the older woman several questions about her injury and the pain she felt, then directed his men to arrange the stretcher. He looked at Bonnie with her blonde hair in a pompom on top of her head. She was still in pink silk pajamas with a matching robe. "We should take her to the hospital for an x-ray just to be sure." They put a blanket over the older woman and used the towel to lift her enough to slide a bigger blanket beneath her. He was glad for the extra team members who tagged along for the call. They carefully transferred Bonnie's aunt to the rolling gurney. She might have been a small woman, but she was dead weight at the moment and with a possible broken hip, they needed to be careful.

As they rolled her through the living room, Bonnie looked down at her pajamas. "Do I have time to change?"

Raphe smiled at her with reassurance. "You have plenty of time. Do whatever you need to do, and you can meet us at the hospital when you're ready. Don't worry, your aunt is in good hands. We'll make sure she gets taken care of."

Bonnie's worried look said she didn't know whether to trust him or not, but he didn't have time to placate her. He joined his men and made sure they strapped the patient in securely. The new engineer took the driver's seat and Raphe switched places with one of the younger EMTs. He held the older woman's hand as they drove away from the house, leaving Bonnie staring after them, her pink robe fluttering in the breeze.

The injured woman looked up at him with a wide toothy smile. Her dentures were slightly askew. "My, my, you sure are a sight for old eyes."

Raphe smiled at the flirtatious compliment and patted her hand again. The woman was at least eighty. "Don't you worry Ms. Bush. We're going to get you all taken care of. You have nothing to worry about."

She slid her teeth out and sucked them back in, flashing her gums at him in the process. "No lumps, no bumps, you want a smooth blow job?"

Raphe almost fell off of his jump seat. He'd heard a lot of propositions in his adult life from women of all ages, but this one took the cake. Bonnie Bush's aunt, Mrs. Rosie Anne Bush, was one of the feistiest and most flirtatious women he'd ever met outside of Mona Calhoun. Bashful wasn't in her vocabulary, and though he thought most of what she said was for shock value and fun, he had a feeling she'd had some success somewhere in the past. The way she was laying down track in every direction said she'd gotten lucky on that line before. The newest recruit, Todd Vinton, was extracting Rosie's fingers from around his bicep, one by one. Thank God the doctor who greeted them was a female. His men were full of smiles and polite banter with the patient, but it was time they said goodbye and let the hospital staff take care of Rosie.

Bonnie came rushing into the ER as Raphe and his crew were leaving. Her hair was still in a pompom and her thick glasses shoved high on her nose. She wore jeans with a yellow t-shirt and canvas tennis shoes without socks. She still wasn't his type, but he had to admit her figure, for someone who sat behind the Library's circulation desk all day, was rocking. High breasts, small waist, and curvy hips.

I wish she'd ditch those glasses, so I could see her pretty face.

Bonnie grabbed onto his bicep as she screeched to a halt. "Where is she? Is she okay? Have they done the x-rays yet? Is it broken?" For someone who barely said a word to him before, she shot out questions quicker than a guest on Jeopardy with a million-dollar bank.

He tried not to chuckle. Bonnie was obviously worried about her aunt, and that warmed his heart. He understood love of family. If it was his nana, he'd be rushing in as well.

"They just rolled her to an examination room in back. The lady at the front desk will help you out."

She tossed out a thank you as she hurried toward the sign-in desk. Raphe wasn't sure if it was for delivering her aunt safely to the hospital or pointing her in the right direction. He'd helped another person and that made him smile. Making a difference was why he'd signed up for the job.

Chapter 7

Nina trained all morning long. She learned how to prep bread, make batter for cupcakes, and cleaned what felt like a million tables. Maria rode her hard for her giving Melvina's brother-in-law a difficult time. Nina didn't complain. Even though she'd been depressed and irritable since she arrived, Jose and Maria had been good to her. She could tell that Maria's patience was running thin and Nina wanted to make up for her bad behavior. It didn't matter that the man who'd walked in before Raphe yesterday had given her a tough time. It didn't give her the right to give someone else grief or assume they were going to be rude.

Nina bused tables, wiped the counters, took out the trash and swept the dining room floor. It was good, honest work that kept her from thinking too much about what she was going to do with her life. She couldn't live with the guilt of breaking up with her ex the night before he died in the fire. Realistically, she knew the fire wasn't her fault. They hadn't been right for each other from the beginning. It was just rough that his family kept phoning her and treating her like their daughter-in-law. In their time of grief, she didn't feel like it was right to share that she'd rejected their son.

The bell dinged over the entrance and the object of her punishment made his way to the counter. His blue uniform was sexy, and his tousled hair made it look like he'd done some grunt work himself today. She made her way to the counter, where Maria cut her off and went to greet Raphe with a smile.

"Mr. Nash, so good to see you. The usual?" Maria turned over a cup and filled it with coffee from the freshest pot.

Raphe nodded, combing a hand through his hair as he let out a sigh. "Thanks Maria. Hey, add two plain hamburger patties then wrap it all up to-go. Lulu's at my apartment and I need to check on her before heading back to the fire station."

Nina's heart sank. He was a fireman. Of course, the blue uniform should have reminded her.... She remembered talking to one of the firemen when she arrived back at her charred apartment building the night of the fire. It happened six months ago but it still felt like yesterday. Nina had stayed at a friend's house the night of the breakup, and she'd come back to pack some things the night after. The building was still smoldering, and they didn't allow her in. She was bordering on hysterical, crying and fraught with worry, but the men who were yelling things like—*pull yellow, crosslays, and pump something or another*—didn't have time to tell her all the details.

After Nina willed herself to calm down, she saw the chaos around her—the other people from her building who'd lost just as much as she had. Recognizing a neighbor—she ended up helping the woman and her kids. A fireman had saved their lives and had gone back for their puppy. They were so worried about their dog and the fire they didn't even real-ize the other problems they faced. That's when Nina's social work skills kicked in. She calmed the mother and kids and found them shelter for the night along with several other families. She'd been so busy and focused on helping, that it barely registered when one of the firefighters handed the puppy to the kids. Cameras flashed, and ash covered faces were lit in the crowded chaos. Nina stood mesmerized by the lights as she watched the family reunion. The puppy washed the kids' faces with kisses, and the children cried with joy. Nina remembered how her heart ached. Stricken with the reality of her own loss, she'd stood alone, lost in the sidelines with other bystanders.

Staying busy that night distracted her while she waited to hear news of her ex. When she finally did find out Derek had perished in the fire, Nina crumpled to her knees in shock. She should have been grateful for the firemen and their service, but she'd felt angry instead. Lives were lost that night and Derek's was one of them. Since the fire, her grief had begun to dissipate but her overwhelming guilt had not.

Raphe glanced at her with a wary look. "Hey, Nina. You all right?"

She shook herself from the blazing past that consumed her thoughts. She tried not to stare at his uniform. "Yeah, I'm okay, thanks." She picked up the pot and topped off his coffee, spilling some over the edge and onto his hand. Raphe pulled back and winced. "Sorry!" She skittered back with a hand to her mouth.

Raphe's eyes held concern. "You sure you're okay? You look spooked." His voice was soft, like he was talking to an injured animal. She was injured inside, but she didn't need him digging into her world to find out just how much. She hated the looks of pity she'd received after the fire from so many co-workers and friends. She didn't need anyone's sympathy. She needed space.

"I—I'm fine, just clumsy today is all. Sorry about your hand."

Raphe gave her a look that said she was forgiven. His eyes shone with interest. "Sorry enough to be my date on Friday for the Fireman's Ball? I still don't have a date."

Nina let her guard down, giving him a half-smile. *He never gives up.* Maria came around the corner with his to-go order and she gave Nina a scowl.

"Mr. Nash, here's your order. There's your usual lunch, Lulu's burgers and I even threw in a couple of cupcakes we made this morning. Would you like a box to take back to the station for the men?" Maria held the bag out, then thought to throw some napkins and condiment packages in. Flushed, she added, "And women. Melvina told me there are three at the station." Her voice held admiration.

Raphe nodded, "Yes, indeed, but Martha is on pregnancy leave and the other two aren't on duty today. I'll say no on the extra cakes. Some of the guys are getting a little out of shape." He winked, patting his flat stomach and then turned toward Nina.

"So, how about it? You're not going to leave me hanging, are ya?"

Nina leaned against the counter, sizing him up. Maria gave her a look of disapproval.

"I'm sure, Mr. Nash…." She used his formal name, as Maria had. "That you, of all people, don't have issues finding a date."

Raphe chuckled. "You've got me all figured out, don't you?"

Roberta slid between them, digging beneath the counter for straws to fill her apron. "Careful with this one. Darcey didn't figure him out so well." She gave Raphe a surly smile, with a glint in her eye that said she was on team Darcey.

It was Nina's turn to laugh. She picked up the cups from a nearby seat at the counter and dumped them in the washtub. Arching an eyebrow at him as she passed by, "Well it looks to me like you're the love 'em and leave 'em type."

Raphe let out a sigh. "Well there's no harm in finding out. Come with me to the Fireman's Ball and I promise you I'll be a perfect gentleman. You'll meet a lot of people, which is good because you're new in town…and I'm bettin' you like to dance."

She contemplated his offer. She hated to admit, she'd wanted to say yes the first time he asked, but something inside stopped her. *Am I afraid to let go and have fun, or am I worried this guy might just break my heart?* He was the tall, dark, and handsome type—the type any woman with a pulse would say yes to, but she'd been through a lot recently and couldn't afford more emotional turmoil. She wasn't sure if she was ready to risk more.

It's just a dance, Nina. Get it together and get out of the house!

Maria and Jose could really use a night alone with their kids. Nina was sure they needed space as much as she did.

Pressing her lips together and tilting her head, she said simply, "I do like to dance."

Raphe's tongue pressed against the inside of his cheek as he nodded slowly to her. "Is that a yes then?"

Nina tried not to smile too broadly. She liked watching him sweat. The Adonis had probably never worked so hard for a date in his whole adult life.

"What's the attire?" Nina didn't have a lot of spending money to buy a dress for one night. She had bought a couple changes of clothes after the fire, enough to fill a medium-sized suitcase, but she didn't exactly have a formal gown for a ball.

"The theme is Havana nights. My brother Ran and the Tomball Cats are playing, and they've been practicing. It's the best Cuban playlist I've ever heard, and I can't wait to cut a rug. It's still black tie, but women can wear just about anything on these occasions." Raphe's words were breezy, like it was no big deal, but to her it spelled dollars. Getting something nice with Latin flare could be difficult unless she went back to Houston and raided her friend, Johana's closet. Johana was a pageant queen several times over and held the key to a wardrobe that'd make most Hollywood actresses swoon with envy. Johana's father had big oil money and she attended a lot of fundraising events in the city.

Nina's pause made Raphe look uncomfortable. She wondered if he thought she was looking for an excuse to back out. He really was hand-some, and she supposed he was worth a drive to Houston to beg entrance to Johana's closet. She gave him a smile as she grabbed her ticket book and wrote down her cell number and address, trying not to think of the woman at Bubbles who'd slipped a note in his rear pocket the night before. She handed him the ticket. "You can pick me up at this address."

Raphe smiled, leaving a twenty on the counter for the to-go food. "I'll pick you up Friday night at seven."

The door dinged as Raphe sauntered out and Nina wondered if the spring in his step was for her. She doubted it. She was just another entry in his little black book. Well, why should she complain. It wasn't like she was sticking around this one-horse town. Once she got herself together, she was out of here. She thought of Carlos's offer again. Maybe she should just call her brother and book a flight.

Raphe studied Lulu, who sprawled on his couch, belly up. It was after ten and he'd missed Lexi and the boys. He'd given Lulu the hamburgers from the diner at lunch, and no telling what Lexi and the boys had given her for dinner, but her belly was swelled to satisfaction. He wondered if he should take her to the vet to get a pregnancy test or something. What did people do for a pregnant basset hound? Were there checkups involved in the first week? He checked Google on his phone and looked up how long a canine pregnancy lasted, and the answer was about two months. That wasn't even one trimester. Dogs were quick breeders. Lulu would be a quarter of the way through her pregnancy before Melvina and Riley even made it back. He contemplated telling them over the phone, but he really hated to spoil their honeymoon. They'd had to wait a year to enjoy this time together.

"Nope Lulu, we better leave 'em alone. They might be makin' puppies themselves." Raphe knew that Melvina was forty-two now and probably wouldn't have children, but women were having children later in life. He wouldn't rule out an extra niece or nephew yet. Riley was forty-two, Raphe was thirty-eight, and Ran was thirty-five, but Lexi was the baby and she'd already had three kids. Time sure did pass in a flash. It seemed like only yesterday he was a smooth-faced kid joining the academy.

Raphe always thought he'd have a family of his own one day, but his work schedule and recreational life hadn't left much time to settle down. Truth be told, he'd yet to meet a woman that he wanted to spend every day with. That seemed to be a necessity if he was going to raise children. He thought about some of the women he'd dated over the years. Sure, they were pretty enough, educated, and from good families, but every time he felt their hooks dig into him, he made a leap to the next pretty gal he fancied. He thought about Sheila, who'd been covered in chocolate by Melvina's dance fiasco with Riley. That redhead was some kinda feisty. He'd seen her face on a commercial during last year's Super Bowl game. She'd been smoking hot but didn't have any real personality. He admitted he was envious of the relationship Riley had with Melvina. She was pretty, smart, funny, and kind-hearted. Melvina and Riley fit together like cake and ice cream, one melting into the other, making the perfect relationship mix.

In retrospect, maybe his move to Magnolia had more to do with wanting a more settled life than he'd had in the big city. Houston was full of nightlife and great food. There was never a dull moment, but it left him feeling empty at the end of the day. He liked the folksy feel of small-town Magnolia and its lively residents, like Mona, the chief, Rosie Bush, her shy librarian niece and yes, even the hot-tempered Latina whose name haunted him even now. Nina, a beautiful name for a beautiful woman. She didn't wear much makeup and yet she looked flawless, like she could be in a Revlon ad. He shifted on the couch as he felt the blood in his body running south. Lulu groaned, rolling over in protest from the disturbance. She gave him a tired yawn.

"Yeah, I agree. Time for a cold shower and bed."

Chapter 8

Nina sat beneath a mound of sequined dresses as Johana tossed more onto the pile. Nina let out a breath, blowing a loose feather toward the ceiling from the flamingo pink gown on top of the stack. It floated to Johana's bed, where Nina had been sitting watching sparkles fly for the last ten minutes.

"Tell me all about this tall, dark, and handsome man you accosted in the diner. Did you meet him before, at the fire?" Johana's question was hushed, like she was afraid Derek's soul could hear them. Nina cringed inwardly. She did feel guilty going on a date with Raphe, especially since he was a fireman, and Derek was killed in a fire. It wasn't the firefighter's fault that night. Those men and women saved a lot of lives while risking their own. If Derek was looking down from above, he was cursing the fact that she was going out with a fireman to be sure, but then Derek had been a cheat and a liar. Regardless, she still felt guilty about being mad at him.

Nina shifted the gowns to her side, holding up a peacock-blue concoction with Latin flare. The half mermaid bottom with the scoop up the front would show off her tanned legs, courtesy of the community pool in Jose's neighborhood. Nina wished all her days could be beach towel-romance novel days.

She stood up and twirled around in front of the full-length mirror, pressing the chiffon fabric to her waist and shoulders. "I think I like this one. Mind if I try it on?"

Johana's head bobbed as she smiled, giving Nina a theatrical wink. "Oh girl, that color is so you!"

Nina hardly recognized herself as she emerged from the bathroom and turned in front of the mirror again. She felt like a brunette Cinderella. Raphe was every bit a handsome Prince Charming, but Nina didn't think there was a happily ever after in the cards. As a social worker, she didn't exactly mix it up with the glitterati. Derek had never been a fan of swanky parties or charity balls. He loved sports bars and low-key restaurants. Not because he didn't have the money for it. On the contrary, his job as a consultant had paid extraordinarily well, and the lavish condo apartment they'd lived in was his. It was also the reason why his insurance hadn't covered any of her material losses. The fact that she wasn't listed as an owner or wife meant she got zilch.

She'd lived off her meager savings and emergency-leave pay, depending on the help of friends and family until now. She hoped her temporary job at the Cupcake Diner and Dive would replenish her dwindling funds and allow her to lease her own apartment soon. She smiled at her reflection as she held up her hair. She missed dancing with her friends in a night club or going out for dinner to a nice restaurant. The thought of wearing the gown at a swanky event with Raphe made her pulse race. She imagined just how spectacular he would look in a tux or better yet, in nothing at all. If he tried to get her into the sack, would she let him? Bonnie's voice rang in her ears…*I bet he's some kinda good in bed.*

"You okay, Nina?" The concern in Johana's voice brought her back to reality.

Nina sucked in a deep breath of air, then smiled at her friend. "Yes, I'm fine. It's just been a long time since I danced with a man. I wonder if I'll remember how?"

Johana hugged her and Nina tried to tuck her unraveling emotions away.

"It's okay to have fun again, Nina. It's time. Besides, dancing's just like riding a bike. You'll know what to do when you hit the floor in Lucky Cleo."

"Lucky Cleo?" Nina was perplexed. "Is that a dance?"

Johana pointed at the dress. "Honey, when he sees you in that dress, you are sure to get lucky, and Cleo because unless you let go a little bit and have fun, you are going to be the queen of denial."

Nina swatted a hand through the air. "Johana, you talk in riddles. I'm not in denial. I'm going to have fun. I'll be calling this the Lucky Peacock. You wait and see."

Johana put her hands on Nina's shoulders, staring at her intently. "My friend, you have been in denial for years. When you agreed to marry Derek, you were denying yourself the chance to find someone you could be truly happy with. Instead, you played it safe because he asked you to marry him. You invested years of your life with that jerk. Destiny and Derek's cheating tore your life apart. But that doesn't mean you can't move on and finally find happiness."

Nina cleared her raspy throat and shrugged off her friend's hands. She turned and began to unzip the dress, being careful with the delicate fabric. "I don't want to talk about this right now. I really don't need to be social worked."

Johana sat on the bed, looking at Nina's reflection in the mirror. "Alright, but I need to say one more thing before we close the subject. I know it wasn't right and it sure wasn't fair to Derek, but fate has a way of righting wrongs. It was Derek's time and you didn't have anything to do with that fire, nor was it your fault that he died. You had already made the choice to move on. Now it's time for you to forgive yourself and live. You didn't do anything bad, Nina, and your life shouldn't stop because you feel guilty about something you had no control over. You're putting your career on hold, your life on hold…for what? He's not coming back." Johana's face was a canvas of concern, worry and dread.

Nina just couldn't seem to bounce back, and it was obvious to her close friend that she was suffering. The tears Nina had been holding back for what seemed like forever slid down her cheeks. She swiped at them with the backs of her hands. Shoving her t-shirt over her head, she grabbed her purse and folded up the evening gown.

"I can't do this today, Johana. I'm a social worker. I see the best and the worst in people. I know what's what and I know the truth in my heart, but my feelings have scars and they need time to heal, so quit picking at them, please." She paused, staring at her friend, who looked slightly ashamed for bringing it all up. "I'm truly grateful for your help and concern but it's still too soon for me." She swallowed and forced a smile, trying to pull it together. "I have to get back to Magnolia. I'm on the dinner shift and I'm going to be late."

Chapter 9

Raphe took Lulu around to the back of the café and in through the back door to Pop's office. Melvina's brother, Eli, sat at the desk with his feet propped up on a nearby folding chair. Melvina's older basset hound, Humphrey, was sitting close by. Due to Lulu's condition, Raphe had been in charge of watching after her and Eli was keeping Humphrey safely at bay.

A loud woof pierced their ears as Humphrey jumped from his doggie bed to cavort with Lulu. Eli shot up, danced around the chair that spun and clattered onto its side. At the same time, Raphe hopped over the chairs on the opposite side of the desk, catching his foot in one of the lower rungs. He met the hard tile floor with a thwack and Eli made a leap over his flattened form. They both called out after the two mutts as they skedaddled out the open office door toward the kitchen. The dogs made their way down the cook's line, through the dishwasher's area and out into the diner.

Shouts over dishes breaking and gasps of surprise were heard throughout the restaurant. Raphe found his footing and gave chase. Roberta sat on the floor in the middle of the cook's doorway leading to the dining room. A nest of French fries clung to her blonde tresses as she sat among a turned-over tray of broken dishes laden with disassembled food. The waitress glared at him, but he didn't wait for her to find her voice. He leapt over Roberta, running after Eli and the hounds.

"Close the door!" Raphe and Eli called out in unison to the diner patron with his wife, who were making an excruciatingly slow exit. Her walker with its florescent yellow tennis balls blocked the door from closing. Lulu ducked under the hem of the older woman's skirt and Humphrey barreled through, spinning the elderly woman into her husband's arms. Eli caught them both as the couple reared backward toward the black-and-white checked tiles.

"Raphe patted Eli on the back before jumping over the walker like a front runner in a steeplechase competition. "Good catch, my man." He didn't look back to see if Eli managed to untangle himself. Raphe knew he had to catch the dogs before they made it to the highway.

Lulu's leash floated out behind her like a long pink ribbon caught in the breeze of her escape. Raphe called after them both as they crossed over the road in front of the café and made their way through the park across the street. It was a decent size park, but another, busier highway was on the other side of it. Raphe gave it all he had, pumping his legs and trying to control his ragged breathing. Tires screeched and he tapped the hood that almost clipped him, calling out, "Sorry," as he waved a hand in the air. He barely glanced at the driver with the double thick librarian glasses. At least Bonnie had quick reflexes. He'd have to thank her later for not running him down.

Raphe rounded the merry-go-round and headed toward the swings. A large rabbit had somehow got caught in the action and Lulu was on full tilt. Raphe rattled his way between the chains, tripping as one of the swing's snagged his foot. The muddy track beneath the seats squished into his shoes and he winced but forged ahead.

The mud slowed him down and he banged his knee as he tried unsuccessfully to hurdle a hobby horse. His muddy shoes slipped in the wet grass and he lost one as he neared the open road ahead. He heard tires screech and he was almost too afraid to look. Then he heard the familiar voice, "Why, Humphrey and Lulu, what would your momma say if she knew you were running wild around Magnolia?"

Raphe bent over with his hands on his upper thighs, trying to catch his breath and think up a good enough excuse to tell Melvina's best friend about why he'd let the dogs run away. He gathered his wits and approached the sporty white Jaguar. Mona had opened the passenger door and Humphrey and Lulu had hopped right in. Raphe expected a withering look, but Mona didn't own one of those. Her expression was one of pure amusement at his expense.

"Raphe Valentino Nash, what in the world are you doing out here with both Melvina's mutts runnin' wild? Aren't they supposed to be separated?" Mona's artfully defined thin lips pursed in mock annoyance, but her eyes sparkled with mischief.

It was at that moment, that Raphe noticed Humphrey mounting Lulu from behind on Mona's tan leather seats. "Oh no! Humphrey, Lulu, stop!"

Mona glanced sideways at her canine passengers. "Oh, hell Raphe, I just bought this car yesterday!"

Raphe sat at the bar, in Bubbles, shaking his head in despair. Ran was quaking with deep, belly-rumbling guffaws "Melvina and Riley are gonna kill you," Ran said between hoots of laughter. "You might as well move back to Houston."

Raphe held up a hand to the bartender, signaling another round. "It wasn't all my fault. I wasn't expecting Humphrey to be at the restaurant with Eli."

"Why not? You take Lulu there all the time."

"Because I take Lulu there all the time. He should've known this might happen."

"If anyone has a right to bring a dog into the café, it's Eli. He works there. You just mooch there."

Raphe scowled at his little brother. "I don't mooch there. I pay well for the food I order, and I tip well too. Just ask Roberta and the gals who work there."

Ran shook his head, trying unsuccessfully to smother a smile. "I wouldn't try talking to Roberta right now. I think she has a bill waiting for you over the broken china. Probably for lost tips, too. That was a table of ten Lulu upended." He chuckled again, then took a swig of his longneck.

Raphe frowned. "Yeah, I feel bad about that. I'll have to go apologize eventually, but Roberta's been mad at me ever since Darcey quit."

Ran tore at the label on his beer, peeling it off in one long piece. "Yeah, that didn't go over so well for you did it?"

Raphe looked at his younger brother with eyebrows raised in disbelief. "You know that peelin' labels is a sign of sexual frustration, don't you?"

Ran smiled, "Speak for yourself."

Raphe scowled. "You're not exactly the best person to talk to when a guy's havin' troubles."

"Maybe you should talk to a social worker or somethin'. I hear there's a really nice-looking one who's helping out at the diner." He paused, smiling like a cat who just cornered a fat mouse. "Oh, wait, you're banned from talking to the gals at the diner." Ran's laughter rang out across the mostly empty bar. It was only two in the afternoon, but it was Ran's day off and Raphe had switched shifts.

Raphe made an irritated grunt. "Wait? Are you talking about the new gal? Jose's cousin?"

Ran nodded.

"I'll have you know I can talk to whomever I please," he said, puffing his chest out, then letting it deflate. "I just can't ask any of them out."

"You mean you're not supposed to." Ran gave him a wicked smile.

Damn it! He knows.

"Well, in my defense. Maria said she was just helping out for the day and I asked Nina out later that evening."

Ran set his beer down and shook his head at Raphe. "And she turned you down."

Raphe shook his head in wonder. "Where do you get all this?"

Ran laughed. "It's a small town, Raphe. People talk. In fact, it was said by Mac Green to the chief, who told Mona…"

Raphe put his hand up to stop his brother. Once any news got to Mona, it would travel around Magnolia before sundown. "All right, I admit it. I asked her out at Bubbles, and she said no, but the second time I saw her at the diner, she said yes."

Ran nodded while continuing to chuckle. "Let's see, you've gotten Lulu hooked up twice in your first week of dog sitting, ruined the carpet in your boss's office, ruined the interior of his girlfriend's new car, and now you're gonna break the cardinal rule of not dating waitresses from the diner."

It didn't sound so good when Ran went through the list of events that had piled up so quickly in the few short days since the happy couple left.

Raphe decided to change the subject. "Who are you taking to the ball?"

"I'm playing in the band. You know that."

Raphe scratched his head. "That's never stopped you from bringing a date before. Your old girlfriend used to go to every gig, remember?"

Ran whooped at the game on TV. The Rockets had scored, taking the game into overtime. "And that's exactly why I am going stag."

"I thought you liked Olivia hanging around. She was cute."

"That girl had married-with-kids written all over her. She had a schedule book that she carried around in her purse outlining her entire life. She even scheduled bathroom breaks!"

Raphe was surprised. Ran had dated her for two years. "Then why did you date her for so long?"

Ran rolled his eyes. "Two years isn't all that long. I actually do want to get married, just not on someone else's calendar. I gave it a chance and tried to make it work, and then I thought about being another entry in her schedule. It made me realize that Olivia and I weren't cut out for the long haul."

Raphe knew it was the perfect time to make his pitch. "Well you are in luck, because I've got just the girl for you."

Ran shook his head, holding up his hands. "Oh no, I'm not ready to be set up, and especially not by you."

Raphe put his hand over his heart in mock pain. "That hurts little brother."

"Who are you callin' little? I'm four inches taller than you."

"Look, I hear there's this hot little number at the library. Her name's Bonnie. She's new in town and it would really mean a lot to our dear sister-in-law, Melvina, if—"

Ran cut him off, "You mean you still haven't manned up and asked her yourself? Riley told me that you were supposed to ask her."

Raphe threw his hands up in the air. "Is nothing sacred in this dagburn town? Geez Louise." He blew out a sigh and then took a large drink from his longneck. "I think I'm gonna need something stronger than this to get through today." Raphe motioned to the bartender and told him to set them up with tequila shots. "Truth be told, I tried to ask her out, but she shut me down. Twice."

"She told you no?" The shock on Ran's face almost made up for the poor conversation. "Maybe I do need to meet her. She sounds like she has standards."

Raphe frowned. "Thanks a lot." They both tossed back their shots. "She didn't exactly say no, but she didn't say yes either, so I asked Nina instead."

Ran was toying with him. He already knew that Raphe had asked Nina out, so why was his brother giving him such a rough time? He pointed a finger at his younger brother. "You knew all this already. You just wanted to twist the blade in a little deeper. You and that gossiping Eli should be ashamed. Is that the way you comfort a family member who's already had a crap day?" Raphe shook his head in mock disgust.

Ran clapped him on the shoulder, giving him a rough shake, with a broad smile across his tanned face. "It was Mona, and you know you can always count on me."

Raphe scoffed, "For what, is the million-dollar question."

Chapter 10

Nina counted her tips, feeling pretty excited by the results of her efforts. Two-hundred and twenty-eight dollars on a weekday shift? Sure, she'd worked from six in the morning until two in the afternoon, but she'd never seen two-hundred dollars cash from a day working for CPS. It wasn't like she'd ever taken a calculator to break down her salary to an hourly wage. As a social worker for the state, she'd worked too many hours to count. Twenty-five dollars an hour cash in tips and take-home looked pretty good to her right now, and it was only Thursday.

She wondered what the weekend would bring. She'd asked for Saturday off just in case she was a little hung over from the ball Friday night. Not that she was a big drinker, but she planned to let her hair down and have a good time tomorrow. Images of Raphe dressed in a tux, twirling her around the dance floor in the Lucky Peacock made her stomach flutter. Other thoughts of Raphe shuffling her to his bed and her tearing off his tux also made her gulp. Would she let him take her to his bed if he tried?

I really need to get laid.

Why else would she be standing in front of the library, daydreaming about hot, meaningless sex with Raphe Nash? She climbed the steps to the old brick building with its concrete scrolled trim and big white columns along the stairs. She wanted to celebrate her tip windfall with her new friend, Bonnie.

As she entered the library, Nina saw her cousin, Maurice. He was starting high school soon, and ever since Melvina took him under her wing, he often volunteered to help out at the library. He'd told her that it was his way of giving back. Maurice talked highly of Melvina for starting the literacy program and not giving up on him when he had wanted to give up.

"Hi Maurice. Did you just get here?"

He flashed a youthful smile. Maurice was growing tall and losing all his baby fat. His face was now smooth plains and angles with thick dark lashes like Maria. He had the physique of his father and would obviously be a heart throb by the look of the three girls sitting at the library tables pretending to read.

"No, I'm actually on my way out. The Firecrackers have a meeting this afternoon."

"Firecrackers?" Nina raised an eyebrow.

"Yeah, it's some of the kids who joined the mentor program. A group of us split off and volunteered to wash the firetrucks twice a month to help the department to show our thanks. We were going to call ourselves the Fire Hydrants, but then people would think of dogs peeing on us, and that didn't seem cool."

Nina tried not to laugh, but he was such an adorable teen. The way he swiped his thick hair back from his forehead and puffed his chest out with pride. He was a smart kid and had a big heart. Nina felt like his aunt because of their age difference. It felt odd to refer to him as a cousin, considering Jose was a few years younger than she was, and he already had a teenage son. Her heart clenched and she pushed her feelings away. She would not feel sorry for herself and all the years she'd wasted on the hope that Derek would change.

Now, she was mourning his death and the guilt she still carried threatened to suffocate her if she didn't let it go. She knew Johana had hit the nail on the head the other day, but she couldn't face it right now. She just wanted to go out, dance, and have some fun.

Nina swallowed the sudden lump in her throat and smiled at her young cousin. "Yeah, I think Firecrackers has more pizazz to it."

Maurice glanced back at the table with the three girls, who all began to giggle and snicker. He blushed, looking back at Nina. "I better go before I'm late."

Nina bit back a grin. He wanted to talk to the girls before he left. She gave him a wave in their direction, "Don't let me hold you up. I'm just here to find Bonnie."

He waved and turned toward the girls, then called out, "She's in the auxiliary room."

"Shh!" The librarian hissed from the information desk.

It was the one constant rule that never changed, no loud talking in the library. Nina never really understood it. People talked in bookstores and coffee shops all the time, and it didn't seem to matter. The seats were usually filled as people read or worked on their laptops. She didn't see the big deal about the "code of silence." Maybe if the library opened its doors to a Starbucks café and allowed people to chat over novels, it wouldn't need a fundraiser to keep it going.

Bonnie was cleaning up a marker massacre on the utility tables that lined the room.

"Wow, what happened in here?" Nina gasped.

Bonnie shook her head. "Mrs. Davis's preschool class paid us a visit for story time, and they asked to work on art projects afterward, to draw story characters while the images were still fresh."

Nina smiled. "Well, the markers were fresh, too. Will that come off?"

"Most of it's water-based, but we're used to this sort of thing with preschoolers. It's why we haven't upgraded the tables in a long time. It'd be a waste of money."

"Maybe you should cover them in newsprint or butcher paper before they come in. Then they could draw to their hearts' content." Nina walked to Bonnie's bucket of soapy water and grabbed an extra sponge.

Bonnie looked at her with wonder. "You are a genius! Now why didn't I think of that?" She paused with her hand on her hip, looking at all the tables left to clean. "I am so gonna do that next month before those little terrors come back."

Nina laughed as she scrubbed another table. "Well let's scrub these for the last time then and head over to Bubbles. You look like you could use a drink and I feel like celebrating."

Bonnie gave her a mischievous glance. "Did you let Raphe take you out? Did you get lucky?"

Nina's mouth opened, then closed as she looked up with a smile. "Not yet, but I did say yes to the ball."

Bonnie scrubbed the last of the tables, smiling at Nina. "Good! I knew Melvina asked him to ask me, since I'm new to town, but I don't want a pity date."

Nina looked at her with concern. Had she stolen Bonnie's date for the ball? "Oh no, Bonnie. I'm sorry."

Bonnie held her hand up with the colored sponge in it. "He didn't. I just heard he was supposed to from Mary Lou Owens, who told her brother Manny, who told Eli, who mentioned to…well, never mind, but the truth is, I was avoiding him asking me, because he's just not my type."

Nina nodded, throwing her sponge back in the Crayola bucket filled with sudsy water. "I remember you drooling over the motorcycle guy the other night." Her eyes gleamed. "You like bad-boys, don't you?"

Bonnie looked like her ears might go up in flames. They were as pink as Nina's Flaming Flamingo fingernail polish.

"Well then," Nina said, "all the more reason to hurry over to Bubbles. Maybe Bad Boy might show up again tonight. Only one way to find out."

Bonnie eyes lit up with excitement. "Let me tell Lisa I'm leaving. You know, we used to have a librarian named Nina, but she retired last year."

Nina smiled, standing in her best librarian pose. "Do we look alike?"

Bonnie snorted, then chortled and made her way to the front to find Lisa.

"I'll take that as a compliment." Nina chuckled.

Chapter 11

Raphe felt Ran nudge him as Nina entered the lounge with the new librarian. The ladies started walking toward the opposite end of the bar, but Raphe stood up and waved. Bonnie looked like a deer caught in the headlights. For a minute he thought she would bolt for the exit. Nina clamped onto Bonnie's arm and whispered something to her as she propelled the petite blonde in their direction. Ran and Raphe stood, making room for the ladies to join them at the bar.

"Hi Nina, Bonnie." Raphe beamed. "This is my little brother, Ran. Ran this is Bonnie, the new librarian in town and Nina, Jose's cousin."

Ran nodded and said the proper greetings. Nina smiled and Bonnie looked at the floor. She was holding onto Nina like a small child with their mother.

"Can I offer to buy you ladies a drink?"

The shy librarian studied her shoes, and Nina gave her a nudge.

Bonnie chewed her bottom lip as she looked at Nina, who smiled encouragingly. "Yes." The ladies said in unison.

Raphe couldn't help but notice Ran's interest in Bonnie. But he was surprised by the librarian's behavior. After spending time with her and Nina the other night and then seeing her care for her aunt the last time they'd met—well, she seemed so normal and really nice. Bonnie was a natural beauty, who hid behind her glasses and ultra conservative clothes, but Ran seemed to like the combination.

Raphe decided to derail the awkwardness with a diversion. "How is your Aunt Rosie?" he asked Bonnie. "Did she come out of the hospital okay?"

Bonnie's gaze came level with his. She gave him a small smile that confirmed she was among the living. "Yes, thank you. I hope she wasn't too much of a handful in the ambulance. You and your men were great. She had nothing but good things to say when I drove her home. Luckily, it was just a bruise."

Raphe thought about the pinch on the rump he'd gotten as he bent over to assist the other EMT in lifting her out of the ambulance. Plus, the offer of a smooth blowjob without the hindrance of teeth. He tried not to cringe at the memory, but something on his face made Bonnie grin, making her more like the ponytail, pompom gal he'd seen in the hospital. Now if she'd just throw away those glasses.

"She goosed you, didn't she?"

Nina looked shocked and Ran choked, spilling beer on the bar.

Raphe tugged at his collar, feeling heat rise along the back of his neck. "She's uh… a very friendly lady, your aunt."

Bonnie laughed and slapped her leg. "Rosie will stop at nothing when it comes to good-lookin' men."

Raphe smiled. *So, she does think I'm handsome.*

"Oh, don't get to thinkin' you're too pretty cowboy. Big. Tall. She likes 'em all." Grinning to show she was teasing him, she waved at the bartender and asked him to bring a round of tequila shots.

Nina's eyebrows shot up, but she didn't protest. "I'll buy this round, since I told Bonnie the first round was on me. I had a good day at the diner." She smiled.

It was on the tip of Raphe's tongue to ask how many patrons she'd accosted to get the wad of bills she pulled from her purse. He thought of how she'd gone off on him when he'd asked for coffee. Instead he held up his hand to the bartender and told him to put it on his tab. "I hope you won't rob me of the pleasure."

Nina and Bonnie nodded their thanks and the bartender lined up the tequilas with lime and salt accompanying each cocktail napkin.

Raphe thought of the body shots he'd done in Cancun last year. Images of running his tongue between Nina's breasts made him shift on the barstool as he reached for the shots. Handing one to each of them, he noticed Ran's rapt attention on the usually meek librarian. Bonnie in turn was staring over the rim of her shot back at Ran. "To the new gals in town. May all their days in Magnolia be full of good livin'."

They clinked glasses and Bonnie muttered something that sounded a lot like, "To smooth blowjobs."

Raphe sputtered a bit, and Nina smiled. "Can't hold your liquor?"

She passed him a clean cocktail napkin, and he wiped his mouth. Arching his eyebrows, he looked at Bonnie. "Do you have any plans tomorrow night?"

Nina frowned. Raphe quickly explained himself. Bonnie was still staring dumbstruck at Ran and for once, his brother was speechless. "Ran here has to play in the band for the Fireman's Ball tomorrow night, but he was just complaining that he didn't have a date. I was thinking that if you didn't have plans, Bonnie, you might take pity and accompany him."

Ran finally woke up. "I would love to take Bonnie, but she might get bored after the dinner was over and I couldn't spin her around on the dance floor." Raphe looked hopefully at Bonnie, who seemed to flush with excitement, but she stayed silent. Maybe it was the tequila that had turned her cheeks rosy red.

Raphe turned and ordered another round of shots. "Well, Nina and Bonnie are friends and you have two seats at my table, Ran. I could keep both ladies entertained while you play. Besides, Bonnie, it's Friday night. You don't want to sit home while everyone in Magnolia is cutting a rug and drinking champagne at the Solarium's hotel ballroom."

Bonnie smiled nodding. *Was that a yes?*

Nina nudged her friend. She didn't seem put out that Raphe and she might have a third wheel for the evening. In a way, he was also fulfilling Melvina's request. Besides, Ran looked like he'd just been shot by cupid's arrow. His smooth, lucid demeanor had evaporated the moment Bonnie arrived. Who would have thought Ran had a thing for shy librarians?

Raphe subtly stepped on Ran's foot, and his brother cleared his throat, stepping up to the plate. "If you'd be okay with my playin' in the band half the night, I'd be honored if you would accompany me. I can take a few breaks, while my bandmate Lenard covers for me."

"Yes," Bonnie blurted, her eyes widening.

"All right then." Ran grinned, his eyes gleaming. "I'll pick you up at seven." Turning to Raphe he squeezed his shoulder. "I got band practice in thirty minutes. Can you still give me that ride?"

Raphe didn't want to tear himself away from this moment. The ladies seemed happy and he would love to see Nina after a few more shots of tequila. Raphe had drunk more than he'd planned and Ran had only had the one shot and his beer, so Raphe tossed him the keys. "Sure, I'll give you the lift, but you'll have to drive my truck. You can drop me off at my apartment and come back to get me after practice." He looked at Nina with regret. "I'd stay to entertain you ladies with stories of Ran—like one

Christmas when we were kids, Mom and Dad gave Ran his first guitar and the cat got his tail stuck in it and ran up the Christmas tree—but I need to go take Lulu for a walk."

"That's right. You're taking care of Melvina's dog while she's on her honeymoon," Bonnie said.

Ran laughed, clapping him on the shoulder. "Oh, he's done that and so much more."

Raphe shook his head as Bonnie told everyone about the Lulu puddle in the library, then Ran filled them in on the hookup with Jake in the chief's office, followed by the most recent event of the café dash to the christening of Mona's leather seats in her luxurious new car. Nina laughed so hard she covered her mouth and bent over as Bonnie clucked and shook her head at him. "Melvina is gonna kill you, Raphe," Bonnie giggled and gave him a playful swat on the arm. "You're a terrible dog sitter."

Nina howled with laughter. Raphe didn't think it was all that funny, but the three enjoyed a good guffaw at his expense. Even the bartender chuckled.

"All right, all right. I'm glad I could amuse everyone." He held up his hands, trying to suppress his own laughter. "Hey, I tried to do right by her, but the bottom line is, Lulu's a hussy."

Chapter 12

Raphe's body was on high alert.

He'd heard the tone drop and knew it was a structural fire. He didn't waste time grabbing his PIG and throwing on his gear. The engineer was in the driver's seat and waiting. Within minutes of the alert they pulled away from the curb. The details of the fire weren't disclosed, so they went on a code three with lights on and sirens blaring. He tried to push back the panic that threatened to surface.

You don't even know what building's on fire yet. Calm down and breathe. Hold it together. Your crew has your back and you have theirs.

He was working with the B team tonight, since he'd switched shifts with another guy who was single and not planning to go to the ball. There were several guys from the A and C teams on duty, since several firefighters had changed shifts to make their schedules work for the gala.

"Captain, the chief's just up ahead. What's the situation?" Matt, the engineer, asked.

Raphe grabbed the radio and called out to Manny, "Is the structure fully or partially involved, Chief?"

"Ah, Captain, it's in the barn and we don't know yet. Tell the guys to pull yellow and meet me around back."

The smoke could be seen billowing up over the small farmhouse and a cow ran kicking and bucking across the gravel driveway as Matt screeched to a halt. Raphe gave the order to remove the crosslays from the quint, and the tailboard crew hooked them up to the pump panel. Raphe's team knew what they were doing and worked like a well-oiled machine. They pulled the yellow crosslays across the field toward the barn and Raphe ran ahead to check the structure for any people or animals that might be inside. When he saw the blaze, anxiety crawled up his spine from the pit of his stomach and flooded his mind, but he didn't allow himself to hesitate. Shaking his head to clear it, he was determined to detach himself from the images of the crossbeam pinning him to the floor in the Houston high-rise.

The smoke was now visible from the roof of the barn. The door gaped open and gray smoke billowed out. He moved in cautiously with his PIG ax and unlatched the horse stalls. Water dripped and hissed as it cascaded from the ceiling, sending new columns of steam and smoke billowing toward the rafters. Raphe found a momma duck huddled in a corner of the barn that was farthest from the door. He grabbed a pail off a hook and started toward the duck. Sure enough, she had ducklings. As the mother started to squawk and waddle toward the fire, Raphe intercepted, scrambling to scoop up the ducklings in the bucket. It may have not been the best way to round them up, but it was the best he could think of under the circumstances. The horses were out, and it looked like the rest of the barn was empty. His team called for him and he motioned for them to get out. The barn was coming down and they all needed to evacuate before the structure crumbled.

Raphe handed the pail of baby ducks to one of his crew as the group of firefighters retreated. He meandered into the smoke with his self-contained breathing container and PIG ax. Using his headlamp, he searched the low areas of the barn and found the white duck smudged with soot, taking cover in a stall. She was okay and if he hurried, they'd both make it out.

Several agonizing minutes later, Raphe emerged from the barn, with the duck tucked under his arm like a football. A cheer went up from the guys, who were still holding the crosslays as they tried to douse the remaining embers of the fire. A flash from a camera went off, and Raphe noticed the reporters who'd arrived on the scene.

Manny walked over, passing the duck to the farmer's wife, who was being comforted by several women. Raphe recognized the gals from the Magnolia Blossoms Ladies League. They must be neighbors to have heard and gotten there so quickly.

Manny shook Raphe's hand. "Good work, Captain. Damn stupid, but good save all the same. I'd say you'll be a local hero by this time tomorrow."

Nina worked the early shift at the café so that she'd have plenty of time to make herself look pretty for the ball that night. She felt a little like

Cinderella as she wiped the counter, swept her section and rolled silverware. She was bone tired, but the tips were generous, and she felt satisfied with her work. She'd found a groove and actually enjoyed talking with the patrons. She had to admit that most of the folks in Magnolia were pretty nice. There would always be some oddball lunatic that wasn't satisfied, but that was true with any job. Nina knew she couldn't be a waitress forever, but for right now it felt satisfying to do a job that didn't require her emotions to get too involved. Technically, she wasn't supposed to be emotionally involved as a social worker, but who could go home and forget seeing a child who'd suffered at the hand of a parent? There were many children she counseled who'd been neglected or abused. On the heels of losing all her possessions in the fire six months prior, she admitted she wasn't strong enough to make that separation right now. Working at the diner enabled her to make a living while protecting her heart, and she desperately needed this time to rehabilitate her sanity.

Bonnie breezed into the café and rushed to the counter as Nina counted her checks and wrapped a rubber band around them. All she needed to do was punch the time clock and she was free.

"Did you hear about Raphe saving that momma duck and all her babies?"

"It was in the paper this morning, and you forget, this diner is news central." Nina smiled. She loved the photo of Raphe holding a duck. It was sweet and showed another side of the brawny, super-hot fireman.

Bonnie wiggled her eyebrows. "Well, I thought it was downright sexy as hell. You should hear my Aunt Rosie go on and on about him. I don't want to think what she's doing right now with that new shower massager."

Nina blanched. "Bonnie!"

"Don't ask. With Rosie, it's better not to." Bonnie flopped down on the stool in front of her. "Oh, Nina, what am I going to do?"

"About what?"

"Tonight! I have nothing to wear. What will I say? What will we talk about? Ran's way too hot for me."

Nina patted Bonnie's hand and turned over a coffee cup. Lifting the pot to pour, she stopped herself. "On second thought. You could use an herbal tea." Returning to the drink area, she filled the cup with hot water and a tea bag, then returned, sliding it across the counter to her friend. Bonnie's hand shook as she reached for a packet of sugar, shaking most of it out onto the saucer, completely missing the cup. She stirred the tea bag until it was twirled tightly around the spoon.

Nina sighed. "Just relax. You are every bit as hot as Ran. And he's obviously into you, so you have nothing to worry about."

Bonnie's eyes searched hers. "Why do you say that? It was his brother that put him up to it. I mean, Melvina asked Raphe, so Raphe pawned me off on Ran and oh, Nina…" Bonnie wrung her hands and bounced a little on her stool. "I shoulda never said yes."

The chief and Mona walked into the café hand and hand. They approached the counter where they usually sat and shared afternoon coffee.

Bonnie looked about to cry. "I have nothing to wear. I don't know why I said yes. All I own are library clothes, workout clothes and stay at home with Maxine clothes."

"Did I hear someone in need of clothes?" Mona's eyes sparkled as her skinny lips pressed into a broad smile.

The chief looked up at the diner's vintage teal blue ceiling tiles. "Oh lord, here we go. Maria, you better make our coffees to go."

Bonnie and Nina sat inside Mona's closet on a pink, leopard-print, crushed-velvet sofa. Nina looked at Bonnie, who was looking up at the gorgeous chandelier hanging from the ceiling.

Nina sighed. "Do you think this is what heaven is like?"

Bonnie made an um-hm sound. "If you add a wall of books and a mini bar, I think it is."

Mona smiled. "I had this house built just for me. This closet is as big as the master bedroom. I don't have a wall of books, but I do have a mini bar." She leaned down, pulling open one of the many paneled drawers. It was a minifridge. "Diet coke and rum is all I stock up here. Is that okay?" Both Nina and Bonnie nodded dumbstruck.

"Cuba Libre is just the ticket my nerves need. This closet is a dream, Mona. You are a genius!" Bonnie exclaimed. "And all these ballgowns," she gasped.

"Being rich has its perks." Mona produced two glasses filled to the rim with ice and rum. She then handed each of them a can of Diet Coke. Nina noticed that Mona didn't add any soda to her glass. "I'm also the president of the Magnolia Blossoms. I hope you two will think about joining. We do all kinds of fun things to raise money for the community. There's a Hot

Buns calendar every year and the firemen make it so—" Mona bit her lip and swiveled her hips. "Hot! We do a policeman's carwash twice a year, but it's not as much fun in winter. They won't even take their shirts off if it's cold." Mona huffed. "Of course, the Fall Carnival is entertaining and that is something you won't want to miss! We have a pie throwing contest and Jell-O wrestling." Mona purred.

Nina raised her eyebrows. She wondered if the Jell-O competition was a fireman, a policeman, or a Blossom event. She didn't ask. Mona threw a few more gowns over a white leather high-back chair before exclaiming, "This one's all you, honey." She held it out to Bonnie.

The white sequined ball gown was simply cut but dramatic all the same. The long slit up one side would show off Bonnie's legs and the spaghetti straps were barely there. The only problem was that Mona was a few inches taller than Bonnie.

"What size is it?" Bonnie sat with her hands in her lap, looking afraid to touch it.

"Don't worry about a thing. Just call Ran and tell him to pick you up here. I've got makeup and lots of doodads to doll you up. We'll get Lupita to hem the gown real fast, and I promise you a make-over that will rival that Ambush Makeover TV show." Mona stood, holding the white sequined dress in front of the full length, concave wall of mirrors. She had a whimsical glow about her. "Manuel Rodriguez took me to the Dance for Diamonds silent auction dinner in this dress." She turned to Bonnie. "I hope you have as much fun in it as I did—or out of it." Mona winked.

They all laughed, Nina thinking about her friend Johana and the Lucky Peacock—she refused to call it Cleo. Derek was gone and she was no longer in denial. Nina's eyes were wide open, and she was ready for an evening of adult fun.

They had a second drink in Mona's luxury closet and Nina told them the story of her sitting in the library's men's room and running into Raphe. Peals of laughter filled the elaborate dressing room. Lupita entered and Bonnie stripped down to put on the gown. Nina and Mona stopped laughing.

"Wow, Bonnie. Why are you hiding that?" Nina gasped.

Bonnie frowned. "Hiding what?" She looked down at her bra and panties. The lacy pink bra didn't match the black cotton thong, but with her body, it didn't matter.

"Your body is amazing!" Mona hooted. "Damn, Madame Librarian. Get the whip and pleather panty set. Your gonna shock the hell out of Ran Nash."

Bonnie blushed. "Oh please. I'm not the leather panty type, and my body is average." Nina and Mona's faces were blank with shock as they looked at Bonnie's reflection in the mirror. Bonnie rambled on. "I like to work out every night, so what? It helps with—frustration."

Mona clicked her tongue. "Honey, if I had a body like that, I'd get laid every night—well, I do get laid every night, but you know what I mean. To think, all that bod is wasted behind those awful spectacles and those horrible pant suits with turtlenecks, in summer, for heaven's sake!"

Bonnie was blushing from her ears to toes with all the appraisal.

Nina tried to change the subject. "I think I need to join your gym. Where do you work out?"

Bonnie smiled. "You won't believe this, but there is only one gym in town. It's called Jim's Gym and it sidles up next to the Cowboy Baptist Church."

Nina smiled. "Somehow I'm not surprised."

Mona lifted her shoulders in a shrug. "Small towns have their pros and cons, but right now I think the Nash brothers are a definite pro."

They all smiled in mutual agreement. There was no question that Magnolia had some nice eye candy. Mona poured another round of rum, but Nina held up a hand. "I need to drive back and get ready. Maria steamed my dress and I need to do something with my hair." Nina motioned to her messy bun. "Will you be okay here?" She asked Bonnie.

Mona answered. "Is Santa well hung?"

That baffled Nina. She'd never thought about good old Saint Nick quite that way, but she supposed it to mean yes. Mona was more fun than an evening of Secret Santa and free margaritas. Nina looked forward to getting to know her more at the ball.

Chapter 13

Nina felt awkward being picked up at Jose and Maria's trailer. She wasn't one to put on airs, but Raphe's truck probably cost more than the trailer and the lot they lived on. How did she explain that her living arrangements were temporary and that she'd once had a very posh apartment in an elite high-rise in the city? It sounded like she didn't appreciate her cousin's hospitality, and she really did. It wasn't that she looked down on her cousin's place, she looked down on herself for caring what Raphe thought.

What does it matter? Why would you explain yourself to anyone? Money doesn't make people better. Jose and Maria are a beautiful family. I'm lucky to have them!

She misted perfume over her body and checked her reflection in the mirror one last time. Nina was satisfied with the exotic gown and her up-do. Maria helped her to pile beautiful curls on top of her head, leaving a long tendril cascading over one shoulder to show the length of her long, mahogany hair. Her lengthy bangs were swept to one side, and the shimmering gloss made her lips look fuller. She used a minimal amount of make-up, since she rarely wore any, but the small amount of eyeliner and shimmering shadow made her eyes shine. She looked and felt glamorous in the silky peacock-blue gown.

The doorbell rang and Nina grabbed her turquoise and silver beaded bag. The Cuban theme was chic. Maria had insisted on adding a single blue orchid to her hair. The woman was amazing and helpful. Nina loved her designs and encouraged her to get a cosmetology license to open up her own beauty salon. Maria would be fantastic at it, and there weren't any Latino shops in Magnolia yet.

Nina walked to the small living room where Raphe stood waiting, holding a blue orchid corsage. *How did he know?*

His jaw dropped a little, then he quickly recovered with a smooth southern grin. "Wow, you clean up nice."

Nina grinned back at him, lifting one bared shoulder. "I do what I can."

"Well you look gorgeous and I will be the envy of the ball tonight." His rich voice vibrated with sincerity. Maria and Jose looked on like proud parents. Maurice and his younger sister, Maurine, looked up from doing their homework. Both smiled and Maurice's voice carried with excitement. "Hello Mr. Nash!"

"Howdy, Maurice."

"You know my nephew?"

"Yeah, through Melvina. He and I both share a love of her cupcakes, and Maurice is one of the best firetruck washers around." He winked at Maurice.

"Oh yeah, the Firecrackers." Nina smiled lovingly at her nephew.

"You look really pretty Cousin Nina," Maurine said, her eyes wide.

"Thank you, Maurine," Nina hugged both kids. "I have your Mama to thank for that."

"Ready?" Raphe slid the wrist corsage over her hand and then held out his arm for her. Nina glanced back at Maria and mouthed, "Thank you," then blew them all a kiss.

Something was definitely wrong. Nina couldn't help noticing Bonnie wasn't herself as the night progressed. Bonnie looked like a Barbie doll in her skin-tight dress with pushed up cleavage on bodi-licious display. Her breasts crested the top of her bodice as if the girls were going to jump out of a cake. Her hair trailed down her naked back in loose curls, and baby's breath adorned the clips that swept her long tresses back from her face.

Ran was practically tripping over himself to accommodate his date, pulling out her chair, hanging up her wrap, fetching a drink as soon as her glass was half empty. That might have been the problem, but Nina had only counted three glasses of champagne and the flutes were small. Bonnie managed to samba, rumba, and get down with the best of them after her trip to the ladies' room with Mona, but later on shut later on she got sloppy. She kicked her shoes off on the dance floor as Ran took a break to dance with her. She shimmied her shoulders, almost giving the ball her Full-Monty rendition, but she caught the edge of her bodice just in time to shimmy it back into place.

Where did the shy librarian go?

Bonnie grabbed Ran in a full lip lock that made his eyes widen in surprise. He had to go back to the stage, but Raphe stepped in, giving her a turn around the dance floor. She pulled away, spinning like a top halfway across the ballroom before smashing into Mac Green and his wife, who were just out of couple's therapy, again. Bonnie held onto Mac for dear life so that she didn't fall into the nearby dessert tray being held by an awestruck waiter. It was touch and go for a moment. Bonnie tipped toward the waiter and Mac reeled her back in, then Bonnie found her footing and righted herself. Reaching out to apologize to the waiter and to the Greens, she swayed precariously before giving up the ghost and falling on top of Mac's wife, Katie.

Raphe pulled recovery duty, escorting Bonnie to the table. Bonnie's eyes looked glazed and she slumped a little in her chair as Ran played the second set of the evening. Raphe, Nina, and Bonnie sat at a table with the chief and Mona, plus two other firemen who had young wives. They were very pleasant to talk to during dinner, but now they were abnormally aloof. Bonnie lifted her champagne and drained it in one gulp. Nina wondered if she had a drinking problem that no one knew about. The change was perplexing.

Mona looked uncomfortable and was picking at the chief's sleeve. "Maybe we should call it a night. Bonnie said earlier she had a headache and Ran has to play in the band until midnight. She can catch a ride home with us."

The chief looked at Mona, concerned. "Anything you want, darlin'." It was obvious the chief was enjoying himself but would do anything for Mona and now that included taking Bonnie home.

Mona tilted her head and whispered something in the chief's ear. Nina couldn't hear. Raphe was recounting something about a Miss Kitty drill that was apparently hilarious, and all the chuckles drowned out the intimate conversation between Mona and Manny. The chief's eyes widened, and he suddenly scowled at Mona. It was the first time she had seen an ill moment between the happy couple.

"Mona, I have told you a thousand times to quit carrying around that Pez dispenser. It might have been funny the first few times, but you have no idea what you're giving people!"

"It was a mistake. I swear, she asked for a pain reliever and was clearly so nervous I thought she might pass out. I had no idea a little Xanax would turn her into a lush. Let's just hope it doesn't have the same effect it did on Melvina."

Manny frowned, "What effect is that?"

Mona winced. "Well, besides the choc-la-tastrophe, she threw up on Celia's shoes."

Manny tried to suppress an ill-sounding snort then chuckled to himself. "No, this is not funny, Mona. Get your wrap and I'll go tell Ran we're taking her home."

Did Mona just admit to giving Bonnie a roofie?

Nina excused herself from Raphe's side to visit the bathroom. She waved for Mona to join her. Bonnie waved desperately to join them both but needed help standing. Each of them held an arm to support her. The glittery platform heels wavered beneath the white sequined gown. When they entered the ladies' room, Nina took a look under the stalls to make sure they were alone.

"Mona, did you drug Bonnie?"

Mona's mouth resembled a goldfish, painted up in coral-gold sparkles to match her dress. "I did no such thing. She said she was nervous, and I didn't think she'd make it through the night, so I just gave her something to calm her nerves."

"That's not an excuse to load her up with Xanax!" Nina fussed as Bonnie entered a stall and began to heave.

"She said she wanted one. I just gave her what she asked for." Mona's eyes slid to the mirror. She opened up her sequined bag and started reapplying her lip liner.

The toilet flushed and a groan followed. "It's true. I asked for something for my headache."

Nina rolled her eyes. "Bonnie, Xanax isn't for a headache! And you shouldn't mix any drug with alcohol."

Bonnie came out of the stall with her lipstick smeared and her hair clip lurching to one side. "I know that—now." She staggered to the sink to wash her mouth out with the mouthwash from the dispenser on the counter.

Mona looked crestfallen. Her own chartreuse feathered clip drooped, and her bottom lip quavered. "I'm so sorry, Bonnie. I was just trying to help. You were so panicked, and I didn't want you to miss tonight. Now you're gonna miss the grand finale."

"What's the grand finale?" Nina and Bonnie chirped in unison.

"Well the award ceremony for one, but that's boring. I'm talking about the hot make-out session you were due to have with Ran when he took you home, but I think you better come home with me instead."

Bonnie took another swish of the mouthwash and spit it out. "I don't think that was gonna happen between Ran and me. Besides, I stepped all over his feet during that last number. He hasn't been back to ask me for a dance since. I'm glad you and the chief offered to take me home. I think I'm ready."

Nina was sad for both of her friends. Mona hadn't meant to ruin things. Nina had seen Bonnie go into catatonic mode as soon as a good-looking man entered a room. Maybe Bonnie was right. Ran might be too much for her to handle. What a shame, because Bonnie was a great person and was a lot of fun when she could be normal. Her contact lenses made her look like a super model in Mona's beautiful dress. Nina hardly recognized her as the funny, shy librarian. Ran must have been gobsmacked when he first laid eyes on her. And clearly, Bonnie had fallen catatonic until Mona propped her up on a cloud of Xanax. She looped her arm through Bonnie's to help steady her.

Mona fluttered her false lashes in the mirror and reached in the bodice of her dress to adjust her cleavage to its maximum potential before grasping Bonnie's other arm.

As they made their way from the ladies' room to the table, Nina stopped and turned to Mona.

"You go on and tell Manny to fetch the limo. I'll go ahead and take Bonnie out for fresh air while we wait."

Raphe had never seen a more gorgeous woman than Nina in her teal-blue dress. He was speechless when she sashayed into the living room of Maria and Jose's trailer. Having eyes only for her that evening, Raphe hadn't paid much attention to Ran and his date throughout dinner. Bonnie looked spectacular, as he presumed she would, without her serious librarian glasses. It was entertaining watching his younger brother trip over himself trying to impress the petite blonde, but Raphe had plans to please a certain woman as well. He couldn't wait to take Nina out on the dance floor again and have her all to himself.

He'd dutifully asked Bonnie to dance during Ran's first set, but the meek librarian barely uttered a word. It was like her battery was dead. He'd seen flashes of her keen wit and sharp sense of humor, but now she was like a cold fish. It was awkward, to say the least, and it seemed to put Nina on edge. By the second part of the evening, when Bonnie switched gears and started to rumba with other guests' dates, Raphe started taking inventory. Escorting Bonnie back to the table after the dancing disaster, he discreetly excused himself to check on the Greens. He wanted to express his apologies and blame it on his own clumsiness, but Katie was giving Mac a dressing down over holding Bonnie up by her breasts. Raphe wanted to save Mac, since he had actually caught her under her arms, but the Greens had been in and out of couples therapy for three years now. He wasn't about to get in the middle of things and make it worse.

Sliding past the Greens's table, he stuffed a big tip in the waiter's jacket—the one who'd been the victim of Bonnie's fall. Raphe ordered another round to be brought to his table, replacing Bonnie's champagne with a hot tea. He thought it pertinent to sober her up. She must be susceptible to alcohol, have an allergy, or something.

It looked like all bets were off for anyone getting lucky tonight. Ran would never take advantage of a woman under the influence and the mood was killed even before Nina escorted Bonnie outside. Mona left with the chief and the other two couples seemed to disappear, leaving him sitting alone. He bet he made quite a picture. Black tux, white tablecloth and no date—no anyone! It was like senior prom all over again, except Nina wasn't the head cheerleader who got upset he was going to a different college, and he wasn't the quarterback anymore. *I thought things were going great until things started going south. Was I that far off, gauging Nina's interest?*

In the car, on their way to the ball, she'd given him the look that said, I like you and I want to have fun tonight, maybe more. Had he misread the look?

"Hey handsome, you wanna dance?"

Raphe looked up, surprised by Nina's pretty smile and eyes glimmering with interest. She was giving him that look again. The one that said, if you play your cards right, you might just get lucky.

Despite the fact that she adored both Bonnie and their new friend Mona, Nina was glad to be alone with Raphe. She'd helped Bonnie get into the limo Manny rented for the evening. He'd told everyone at their table that

Mona looked too lovely to be crawling in and out of his truck in an evening gown. It was perfect for Bonnie to roll into and stretch out on the long leather seats. Nina wasn't too worried about her friend. Mona and Manny would take care of her and see to her needs. Nina glanced at her reflection in the large entryway mirrors as she'd headed back to the ballroom and her very hot date.

Nina didn't look any worse for wear by helping Bonnie. The Lucky Peacock fluttered and sparkled beneath the chandeliers. It made her feel sexy and elegant. The champagne had taken effect and she felt confident when she found Raphe alone at the table. He was tall, fit, and devastatingly gorgeous, just like she imagined he would be in a tux.

He looked awestruck when she asked him to dance. Maybe he'd just been lost in his own thoughts, but the slow grin he gave her and the heat that flashed in his amber-colored eyes made her keenly aware of his interest. Always the gentleman, he held her at a respectable distance. Damn, the man knew how to dance. The first number was a waltz and then something more fun and free style played. She'd thought the Latin base might be harder for some men who didn't know how to move their hips. Raphe had it all down pat.

"Did you take dance lessons?"

Raphe smiled. "My momma made sure we were all educated in the arts. She hired a private teacher for my older brother, but by the time it was my turn, dad had caught on to the amorous relationship between Leena and my brother, Riley." His eyes glittered with laughter as he spun her out and rolled her back into his frame. He was better than good. He was fabulous.

"The lessons with benefits didn't get passed down to you?" She smiled coquettishly as she stepped away then sashayed back.

"No. Besides our parents' concern for our delicate sensibilities, Riley, Ran and I don't share." He twirled her in his arms, and they sambaed slowly to the Latin rhythm. "Ran and I took lessons at a studio after school two days a week for all of our junior high and high school years."

She tilted her head back, laughing. "I bet you love Riley for that."

"Actually, it worked out great." He smiled. "It really helped me with my balance and moves on the football field and it helped Ran develop an appreciation for all kinds of music."

His warm hands radiated around her waist as he lifted her up and slid her down his sculpted body. He acted like she weighed no more than a feather. He was hard everywhere. Nina gulped. She was every bit as entranced with him as he seemed to be with her. She locked eyes with him as she slid into place. Their bodies fit together perfectly, and he shifted her side to side with flare. "Did you prefer the dancing to the football?" she whispered.

Raphe's voice was raspy, "I don't know, what do you think?"

She raised up slightly and brushed her hand over his thick brown hair. Putting her lips to his ear, Nina told him exactly what she thought.

Chapter 14

Raphe tried not to speed as he drove to his apartment. He needed to slow down. From the moment Nina had wrapped her arms around him for a slow dance, to the moment she pressed her sweet body against his and whispered in his ear, he'd been on fire with need. Nina's sexy voice and warm breath as her lips brushed his ear was almost his undoing. All the blood seemed to be rushing from his brain to his lower regions, making him lightheaded. He was starting to think he might need to excuse himself for a cold shower first.

Raphe shifted in his seat, trying to will himself to act like an experienced adult instead of a horny teenager. All that back and forth about Leena, the dance instructor, and Riley's affair had set the stage for more than a course in dance instruction. Nina reminded him of Leena. Both were beautiful, curvaceous and sexy as hell. Nina had something else. She reminded him of the picture that comes in the frame when you buy it new from the store. Aesthetically she was perfect and a natural beauty, but there was an undercurrent of warm electricity that told him she was capable of so much more.

As he opened the apartment door, Lulu shot off the couch baying for the entire complex to hear. He guessed that was his cold shower. Nina screeched, then giggled. "Oh hell, Raphe. That scared me half to death. I forgot Bonnie said you had a dog."

"Lulu belongs to my brother and sister-in-law, Melvina." He sighed as he reached down to pet Lulu and make introductions. Nina bent down too, petting Lulu's soft ears.

"She's beautiful, and I bet she's gotta go out." Nina looked at him longingly. He'd been hoping to crash into his apartment and kiss her senseless. He was on fire with the need to taste her full lips and hold her glorious body against his. He stared at her, mesmerized by her luscious beauty. A look of desire radiated from her velvety dark eyes. She leaned slowly toward him and he put his arm out to wrap it around her waist, pulling her into him as she raised up. She clung to his shoulders, as he grasped her waist. His lips slid over hers and she parted them as he moved his tongue against hers to explore. She tasted like golden champagne and sweet chocolate with a hint of coffee. He remembered the sweet tiramisu they'd both eaten after dinner. Nina had sipped tea. She was the best dessert he'd ever tasted and like a sugar addict, he craved more.

Lulu placed a paw on each of his dress shoes, surely scratching up their shine. Raphe groaned, looking down at Lulu's doleful eyes. "I know, Lulu. I'm on it." Giving Nina his most promising look, he rasped, "I'll be back."

As he walked Lulu down the stairs and out to the complex dog area, Raphe took in deep gulps of air. *What just happened back there?* He didn't pretend that there hadn't been a long line of love 'em and leave 'em gals from high school until now, but he'd never shared a kiss that made him physically weak in the knees. His legs felt like water, and he tried to stretch them out as he walked. Lulu loped beside him, staring up at him every now and then. The intuitive dog seemed to ask the same question he was asking himself? *What in the hell are you going to do about Nina?*

When women tried to get close, Raphe had a notorious habit of running. The ones who'd broken it off with him were his favorites. They were in it for the short-term and didn't have their hearts invested. He'd never dated the girl-next-door because those kinds of gals spelled trouble. Nina wasn't the girl next door, but she might be the woman who had the key to his heart. He'd never felt this kind of instant attraction and it wasn't just physical. It was the first time in his life he felt he had everything riding on this one moment, and if he messed it up, he wouldn't get another chance.

Lulu barked. Staring up at him, the basset reminded him he needed to scoop the poop and put it in the waste can by the parking area. "That'll sober a man up." He grabbed the bag clip and tore a small garbage bag from the holder. He cleaned up the mess and told her she was a good girl. As he dropped the stinky package into the can, he looked at Lulu with her tail wagging and tongue lolling out. "Is that what it's like with you and Humphrey?"

Lulu barked twice.

"Hm, well let's just hope he doesn't find out about Jake."

From nerves to pleasure and back to nerves in a matter of seconds. On the ride to Raphe's place, Nina had almost chickened out. What was she doing? This man wasn't the dating type. He had playboy written all over him and she wasn't the one-night-stand type. She'd only had a few boyfriends in her life including Derek, but all of them had been long term and Derek had been the man she was supposed to marry—or maybe not, since she broke it off just before—No! She pushed her torn and guilt-ridden thoughts away. The point was, she didn't know how to do casual.

As much as she wanted her hands to roam all over Raphe's body and to let him pleasure her in any and all ways possible, she wasn't sure she could do it and just go back to her cousin's home like nothing had ever happened. As much as she hated to admit it, her heart had planted a seed from the night she'd seen him at Bubbles, and he'd asked her to the ball, maybe even before then. He'd caught her eye and her temper at the diner. She remembered the red-hot jealousy she'd felt when that woman had given Raphe her phone number in Bubbles. Even Bonnie had seen how it affected Nina's mood.

Nina lingered over how he'd taken her into his arms and kissed her. His lips were soft and yet demanding as his teeth nipped at her bottom lip. She could feel the slight scrape of his stubble as he brushed his cheek against hers with a groan before Lulu insisted on her walk.

The basset hound was adorable. Nina had really wanted a dog, but Derek hadn't wanted the responsibility. Since the high-rise condo burned up in the fire, she was relieved she didn't have a dog. It was enough grief and guilt losing Derek that way. He wasn't who she wanted to spend the rest of her life with and she realized that now. It didn't keep her from making comparisons between Derek's ability to be a good husband and father and Raphe's potential. *Would he even consider a relationship?* He seemed pretty popular with the women at the diner and the bar. *Would he want children?* Not every man felt the need to procreate. *If I sleep with him now, will I ruin the chance at something more?* Derek hadn't been ready to settle down, though he had knelt before her and promised the world. Nina still felt guilty for what happened, though none of it was really her fault. She desired Raphe. Had enough time passed to heal old wounds?

Nina sighed and flopped down on Raphe's leather couch. The champagne and the excitement of the evening had caught up with her. Not to mention her tumultuous thoughts about Derek and Raphe. She tucked her feet beneath her and curled into the afghan throw as she waited for Raphe to return with Lulu. She thought of his amber eyes and his soft lips as he brushed them against hers. Closing her eyes, she touched her own lips and smiled.

Chapter 15

Sunlight streamed into the room, flooding the bed and waking her. She stirred, stretching her sore limbs. Nina felt like she'd spent two hours on the treadmill. Memories flooded her mind of Raphe dipping, twirling and swaying her to all the Latin music. She sighed as she thought about the fun they'd had at the ball. Raphe was gorgeous in his tux, and Nina loved the way he felt pressed against her. Realization flooded her senses. She was alone, not in her own bed, still wearing the Lucky Peacock that obviously wasn't so lucky, and a basset hound was belly-up beside her, snoring like an old man.

"Lulu, honey, where's your handsome dog sitter?"

As if hearing her inquiry, Raphe appeared, standing in the doorway. He held two steaming cups of coffee and a smile that made her panties melt. *Oh God! I must look like I've been run over by the Cuban dance team.* Nina ran a hand through her hair. Pins dangled every which way, but the up doo was still half up. A long tendril fell over one eye as she sat up. Her dress had shifted in the night and one breast was fully exposed. Nina wiggled to try to fix it, but she was wrapped in it like a mermaid in a fishing net. Raphe moved to the bed, setting the coffees down and extending a hand to help her up.

"How in the world did I sleep in this thing?" She tugged at the gown in frustration as she covered her nipple with her other hand.

"I did try to wake you when I came back with Lulu, but you were so sound asleep that I decided to let you rest. I didn't think it very gentlemanly to undress you, so I'm sorry about the—um, dress." He didn't try to look away from her cleavage as she adjusted her bodice. Something tantalizing lingered in his gaze and she felt sparks of energy ignite in the pit of her stomach.

Raphe cleared his throat as if bringing himself back to the present. "Sorry, all I have in the apartment is coffee and bagels from the bakery. I don't keep tea, but I'll go out and grab something else if you want it. I left a new toothbrush and a few toiletries in the bathroom for your convenience and I've got a t-shirt if you want something else to wear." His smile was lopsided as his head tilted to the side. He picked up a tendril of her hair that was still trapped in a bobby pin. "I doubt my warmup pants would fit you, but you're welcome to peruse my closet."

Nina thought he looked even sexier now in the morning light. He'd showered and shaved and smelled of fresh soap and minty toothpaste. It made her self-conscious of her own bedraggled state. His eyes twinkled with amusement as he moved toward her, like he was about to kiss her. She smiled at him and held up one finger.

"Give me ten minutes and hold that thought."

Raphe thought he might spontaneously combust from sexual frustration when he found Nina asleep on his couch. Lulu had just loped over and flopped down next to her, giving him the look that said, "Buddy, your night is over. Hang it up. You're done." Raphe had shaken Nina gently, asking her if she'd like a t-shirt or would she like him to drive her home. He hadn't wanted her to answer, so he didn't try too hard to wake her. Instead, he picked her up and moved her to his bed. It was a one-room apartment, and he wasn't sleeping on the couch. Ever the gentleman, he took off her shoes but left her dress on. He'd hoped she would wake up and take it off or ask him to, but his hopes were dashed as she'd delved deeper into the mound of pillows. She'd started a symphony of soft snores that were shortly joined by Lulu at the foot of the bed.

He smiled at the memory of Nina sleeping snuggled at his side. She'd wrapped her arm around him, delving her face into his chest. He wondered if she was used to sleeping with someone. He'd never asked if she had a boyfriend, but he assumed she would tell him if she did.

He took Lulu out for a walk, giving Nina some privacy. Raphe thought about Nina in his shower, using his towels and maybe looking through his medicine cabinet for some aspirin. He should have thought to leave some out. When he returned with Lulu, he filled her bowl with kibble and perused his almost empty fridge. He'd done this once before this morning and knew the contents already. Beer, water, a bag of bagels and a carton of half and half.

"Anything good?" Nina peered over the counter that separated the kitchen from the rest of the apartment. Raphe turned, taking in his lovely guest wrapped in a towel.

"I guess the t-shirt didn't fit?"

Nina gave him a flirtatious grin. "Would you rather I was wearing it?"

Raphe let go of the refrigerator door. "No ma'am. I am all about one-hundred percent Egyptian cotton." Coming around the bar, he closed the distance between them, taking her into his arms. The blinds were open, and light streamed in through the many windows of his corner apartment. He'd picked this unit for all of the wonderful light. He loved looking at Nina and was happy his first time exploring her would be so illuminated. There was something more erotic about sex in bright light.

His heart raced as he leaned forward, brushing his lips over hers. She returned his ardent attentions with equal passion. As his hands found their way to the back of her neck, he wound his fingers in her hair, pulling her head back to expose her soft flesh to his lips. Nipping softly at her ear, he rained kisses down her long neck to the base of her throat. The towel unwound, sliding free to the floor. Raphe was momentarily paralyzed by her beauty. As much as he loved the light filtering through the windows highlighting the smooth curves of her body, he wanted nothing more than to lay her in his bed and slowly explore every inch of her being. Uttering a low growl, he swung her up in his arms, curling her stomach to his face and kissing her delectable navel as he started toward his bedroom.

Nina decided it was time. Her body craved what Raphe was offering and who cared if it wasn't with a promise of forever. She was thankful for the toothbrush and toiletries. The champagne had left her with a bad case of morning breath and after she shed the not-so-Lucky Peacock, a shower was in order. Standing beneath the hot spray of water, she lavishly ran the bar of creamy soap over every surface of her body. After wrestling with her churning thoughts the night before, she decided she didn't want to think too hard about anything right now. She wasn't sure she was staying in Magnolia anyway. What she did know was that Raphe lit her on fire with a sexual need she'd never experienced before. And with such a powerful need swirling insider her, she had to find out if it was worth the risk of heartbreak. *What if it is? Then what?*

She'd thought she was in love with Derek, but throughout their three-year relationship, Derek had never made her feel the way Raphe did. If she were being completely honest with herself, she'd never experienced this burning sense of desire that consumed her. Raphe had thought of everything except underwear, but since she had made her decision, no big girl panties were needed.

Raphe set her on the bed and dropped beside her. She shifted to her side and twined her arms around his neck, pressing her body against his. He groaned in reply, roving his hands over every inch of her skin, making her gasp with pleasure. They groped each other with animal need, latching onto each other. Nina grasped his thick head of hair. The silky mocha strands slipped through her fingers as she moaned beneath him. He felt like heaven pressed against the length of her naked body, except that he was still dressed.

"Take it off," Nina gasped, tearing at his t-shirt as he tried to guide it over his head. He was gorgeous, just like she knew he'd be. Perfectly sculpted pecs and a taut stomach, he was every woman's fantasy. She unfastened his jeans, pushing them down as he resumed kissing her. "I—I can't wait. Take them off."

Raphe chuckled but pulled away momentarily to shed the denim that separated them. Flesh to flesh, his shaft radiated heat against her core. She wrapped a leg around one of his, pulling him closer to her need. He groaned and his member flexed with pleasure. He pulled back so his lips could roam lower. He laved at her breasts, suckling, nipping and teasing until she bucked beneath him. The invitation to enter her was met by his hands first as he rubbed his fingers over her sex, entering her wet heat after just a few short strokes. Her breath caught when she felt his hot breath between her legs. This was really happening.

She was in bed with the man of all her fantasies and he was pushing every button she had. Arching at the touch of his mouth between her legs, she whimpered. Not sure she could handle the pulsating swirl of his tongue and the suction of his lips to her flaming bud, she tightened her thighs around his head. "Stop, I'm going to...." She withered and trembled from the sheer sexiness of his devilish grin, as he looked up from between her legs.

"No way and good," he responded breathlessly.

Nina moaned, throwing her head back and letting out a guttural cry of satisfaction as her entire being tipped over the edge, soaring to the height of surreal pleasure. The throb between her legs pulsated in the aftermath and she jerked slightly as his lips pressed a soft kiss to her happy button.

Raphe chuckled as she let out a gasp and then a squeal of pleasure. "Oh, my God, I think I just died and went to heaven."

Raphe raised up and pushed himself on top of her once more. "Honey, you haven't even seen the gates." Taking her mouth in a long, deep, breathless kiss, he settled himself almost to her entrance. Breaking the kiss, he leaned far right to the nightstand and cursed softly. "Damn."

Nina was too limp to protest. She waited as he rolled to his side and off the bed. "I'll be right back."

Raphe cursed again as he held a small, tattered box of condoms.

He returned to the bedroom and sighed as he looked at Nina's naked form sprawled on his bed, flushed by the pleasure of her orgasm. Her glittering eyes spoke volumes of her anticipation.

Aware of his naked hardness, Raphe held the box up with dismay. "Lulu must hold a grudge."

Nina laughed. "Or she's the jealous type."

Raphe's eyebrows arched, "Who wouldn't be envious of you? You're gorgeous." He lay down next to Nina pulling her into his arms. Kissing her lightly, he tried to control his need. He wasn't stupid. As much as his body said go, his brain said, "hold it right there, fella. Rome can be built another day."

Nina rolled on top of him, seemingly unaffected by their sudden plight. She moved down his torso, giving him the same slow attention, he'd given her. This isn't what he wanted—well, actually he did want this, but he also wanted to be deep inside her, hearing her breathlessly calling out his name. She was soft, curvaceous, and he loved her thick mahogany hair and gorgeous brown eyes. He'd never been with a woman so lusciously beautiful and real. Most of the ladies he'd been with were beautiful but missing that kind of emotional connection he also craved. Nina was smart, funny, and caring and all wrapped up in a super sexy body. He'd never shared this kind of passion or wanted to be with someone so badly.

Fear prickled at the back of his neck, distracting him for a moment. When the heat of Nina's mouth covered the tip of his erection, he sucked in his breath and tightened his grip on her hair. She responded by taking him deep into her mouth where he could feel the pressure of her throat. She

wound her tongue around his shaft and lifted it back up to the tip repeat-
edly until he could take no more. He lifted her head and she grasped him
in her palm, pushing him at a tempo that had him arching underneath her
as she straddled his legs. He came hard and his member pulsed with the
lingering sensation of her stroking him with her tongue. Nina leaned down,
kissing him with need. She slid her wetness over his hip as she held onto
his shoulders and nuzzled his neck. Her hair trailed across his face and he
drank in her scent.

"I want you so bad."

Her words were his undoing. Like a crack addict, he rolled her onto her
back and hovered above her. "Are we doing this?" he whispered, gazing into
her eyes. He knew there was more to this moment than just sex. He didn't
know if it was a lifetime more, but he knew from the small sip they'd shared
that he wanted her in his life, with her by his side for a long, long while.

Nina's eyes held concern, and she hesitated for a moment. She closed
her thick, dark lashes and opened them slowly. Her gaze mesmerized him,
took hold, and wouldn't let go.

"Yes." She wrapped her legs around his hips and guided him home.

Chapter 16

"Does your job ever give you nightmares?"

Raphe looked down at Nina, who was curled up against his chest. Her sultry eyes looked somewhere between sleep and another round. It was almost dinnertime and they'd completely skipped lunch, sharing only a bagel between interludes just to keep from passing out.

"Does yours?" he countered.

Nina's lips quirked up in a smile. "I asked you first."

Raphe took in a deep breath. Should he be honest? He hadn't told anyone about his fear after that night. "Sometimes. I lived in Houston up until about six months ago. There was a fire in a high-rise in the Galleria area. We couldn't get there in time and the entire upper three floors were engulfed in flames when we arrived. I was able to rescue a woman with her three kids and I went back for more, but a rafter gave way and I was pinned. My air was low, and I took in too much smoke. My men saved me, but we lost the guy who lived in thirty-thirteen. The ladders couldn't get that high and we had to go down. We couldn't save him."

Raphe took another deep breath and let it out slowly, trying to focus. He felt his temperature rise and his palms begin to sweat. "I know if my men had tried to go back, we would have lost someone, but I can't help thinking, what if I hadn't been injured? A man is dead because I didn't see that rafter coming down in time."

He paused again, shaking his head. He was reliving it as he held her in the crook of his arm. "I don't know if I can forgive myself," he whispered brokenly. He felt emotion pool in his eyes, but he wasn't a man to succumb to tears—not with Nina, hell, not even alone. His heart ached for any lives lost during any emergency, but this one was a stake in his heart that he would have to bear alone. He didn't even know why he was telling her this. He hadn't even told Ran or Riley.

Nina's face looked as ashen as he felt. "Six months ago…in Houston…T-thirty-thirteen?" She began to tremble, and tears streamed down her cheeks as she pulled away from him. Grabbing at the sheets, she stumbled to the bathroom.

He followed her, wondering at her reaction. Knocking softly on the door he called out to her, "Nina, are you okay? What's wrong? I'm sorry if I upset you. My job can be pretty gritty. I still feel this irrational guilt about that fire. My crew had to save me and then it was too late. It was too high up." He hated the way he sounded. Like he was making excuses for the loss of life. But her reaction flummoxed him. She knew he was a fireman, knew the risks he faced…He scrubbed his hands down his face. He'd made himself vulnerable and she jabbed him in the gut. Why was she so upset?

Nina emerged from the bathroom fully dressed in the blue gown with her diamond-studded bag in hand. He moved out of the way as she stalked to the door. He went after her, calling her name, reaching for her arm but she shook him off. She uttered no words, no explanation, just a guttural cry as she rushed out without a second glance.

Chapter 17

Rosie Bush put on a pot of tea while Nina sat biting her thumbnail waiting for Bonnie. Still in the Lucky Peacock, Nina crossed her legs and swung her foot back and forth. Rosie clattered around with the teacups and silverware, placing sugar and creamer on a big silver tray.

Rosie sighed loudly then hollered, "Bonnie! Get your bush out here before Nina faints on the floor from the gossip she's gonna tell us!"

Bonnie appeared at the doorway to the kitchen, holding onto the frame with one hand and her head with the other. "You mean, *you* are going to faint from nosiness." She looked at Nina, rolling her eyes. "We call her Nosey Rosie for a reason."

Nina let out a soft, nervous chuckle. Bonnie's humor turned to concern. She sat down across from Nina at the kitchen table. "Hey, what happened? I thought you must have gotten lucky with the Peacock last night."

Rosie snorted. "Is that what you kids are calling it these days? Back in my day we just called it like it was, C-O-C-K." She laughed at her own humor, but when Bonnie threw her a scowl, she zipped it. Rosie brought the tray to the table and poured them all tea, then uncapped a large unlabeled bottle of amber liquid. "Here, sweetie, have a little nip. Looks like you could use a little fire in your loins. Anyone who goes out with a hot fireman and doesn't get laid has bigger issues than I can solve."

Nina and Bonnie glared at the old woman in unison. Rosie splashed everyone's cup with the amber liquor and held up both hands. "All right, all right. I'll leave you ladies to it." Rosie scooted her walker to the next room and turned on the TV.

"So, what happened?"

Nina sniffed and took a sip of the hot tea, then blanched. "What the hell was that stuff, turpentine?"

Bonnie took a large gulp without flinching. "You get used to it after a while. It's Rosie's homemade moonshine."

"Why is it that color? I thought moonshine was clear." Nina gasped, trying to recover her voice. Her throat burned like fire.

Bonnie shrugged her shoulders. "Who knows? I gave up asking Aunt Rosie '*Why*' questions long ago." She winked. "I got too afraid of the answers."

Nina laughed at that. "I can believe it." Taking another sip, she sputtered and looked up at Bonnie, wide-eyed. After she calmed herself with the water, she thought to apologize for barging in unannounced. "I didn't have a ride and when things went south, I just had to get out of there."

Bonnie listened as Nina told her about the lackluster night, but incredible sex marathon day and then what Raphe had confided about the fire. She'd already told Bonnie about Derek and about her guilt for breaking off their engagement the day before he died. If she hadn't broken it off and gone to Johana's place would she have perished with Derek or would she had been able to save him? She'd torn herself inside out with all the what ifs. Sharing her pain with Bonnie had given her some relief. Bonnie didn't judge her—didn't know Nina's whole life and all the mistakes she'd made. There was something liberating about unveiling secrets to almost strangers.

Nina supposed it was the reason why she'd shown up on Bonnie's doorstep. The town wasn't that big. She could have walked to the café and borrowed Jose's car, but the idea of facing family right now was too overwhelming. She felt like a failure all over again. First the break-up and then the smothering love and attention from Derek's family and her inability to tell them the engagement was off before the disaster. Now she'd slept with the man who was responsible for Derek's death. *Oh, God what a mess.*

"He said thirty-thirteen?"

"The hell you say?" Rosie gasped from the doorway.

Bonnie pointed toward the TV room. "Aunt Rosie!"

"Are you kidding me? This is better than my damn soap opera."

Nina snorted with suppressed laughter. "Bonnie, let her stay. At least she makes me laugh—I need that. It sure feels better than crying."

Rosie fluttered back in and flopped down at the table, uncapping the moonshine and topping off their cups. "Oh honey, you're too young to cry over men. You are at a prime age and beautiful enough to have them all panting at your feet. That Mexican blood is cali-ent-tay," the old woman whooped.

Nina would've been offended if she hadn't been obsessing about the fire.

"Aunt Rosie! Nina's parents were from Colombia." Bonnie gave her aunt a stern look then apologized to Nina.

Nina shook her head with a deep sigh. "Don't worry about it. I'm used to the assumption."

"What's the big deal? Is she prejudiced against Mexicans?" Rosie waved them both off from answering. "Forget about all that." Her voice turned serious, and she grasped Nina's hands in hers. "Look honey, from what I hear, you are not responsible for any of this tragedy and neither is Raphe. It sounds like he was just trying to do the right thing and got stuck in the wrong place. He almost died trying to save your ex-fiancé's life." She paused and looked back at her niece with a sultry wink. "Ain't nothing sexier than that. Imagine that hot male body in that tight uniform, rushing into a burning building to save you."

Bonnie put a hand to her head like she was fighting off a migraine.

I bet she has a lot of headaches living with Rosie.

Bonnie chuckled. "Rosie, you should have been a romance writer with that over-sexed imagination of yours."

Nina smiled at her new BFF. "She's right. He does look amazing in his uniform and even better out of it." She didn't share blow by blow details of her romp in the sack with Raphe, but she gave enough description of her afternoon to delight Rosie's old ears. It must have been the moonshine that loosened her tongue.

Raphe slid into a booth at the diner, checking out the other tables around him. Ran had called and asked him to meet for a brother to brother talk. That had Raphe concerned.

Maria greeted him with a cup of coffee and a smile. He told her to hold off on his order as he waited for Ran. Relieved it wasn't Roberta waiting on him, he sank back into the tufted tangerine upholstery with a sigh. Roberta was always full of gossip and chatter, and right now, he wasn't in the mood. Moments later, Ran breezed into the diner and flopped down on the opposite side of the table. His eyes were still puffy from sleep or lack thereof.

"You just wake up?" Raphe turned Ran's empty cup upright as Maria approached. By the look of him, Ran could use the caffeine.

Ran shook his head. "It was late after we broke down all the equipment and put it into the truck. I drove home, but I couldn't sleep, so I took a drive."

Raphe was surprised. There wasn't much to do in Magnolia after ten o'clock, let alone two in the morning.

Ran looked sheepish, "I met some of the guys at a strip club in Houston. They'd invited me before I left the hotel, but I wasn't interested. After Bonnie left with Manny and Mona, I didn't know what to think. That's why I called you. I need to know what happened."

"I would rather hear about the strip joint." Raphe's grin faded at his brother's nervous tension. Ran gripped his coffee cup like it was a lifeline and his knee bobbed under the table, making the cutlery jiggle.

Raphe looked at him with mild annoyance. After a few moments he pointed at the cutlery. "You mind?"

Ran halted, leaning forward to whisper. "Thing is, I saw your ex."

Raphe's eyes widened, thinking about the model he'd dated on and off. "Sheila?"

Ran looked over his shoulder nervously. "No, Darcey!"

Raphe blanched, almost spilling coffee down his shirt. "What? Are you serious?"

Ran nodded. "I wasn't there to get dances or anything. I just couldn't sleep after Bonnie rushed off, so I went to hang out with my guys."

Raphe smiled knowingly. His brother looked guilty. "You got a lap-dance, didn't you?"

Ran put his hands up. "I didn't want one, but clearly if she's there, the girl needs money. What was I supposed to do?"

Raphe laughed heartily. "So now you've broken the cardinal rule, is that the reason you called the meeting?"

Ran was silent for a minute. He looked perturbed but mostly guilty. "I didn't sleep with my brother's ex-girlfriend, so I didn't break the rule." He looked over his shoulder again as Maria approached to take their order. Both of them ordered the brisket burger with fries. Maria left to put their order in, and they continued their conversation.

Ran leaned in and whispered. "Besides, who's breaking the rules? You promised Melvina you wouldn't take out anymore of her waitresses and you promised to keep Lulu safe while they were on their honeymoon."

Raphe blew out a sigh. "Technically, Nina is not one of Melvina's waitresses since she's only temping until Melvina and Riley return. Only Melvina can hire her, so she's just working for tips at the moment. And as far as Lulu is concerned, no one should ever trust me with any female's reproductive system." He tried not to think about the irresponsible sex he'd had with Nina only hours before. He'd never had unsafe sex. It had been drilled into Raphe and his siblings by their parents. They'd had a full quarter of sex-education classes in junior high and high school. What could he say? He'd been consumed with lust, and now that the fire had been harshly put out, he worried about the repercussions, especially since the beautiful woman he was senseless about had run out of his apartment like he'd kicked her dog or worse.

Ran scoffed, then looked at him curiously. "Did you get someone pregnant?"

Raphe threw up a hand, running it through his hair. "You're changing the subject. This was about you and Bonnie or you and Darcey. Which is it?"

"Oh, I think we know who's changing the subject here. Spill the beans."

Raphe shook his head, glancing around the diner. It was close to closing time, so it was mostly empty. "I had sex with Nina last—today. She passed out on me last night. Anyway, Lulu ate my box of condoms and I lost control. I couldn't wait to run out and buy more, heat of the moment and all. Then, since we'd already broken the seal, we let loose and went for a marathon day of it." Raphe ran a hand over his face, trying to wash away the emotion that surfaced. He felt another wave of heat burning in his loins. He squirmed in the booth, adjusting his jeans.

Ran smiled, "Damn, and I thought I was in for it."

Raphe tried not to smile but failed. The memories of his hot afternoon with Nina were too good to dismiss, even though what followed afterward had him tied up in knots. "Yeah, I guess comparatively, I stepped in it. So, what's eating you about last night? Do you want permission to date Darcey?"

Ran looked shocked. "No, I really like Bonnie, but she skated out of there without even saying good-bye. Mona waved at me as she left, but Bonnie never looked back when Nina escorted her out. What was I supposed to think?"

Raphe nodded. "I can clear that up. Mona offered Bonnie a little Xanax to take the edge off her nerves. Mixed with the champagne, she dove into Mac Green and his wife, who'll probably be back in couple's therapy for another few years. The chief and Mona decided it was best to take her back to her aunt's at that point."

Ran perked up, "So I wasn't the reason she found another ride home?"

Raphe nodded. "She was high as a kite."

Ran looked concerned. "She hasn't answered my texts, should I stop by her aunt's to check on her?"

The diner doorbell clanged, and Raphe's face lit up with a broad smile. "I think she's all right. Maybe you can ask her now."

Chapter 18

Nina knew it was a bad idea to walk to the diner, but none of them could drive from all that tea and moonshine on an empty stomach. She didn't count the few bites of one of Rosie's homemade brownies because it tasted a little like an ashtray. Soon after, they all got the munchies and a hankering for burgers and fries.

The diner was less than a mile from Rosie's and Bonnie assured Nina they could push Rosie in the wheelchair that the rehab place had set her up with. The first few blocks they made without a hitch, but when a coyote yowled from close by, they gunned it for the main road since it was better lit.

Unfortunately, a pick-up truck had made a quick turn and they scooted to the side of the road to let it pass. The high beams temporarily blinded them, and Nina made the mistake of letting go of Rosie's wheelchair. She heard a, "wha-wha-whoa-" from Rosie as the old woman's chair rattled off somewhere in the darkness. "Oh my God, Bonnie, we've lost Rosie!"

"What do you mean we? You were pushing her," Bonnie accused.

Nina's hands were shielding her eyes from the oncoming pickup, and she blinked, trying to look past the bright headlights, scanning the road for the wheelchair. She couldn't see anything. A horn blared and Nina yelped, making out the shadow of Rosie's chair in the center of the road. Nina broke into a run, grabbing hold of the back of the chair just in time to give Rosie a big shove. The truck lurched in the other direction, nearly hitting a row of mailboxes on the other side of the drive. Nina and Bonnie watched with wide eyes as the wheelchair went airborne with Rosie strapped in it. Bonnie gasped. "You pushed Aunt Rosie into the ditch!"

Bonnie and Nina slogged through the mud to get to Rosie's upended chair. To her credit, Rosie was howling with laughter.

"I told her to lay off the hooch." Bonnie poked and prodded Rosie's limbs in the dark, feeling around the chair to see if anything was broken. "Aunt Rosie, you okay?"

Rosie let out another hoot and then a loud toot.

"I think she might have soiled her pants," Nina waved a hand in front of her face.

Rosie went into another tirade of giggles. "Naw, it was just a brownie fart."

It took a few minutes to turn her right side up and fish her wheels out of the muck, but somehow, they managed to wiggle their way back to the road. The main street was well lit, and a sidewalk graced the thoroughfare. It was then that Nina noticed Rosie's mud-caked bunny slippers. She'd never changed from her pajamas. How'd they miss that?

"Bonnie, Rosie's still in her pajamas!"

Bonnie snorted with laughter. "Oh well, The Cupcake Diner and Dive has seen worse, and I sure as hell am not turning back."

Nina nodded. They'd call a taxi to take them home. She'd called Maria earlier from Raphe's telling her she was okay, so that she wouldn't worry. What would Maria think now when she saw the muddy trio?

As they made their way into the diner, Nina gave Maria credit for not making a fuss over the mud caking their shoes or the grass in Rosie's hair. Maria's eyes were filled with concern, but Nina didn't understand why until she spotted Ran and Raphe.

Bonnie muttered under her breath, "Lord have mercy, my luck's been crap tonight." She turned to Nina. "Tell me the truth. Do I look awful?"

Nina tried not to snort with laughter as she took in Bonnie's orange t-shirt and black velvet warm-up pants that said "Sassy" on the rump. Her hair was in pigtails and dried mud was smeared on her cheek. Like a mother of a preschooler, she grabbed a napkin from Maria's apron and wiped the smudge off Bonnie's face.

Nina smiled. "You look cute enough to eat."

"Don't say that. I'll start thinking you're a lesbian again."

"I think she would have to be bi-sexual since we already know she slept with Raphe." Rosie's voice was loud enough for the patrons in the restaurant to hear.

"Rosie!" Both Nina and Bonnie shushed the older woman at the same time. Maria looked embarrassed. How would Nina explain the situation to her cousin's wife? Coming to the diner was a bad idea. Maria was a sweet young woman who was easily shocked. Nina reminded herself that it didn't matter. She wouldn't be imposing much longer. She intended to call her brother first thing in the morning.

Raphe stood motioning for the women to join them. Nina would have made excuses, but Rosie found her second wind and rolled up to their table on her own.

Bonnie winced. "Here goes nothing."

Ran beamed at Bonnie, taking in her Halloween cheerleader outfit. The contacts were back in their container, but her horn-rimmed glasses looked cute with her pigtails. Ran and Bonnie launched into a private conversation as Rosie started ordering enough food for a football team.

If Bonnie was the Halloween cheerleader, Nina was a fairy princess in her borrowed ball gown and muddy heels. What a trio they made. Too late now, they were already there. Nina's stomach growled. She hadn't eaten anything except the bagel she'd shared with Raphe that morning and the two bites of brownie. "Add a piece of coconut cream pie for me."

Raphe looked at her with concern. "Are you okay? I was worried about you after you left."

Nina felt heat creep up her cheeks. "Sorry about that. Can we talk about it later?"

Raphe nodded. "It looks like you girls might have fallen into one of Magnolia's infamous potholes—or perhaps you were mudwrestling?" He wiggled his eyebrows.

Rosie roared with laughter and regaled them with the story of how they ran out of her special brownies, finished her homemade moonshine, and they'd wanted French fries, so they'd decided it was safer to walk to the café.

"Are these pot brownies we're talking about?" Ran's eyes glinted with interest.

Bonnie blushed and Rosie chortled. Nina jumped in. "No, they were normal brownies, though the ingredients were unique."

"Hell, yes, they were pot brownies! I eat them to treat my glaucoma." Rosie gave them all a theatrical wink.

Nina's jaw dropped with shock. "You didn't tell me they had marijuana in them! I'll lose my license if they drug test me."

Rosie waved a hand at her without concern. "Honey, if you think you are the only social worker who's ever ingested Mary Jane in the state of Texas, you're in for a shock."

Everyone was laughing at the table but Nina. It wasn't like she was going back to her job tomorrow but learning about her incriminating actions was sobering.

Raphe put his arm around her, and she couldn't help but lean against him and close her eyes as he brushed his lips over her hair.

"It'll be okay Nina," he said reassuringly. "I doubt you'll be tested anytime soon, but in the future, I might stay away from Rosie's cooking."

She was having trouble forming the words for a reply. It felt so good to have his arm around her. She'd already missed the smell of him, his warmth, and that charismatic smile. It was difficult to believe she could feel so comfortable with him after what he'd told her earlier…but she realized the truth of it. It wasn't Raphe's fault that Derek died. Rosie and Bonnie had made her see the truth of it. Raphe was trying to save lives and nearly died himself in the process. He had no idea who Derek was and what his relationship was to Nina. Her reaction had been so intense because of the shock of the revelation, not to mention her own feelings of guilt for not being there when the fire broke out.

Raphe was giving himself enough of a hard time as it was. She felt the intense emotion emanating from him as he told her what happened. He'd shared something very personal with her. Trusted her to know the truth about why he'd left Houston and moved to Magnolia…And what did she do? She ran out of there without a goodbye or the decency of telling him the truth.

Raphe didn't need her judgment and she didn't plan on giving it. Besides, he wasn't anyone's Mr. Forever. He was Mr. Right Now, and she was a fool if she hoped otherwise. She could only cope with the now in any case. She was having a hard-enough time dealing with the past and sure as heck couldn't think about the future. No, she would only live in the moment and enjoy being with Raphe like she promised herself when she let him in to begin with. Besides, she'd already made up her mind to move to California, so why not just enjoy the time here with Raphe before she left. She knew going in what kind of guy he was when it came to relationships. *Live for now, Nina. There is no guarantee for tomorrow.*

Maria arrived with a large tray filled with burgers, fries and all the trimmings. Nina ducked her head when Maria set eyes on her. Had she heard about the moonshine and the pot? What must she be thinking now? There's no way she would let her stay on with two kids in the same house and one on the way. Everything was going in the wrong direction. It was like she was caught up in a bad dream, trying to get home, but taking all the wrong turns.

Raphe squeezed her hand. "I'm sure we can work things out. Don't worry about it right now. Enjoy your pie." He gave her a reassuring smile and handed her a fork. She sliced off a large bite and offered it to him. His mouth engulfed her offering, lapping up the extra cream with his tongue then kissed her full on the mouth in front of everyone. Normally, she would have pulled away in embarrassment, but his hypnotic kiss was so tempting, all she could think about was their marathon sex afternoon and how she wanted to do it all over again.

Bonnie cleared her throat. "Now, that's not awkward at all."

Ran laughed. Then grabbed Bonnie to him and kissed her. He didn't give her time to think about it or protest. She didn't. Raphe let Nina go and started in on his plate of fries. Ran held Bonnie tight and continued the onslaught of his lips over hers. She slithered one leg over his and was practically sitting on his lap.

"Wait! Who's gonna kiss me?" Rosie complained. When no one answered, she shrugged and dug into her burger. Juice ran down her chin as she watched Ran and Bonnie kiss, like she had front row seats watching a really good movie. Shouldn't it be weird that Bonnie was her niece? Nina had to admit, Ran and Bonnie were steaming up their side of the booth and it was difficult not to notice.

Maria showed up to fill their drinks. This time she pointedly looked at Nina, her eyebrows sky high as she angled her head at the make-out session.

Nina shrugged her shoulders. "What? They're grown adults. I can't tell them to stop."

Maria let out a huff, turned on her heel, and without a word, returned to the kitchen.

Raphe looked at his empty soda glass. I guess that means we're cut off?"

Nina laughed. "I guess so. At this point I'll have a lot of explaining to do tomorrow anyway. "Bi-sexual, pot brownies, moonshine, and marathon sex. Oh, the things Maria will tell my cousin, Jose, tonight." She shook her head, then rested her cheek on one hand and took in Raphe's beautiful features as she balanced a bite of pie on her fork.

Raphe ducked down and stole her bite. "Bi-sexual? Hm, that sounds sexy, but should I be worried?" He looked across the table at Bonnie then back to Nina. "If you take Ran out of the picture, it about checks all my fantasy boxes."

Bonnie and Ran finally broke off their make-out session and began to peruse the menu.

Nina punched Raphe's arm playfully. "I'm not having sex with Bonnie. She said it in front of Maria, but it was just a joke." She paused as his eyes widened, waiting to hear the punchline. She gave up trying to explain. "Never mind, it's a long story."

He ran a finger down her arm, tickling the underside of her wrist. "One I am happy to hear as a bedtime story later. Are you coming home with me? You did say you would explain to Maria and Jose tomorrow… So, does that mean you're free tonight?"

Nina winked. "Only if Lulu is okay with sharing. And maybe we should visit a pharmacy to refresh your depleted supply of safe sex materials."

"You mean the condoms Lulu chewed up." Ran howled and Bonnie looked like she might spit out her soda. She put her hand to her mouth then coughed. Ran gave them a sheepish grin. "Oops, I probably wasn't supposed to know that."

Raphe scowled at Ran. "Not cool, little brother."

Nina smiled. At least he confided in Ran about her. She knew it was a big deal for them both that they went all the way without protection. Each swore it had never happened before and she believed him. That had to mean that there was something more than just hot sex. They both had risked it all, and she admitted now that given the situation played over, she would make the same irresponsible choice. She'd never experienced such intense heat in the moment before. She could have—would have waited for protection for any other encounter she'd ever had…Anyone other than Raphe.

"It's okay. I told Bonnie and Rosie that we slept together."

Raphe smiled. "So, girls do talk about their hook-ups?"

Nina frowned. "Is that what this is?"

Raphe sobered. The table was quiet. "No, I told Ran because…" Raphe paused. Rosie was hanging on every word. A dab of ketchup dripped from the French fry she was holding midair.

Ran cut in. "I was worried about Bonnie. She left without saying a word."

"And that has to do with the price of apples to oranges, why?" Nina wasn't following.

"It's a story we can discuss later. Trust me on this one." Raphe looked from Ran and Bonnie to Nina. She understood he was saving Ran instead of himself. Nina relaxed. She was tired of being mad anyway. There was a fine line between anger and sexual frustration. She needed to release whichever one was needling her right now.

She stood up and flashed Raphe a wicked smile. "Then take me home. And Raphe," Nina paused giving him her most suggestive stare. "Let's *not* talk."

Chapter 19

"Did you ask him?" Nina stage-whispered as she leaned over the circulation desk. It was her lunch break and she didn't feel like hanging out in the diner. She wanted to know what had happened between Bonnie and Ran.

Bonnie looked up, readjusting her glasses to the bridge of her nose. "Ask who what?"

Nina scoffed. "Don't play coy with me. Did you ask Ran to the Sadie Hawkins Dance? And did you get lucky last night?"

Bonnie smiled, looking around the library. "I had Rosie with me. Believe me, as much of a show as that old broad puts on when it comes to men, she's the worst cock-block ever."

They both laughed and were shushed by Lisa, the head librarian.

Waiting a beat, Nina grabbed the book from Bonnie's hand. "I only have twenty minutes left on my break, now give me the skinny."

Bonnie suppressed a laugh, looking back at Lisa, who was checking books into the computer system. "He took Rosie and me home, so we didn't end up getting run over, then Rosie invited him in for coffee. The moonshine was out, remember?" She paused, giving Nina a conspiratorial grin.

"So, the coffee sobered you up and you went catatonic again," Nina guessed.

Bonnie ducked her head sheepishly. "I know. I don't know what's wrong with me, but when a man as hot as Ran is in my presence, my knees go weak and my mouth goes dry. It was downright awkward, and Rosie rambled on until Ran couldn't take any more, I guess, then he left."

"You mean you didn't invite him?"

Bonnie looked miserable. "It's just a dance."

Nina pressed her lips together giving her a sympathetic look. "He's just a man, Bonnie. And he seems to really like you. You don't have to be nervous. Call him up and ask him. Maybe there would be less pressure if you didn't have to look at him."

Bonnie shook her head. "And what happens when my vocal cords lock up on me? He probably thinks I'm an addict after last night."

Nina thought about it. It might be tough to figure Bonnie out for some people. She was painfully shy with men and yet she had an aunt who could make a sailor blush. It was a shame because Bonnie was fun and had a wonderful sense of humor when she felt comfortable. The alcohol and pot brownies definitely lifted her inhibitions, and that was good in a way because Ran got a glimpse of how she could be. But her friend had to conquer this anxiety she had. She couldn't keep drinking and eating pot brownies just so she could get up the nerve to talk to men.

Nina hoped Ran could hang in there to give Bonnie a real chance. Last night had been fun, but Nina didn't do drugs—or she never had before. Nina had to ask the question. She whispered, "Do you do drugs?"

Bonnie looked over her shoulder at Lisa, "Are you trying to get me fired?"

"No, but I need to know so I can help you," Nina whispered.

Blowing out a breath, Bonnie confessed, "No, I didn't know the brownies had pot in them until Rosie told us all at the diner. I've had them before, so I did recognize the taste and suspected it, but it was too late. We'd already eaten them."

Nina arched a brow and leaned farther over the desk. "What about the Xanax?"

Bonnie looked guilty. "Mona said it would relax me and I was desperate to fit in." She groaned, rolling her head back. "I sound like a teenager, don't I?"

Nina tilted her head, studying her friend. "So that's the only time?"

Bonnie nodded. "I should have asked Mona more questions. It was my fault, and I take responsibility for messing up everyone's evening."

Nina winked at her. "You didn't mess up my evening. I did that all on my own."

Bonnie's face crumpled as she stared at the counter. "I haven't had a pot brownie since college and I've never tried anything else illegal. Mona said her Xanax was a prescription. I rarely ever drink, but this new life feels so different than my old one." She smiled at Nina. "I like having friends."

Emotion squeezed Nina's heart. With Bonnie's social phobia of men, she had no doubt been very lonely before moving to Magnolia. Having friends would be good for Bonnie, especially if Ran was one of them.

"Bonnie, you never have to drink or take drugs for anyone. You are beautiful, funny, and smart. Please trust me when I say that you are just fine the way you are."

Bonnie nodded. "My thirty-two-year-old self knows that. I'm a grown woman, for God's sake. It's the socially inexperienced part of me that's scared. I've had such a good time lately. I've never been asked to a dance, not even in high school. I've been on about five dates in my entire life and they were men who lived with their mothers and my mother knew their mother!" She stamped the return card on the back jacket of the book rather roughly. "I've had prime-rib, Nina. I can't go back to broccoli."

Nina couldn't help but giggle at Bonnie's serious confession. "And Ran is prime-rib?"

Bonnie's face said it all.

Mona approached the counter, red heels clattering on the library's tile floor. "Did someone say prime-rib? That is just the dish we need," she exclaimed as she put her leopard-skin purse on top of Bonnie's book. Pointing to an older woman with her in a prim tan suit, she made introductions. "Nina, Bonnie, this is Addy Lablanc. She's the treasurer of the Magnolia Blossoms. I was hoping to find you both to see about helping out at the dance this upcoming weekend. But first, are you ladies ready for my next masterpiece fundraiser?"

Lisa shushed them again. Mona waved to her, giving her a loud, "Hey Lisa, how is Harold Mathison?" Mona gave Nina and Bonnie a sly grin. "That should shut her up. Angela Brittmoore, the orthodontist's secretary, told Ricky Johnston, the florist, who told Peg Larson, the delivery lady, who told Eli that Harold, the orthodontist, is working on making a set of Invisalign braces for Lisa."

Addy was sweating bullets. She brought a handkerchief out of her satchel purse, then mopped at the beads of perspiration.

Bonnie looked at Mona with brows knitted together. "So what? Why would anyone think that was gossip-worthy?"

Mona smiled like the cat who had a canary between its sharp teeth. "Because Angela saw Lisa grab hold of Harold after the fitting and put a lip-lock on him that would make Scarlett O'Hara blush. Apparently, Harold ordered a huge bouquet of flowers and had them delivered to Lisa."

Addy grabbed a literacy brochure from the counter, fanning herself. Bonnie and Nina nodded, though Nina felt guilty listening to gossip about poor Lisa. She wondered what gossip was being spread about her after the last two days. Changing the subject, she asked Mona, "What's the new fundraiser?"

Mona spread her hands wide, like a flamenco dancer on a Vegas stage. "Casino Nights!"

Nina raised her eyebrows and looked at Bonnie. "And I thought I would be bored living in the suburbs. Latin nights, Sadie Hawkins, Casino Nights. Where's the roster? Sign me up. I'm a sucker for roulette."

Bonnie looked confused. "I don't know how to play."

Mona smiled at a handsome young father holding his young son in one arm as he returned a book to Bonnie. "There's nothing to it, sweetheart. You just keep your eye on the ball."

Nina pressed her lips together, wondering why Mona had said that. Roulette was about picking numbers. The ball landed on a number after spinning the wheel.

Tearing her gaze away from the young father, Mona moved on. "I was just wondering how we would get people to spend five-hundred a plate, and I walked in and heard prime-rib. Every wealthy man in Montgomery County loves a good steak and I know just who to call to cook 'em. Can I count on you ladies to help organize?"

Nina started to respond, but Mona turned on her heel and sashayed out. Addy followed, saying something that sounded a lot like, "If these hot flashes don't end, I'm going to shoot myself."

Lisa glared in their wake. Nina straightened up as the librarian approached. "What news did Mona Calhoun bring this time?" Lisa said in low voice.

Bonnie stamped books faster than before.

"Did she say anything about me? Mona's always saying stuff…" Lisa trailed off.

Bonnie airily waved her hand, "Oh God, no. Why would she do that? She's on a mission to raise money for something or another. Casino Nights is the theme."

Lisa's brows stretched as she nodded. "Oh. Okay. When you get done with these, Bonnie, the tables need to be covered in paper for the next visiting class. Great idea, by the way."

Bonnie winked at Nina and she smiled back, "I gotta get back to the diner. Don't forget to make that call to Ran, okay? Bubbles at six?"

A few hours later, Nina received a text from Raphe as she was clocking out to go meet Bonnie.

Raphe: *I hate that I have to work tonight. It's a twenty-four-hour shift. Are you sure you don't mind staying the night with Lulu?*

Nina: *Are you kidding me? An apartment all to myself for a whole twenty-four hours? I'm thrilled.*

Raphe: *You're killing my ego.*

Nina: *I'll be waiting in your bed when you get off. Pun intended.*

Raphe: *I'm counting the minutes. You're the best.*

Bonnie was at the bar with a bottle of Diet Coke and a glass of ice.

Nina sat on the stool beside her. "Taking it easy tonight?"

Bonnie poured the soda over the ice, watching the bubbles fizz over the top of her glass. "Yeah, I'm still hungover from Rosie's moonshine. I don't know how you suffered through a shift at the diner. At least the library is quiet."

Roberta from the diner walked in with a very pretty blonde. Nina waved them over. "Hi Roberta, want to join us? It's ladies' happy hour."

Roberta smiled and introduced her friend Darcey. "She used to work at the diner until...." Her words trailed off as the bartender approached and they all ordered. Nina decided to have a glass of wine. She would nurse it to be social, but she wasn't a hundred percent yet and she still needed to get back to Lulu. She'd let the dog out after her shift at the diner, but she wanted to call it an early night and Lulu was the perfect excuse.

Bonnie smiled at Darcey. "Where are you working now?"

Roberta choked on her margarita. She looked at Darcey and shook her head.

Darcey stood straighter. "I don't care what anyone thinks, Roberta. I make more money than most doctors and lawyers now."

That got Nina's interest. The girl looked like she should be in college.

Darcey pushed a long lock of golden hair over one shoulder, exposing the deep v of her shirt.

Bonnie looked at Darcey's cleavage and blurted, "Dang! Are those real?"

Darcey smiled, swiveling her shoulders back and forth. "Ten-thousand dollars real and worth every penny. Stan says I can write them off on my taxes."

Nina raised an eyebrow, "Stan?"

Roberta hung her purse on the back of her stool, sighing. "He's the accountant in Magnolia who does the diner's taxes."

Bonnie was having a difficult time putting two and two together. "How is that possible?"

Nina tried to sound polite, "I think Darcey dances for a living. She can write off a lot of items we can't."

Bonnie sighed, a whimsical smile on her face. "I wanted to be a ballerina so bad when I was young."

Roberta coughed, dribbling beer down the front of her shirt. "Oh hell." She excused herself to the bathroom. Darcey sat on the vacant stool, leaning forward. Bonnie was mesmerized by Darcey's over-large breasts.

The blonde didn't try to lower her voice. She looked at the man on the stool next to them with a glint of interest. "I'm not a ballerina. I think those slippers are horrible looking. I like platform heels. You wanna see?"

Bonnie nodded and before Nina could say or do anything, Darcey pulled a clear platform shoe out of her bag and plopped it on the bar. The heel was at least eight inches tall.

Bonnie finally caught up. A hand flew to her mouth and she squealed with excitement. Leaning in toward Darcey and Nina, she said, "I've never met a stripper before."

"We prefer to be called exotic dancers." Darcey pushed back her shoulders, and preened with pride, as she looked down at her full breast. "Best thing Raphe Nash ever did for me."

"Wait, Raphe Nash bought you boobs?" Nina thought about his offer to take her dress shopping when she told him she had nothing to wear to the Sadie Hawkins Library shindig.

Darcey shrugged. "In a roundabout way. I'm grateful now, truly I am. Hell, his brother came to see me night before last and took me to the VIP room. Champagne and five-hundred dollars will satisfy me any night."

Bonnie sputtered out her Diet Coke, launching into a coughing fit.

Nina thumped Bonnie on the back until she was breathing normally again. "Wow, I don't know what to say to that, but Bonnie and I probably should get going."

Roberta chose that moment to return. "Are you gals leaving?"

Nina grabbed Bonnie by the arm, dragging her from the stool. "Yeah, we drove here together, and I have to go take Lulu out."

Darcey glanced at Roberta, her eyes questioning. "Isn't that Melvina's dog?"

Roberta looked like she was debating whether to explain or leave it alone. "You don't mind if I take your spot?"

Nina nodded to their vacant seats. "Sure, go for it."

Roberta and Darcey waved as Nina ushered Bonnie's petite form in its catatonic state from Bubbles.

Bonnie found her voice as they hit the parking lot. "What the hell?"

Nina tried to be neutral. "I'm sure there is some other explanation. Darcey doesn't look like Ran's type."

Bonnie's eyes were wide and shimmering with tears. She looked dumbfounded and crushed at the same time. "Nina, that blonde is any man's type for a night."

Nina nodded. She couldn't argue with that and apparently, Darcey had been Raphe's type too. It was probably more than one night if he'd paid for her breasts.

"Did you ask Ran to the dance?"

Bonnie frowned. "I texted him. I didn't trust myself to call him."

"What did he say?"

"Yes." Bonnie didn't look thrilled.

"You can ask him then about what Darcey said—or maybe not."

Bonnie sighed as they walked to their cars. "It's not like we're dating. I can't blame him. Hell, I'd do her."

Nina laughed, but she couldn't resist teasing. "Who's the lesbian now?"

Bonnie snorted. "Tell me you wouldn't."

Nina turned to Bonnie and gave her a look of mock shock. "You mean you think she's prettier than me?"

Bonnie scoffed. "Hell, who could even see her face past those tatas?"

"Well, that answers the question of whether you are a breasts or ass woman."

Chapter 20

Nina waited in Raphe's bed, reading her novel. Lulu was belly up and snoring beside her. She wore her oldest sweats with the holes in the knees and her mismatching sweatshirt with a hoodie. If anything spelled, *ain't gonna happen*, it was her current outfit. She knew that Raphe was a player and she didn't know why it bothered her if she planned on moving to California, but something needled her about him buying another woman a boob job.

Lulu passed gas and Nina scooted to the edge of her side of the bed. "Lord girl, that was rank. What's in that dog food they feed you?" Lulu's tail thumped, fanning the stench as she looked at Nina innocently. The front door opened, and Lulu pounced into action, baying at the edge of the bed. Raphe entered the bedroom smiling.

"All dressed up for me?" He walked toward her, removing his watch and wallet, then laying them on the nightstand. Raphe reached out and scratched Lulu behind her ears.

The flash of his wallet struck a sensitive chord and she stared down at it, giving him a fake smile. "For me?"

Raphe looked confused by her comment. He gave her an awkward look then walked to a window to open it. He breathed in deeply.

Nina blushed, forgetting her anger. "That was Lulu, not me." She stood up, moving away from the gassy pup.

Raphe turned, giving her a teasing smile. "Yeah, right. That wouldn't be why you're so dressed up?" He motioned toward her attire. "Upset tummy?"

Nina looked down at her dubious, mismatching blue bottoms with red piping down the sides and orange and gray University of Texas top. "What? You're not a UT fan?"

Raphe snorted. "I graduated from Rice." He paused, stripping off the shirt to his uniform. "I was on the wrestling team."

Nina gasped as he charged at her, picking her up and taking her back to his bed. Lulu jumped off and went to explore the kitchen. "I have no problem with what you're wearing, darlin'. I would just rather we skip the formalities of clothes and get down to what's important."

Nina tried not to giggle. She was supposed to be mad at him, but curiosity got the better of her. "And what's that?"

He lowered his body over hers and dipped his head to nuzzle her neck as he lifted the sweatshirt up and took one nipple into his mouth. She felt heat pool in her thighs as his hands grasped the outer edges of her breasts, squeezing them together. He laved at one nipple then moved to the other, breathing in deep and letting out a sigh of pleasure. Raphe tugged the drawstring of her sweats. Nina put a hand over his to stop him.

"I have a question first."

Raphe arched a brow. "Sure, sweetheart."

Nina sat up as he rolled to the side. He took a long tendril of her hair and brushed it away from her face. "Did you buy new boobs for a stripper who used to work at the diner?"

Shock registered on Raphe's handsome face. Nina tried not to laugh at catching him off guard.

"Are you asking me if I bought Darcey Gallagher a boob job?"

"I never got her last name. Roberta brought her to Bubbles, and she said that Ran bought champagne and spent five-hundred dollars in the VIP room with her. She said she should thank you for her boobs."

Raphe shook his head as if trying to clear it. "Well, nothing about that is true, except that Ran felt sorry for her and couldn't say no to a dance. I admit I hung out with her when she worked at the diner, but that fizzled out quickly and she quit working at Pop's. Darcey said she couldn't continue to work at the cafe if I was going there. Melvina told her that I was family and she wouldn't bar me from Pop's. I'll be honest, I haven't seen Darcey since." Raphe sighed. "Actually, I've been meaning to talk to you about the Pop's rule."

Nina's brow wrinkled in confusion. "Pop's rule?"

"The diner used to be called Pop's before the remodel. Anyway, after Darcey quit, Melvina said that I was never to date any of her waitresses ever again if I wanted to be served and I agreed. I don't know how to cook, and I want more than a bagel on my days off." He gave Nina a lopsided grin, running a finger over her cheek and brushing her hair back to cup her head. He brought her slowly toward him and brushed his lips over hers. "What are your plans a week from now?"

Nina was confused. Was he asking if she planned to keep working at the diner after Melvina returned or what her schedule would be? "I'm working."

Raphe kissed her neck and pulled her onto his lap. "At the diner? Do you plan on ever going back to your job as a social worker?"

Nina pulled back. The moment was dampened by too much reality. She didn't know the answer, and she didn't want to tell him about the call she'd made to her brother, Carlos.

"I don't know. I just need some time to get back on my feet. The diner's been good for me. My head's in a better place." She thought about how angry she'd been when she first met Raphe. She'd carried around all the guilt and anger for so many months. It had changed her...Meeting Raphe had changed her, too.

Raphe nodded. "I understand. I had my own issues after that fire, and I guess that's the big reason I'm here." He placed his hands on her shoulders and looked her in the eyes, imploring her with his subtle voice. "It kind of seems like fate, doesn't it? I mean we both lived in the city and loved it. Our family is here, so for our own reasons, we sought refuge in a storm and then we found each other." He paused as if thinking about what he intended to say. "I want to be with you, Nina. I don't know what your plans are, and I don't care what Melvina says about the rules. If I have to quit going to the diner, I will. I want you in my life. I just want to know if you feel the same."

Nina gulped. "It's...it's too soon, Raphe." Her gaze skittered away. "I don't know what I'm still doing in Magnolia. I don't belong in a small town. I'm used to the traffic blaring, rude people who steal your parking spot, and grabbing lunch with my friends downtown." She lay on her back, staring at the ceiling.

Raphe twirled a strand of her hair then bent to kiss it. "I'm sorry. I keep upsetting you. The other night and now."

Nina looked at him with unshed tears. "It's not you. I promise." She let out a long sigh as she twisted the edge of the sheet. "The reason I'm staying with my cousin is because my place burned down in a fire."

Raphe's mouth opened in surprise. "Oh my God, Nina. I'm sorry."

"I lived with my fiancé until the night before, when I broke off the engagement. I stayed with my friend that night, but I went back to get my stuff the next evening. When I got there, the whole top of the building was ablaze. I was supposed to be home that night, cooking dinner, like always." She'd managed to keep the tears at bay, but it felt like a rock sat in her stomach. She clutched her middle. "I lived in number thirty-thirteen with Derek, my fiancé."

Raphe didn't disguise his look of shock and pain. He pulled her against him. "Oh, God. No wonder you ran out of here. You must have been devastated, then and now. I'm so sorry." He rolled back onto his back and ran a hand through his tousled hair. She rolled toward him and placed her hand on his chest as she curled into his arm.

"I guess you feel like I failed you. Failed to save him."

Nina shook her head. "It wasn't your fault. It wasn't anyone's fault. It just happened, but for whatever reason, I still feel so much guilt."

Raphe ran his hand over her shoulder, squeezing her closer to him as he rubbed soothing circles over her skin.

"I know. I can't help that the beam fell on top of me, yet I can't forgive myself for not saving him." Raphe blew out a frustrated sigh. "What are the odds?"

Silence fell between them as they lay entwined in each other's arms. A salty tear splashed from her cheek onto Raphe's chest.

"You said you broke up the night before the fire," he said in a low voice. "You obviously weren't happy if you broke off your engagement."

Nina sighed, nuzzling her face into his warm skin. "No, I wasn't happy. Derek was a city-slick type of guy who didn't care about anyone but himself. I didn't realize it until the wedding drew near. My brother from California was flying in to meet him and I wanted to arrange a drive to Magnolia to include Jose and Maria. My parents died in a car accident when I was six, so I don't have much family left. Derek told me he didn't have time to meet them. He barely spent time with his own family. That's when I should have known I was making a mistake. Don't get me wrong. There were other red flags and red-heads." She rolled her eyes, thinking about Derek's partner's girlfriend. "I should have never said yes, but...."

Raphe picked up her hand and started kneading it. Carrying heavy trays at the diner were taking a toll on her. His hands had a magical touch. "Are you happy here in Magnolia?" he asked.

Nina thought about it. "I guess I'm happy right now." She turned her head to look at him. His dark eyes glowed in the soft light from the bedside lamp, but his gaze radiated kindness and concern, not sensual conquest. She knew that he cared about what she'd told him. His touch was nurturing, not sexual. "Where did you learn the art of massage? It feels amazing."

Raphe chuckled as he pulled her back against him, hugging her to his chest. "I think you are changing the subject, lady."

Nina smiled. "I know a better way to distract you from all my secrets." She got on her knees, facing him. She framed his gorgeous face with both hands, loving the slight stubble of his beard against her palms. She combed her fingers through his thick mass of brown hair. She tugged at the back of his nape, pulling his head back as she nipped at his neck. Raphe groaned with pleasure.

Moving her hands to his chest, she ran her lips across his pecs, and delved lower, swiping her tongue across his warm flesh. He grabbed the bottom of her homely sweatshirt and pulled it over her head. She heard his intake of breath as he stared at her naked breasts.

"Well now, at least the sweatpants match better." He grinned before rolling them both to the other side of the bed and taking the top position. "But I think we can find a more suitable ensemble." Straddling his hands on either side of her, he slid his knee between hers. He looked like a lithe panther, crouching over her half-naked body, ready to devour her. She gulped. Nina's mouth was suddenly dry with anticipation. Other regions of her were pooling with moisture. Without warning, Raphe snagged the elastic at her waist and tugged the sweats from her legs in one swoop.

He stared at her naked body, mesmerized. "No underwear? You're killing me. I'm beginning to think this whole outfit was a sham."

Nina couldn't help but laugh. She shrugged cheekily. "Maybe. I was waiting for your answer. You did offer to take me shopping for a dress."

Raphe shed his uniform pants, including his tight boxer briefs. Nina admired his biceps as they flexed with his movements. He stood tall and his taut abs rippled above his engorged sex. Now her mouth was watering. He took a hungry lion's position between her legs, and as if stalking his prey, he let his body slowly come to hers.

He nuzzled her neck, biting a little harder than she expected. The bite sent pleasure dancing down her spine, pooling in her loins.

"What does that have to do with anything? You said you lost everything in the fire. I want you to look pretty. Call me selfish."

She moaned as he dipped lower to her breast, caressing the undersides with his hands as he suckled at one nipple.

"Do you like fake breasts?" Nina asked through heavy breathing. Raphe growled and rolled her on top of him. She sat astride his hips and slid her sex over his hard cock.

Raphe looked up at her with half-closed lids. "I have never seen more beautiful breasts than what I am looking at right now, and I have no inclination to put in an order for something different." He flexed beneath her, almost sliding into her as she moved back and forth over his smooth shaft.

"Wait!" She said, bending over to take a condom from beneath the pillow. A smile spread across his face.

"I knew you were teasing me with that get-up." He let her roll the condom onto him and then place his tip strategically at her entry.

A lock of her long hair fell across her face and his lips parted with anticipation. She couldn't help but tease him. "What's the magic word?"

His eyes closed. "Oh God, please."

Nina guided him into her, letting out a guttural cry of pleasure as she rocked back and forth. Her breasts felt heavy with desire and she couldn't stop herself from getting carried away. Raphe's headboard rocked against the apartment wall and she was glad his bathroom lay on the other side. She didn't like the idea of giving the neighbors a thrill.

Raphe bucked beneath her, holding on tightly to her hips. They ran the gauntlet, grasping at each other and moaning with pleasure. Raphe ran his hands over her breasts as she rode him with wild abandon. On the brink of finding her goal, she leaned down, pressing her torso into his as he gripped her to him, tightening all the muscles in his body. They slid into a blissful climax together, making her head spin and her lungs gasp for air. She lay limp on top of him in the aftermath. Her face buried in his neck. She felt him flex, then glide out of her. She groaned from the loss of their connection. She felt Raphe shift, heard the crackling of another foil package and smiled at what she knew was coming next. Raphe could be as insatiable as she was. Primed and ready, he rolled her onto her back and poised between her thighs.

"Now this time, let's enjoy the scenery."

Chapter 21

Standing in the Galleria in Houston was like coming home. Nina hadn't been back to the city since she moved to her cousin's place in Magnolia. She'd fidgeted on the drive, worrying that seeing the Galleria area again would remind her of the fire and everything she'd lost with it. She didn't plan on letting Raphe buy her a dress, but she really did need a few more clothes and it was nice that he offered to drive her to the city to shop. Her ex wouldn't have taken her shopping if his life depended on it, unless it was for lingerie.

"I've never been shopping with a man before, besides my brother, and Carlos always left me in the girls department as soon as we were dropped off at the mall. He always met me in front of the exit at a designated time."

"Well that's too bad for him. He had the perfect opportunity to learn what women want and he passed it up." Raphe winked at her and grasped her hand, pulling her toward Nieman's. Nina dug in her heels, pulling him to a stop.

"Whoa, hold up. I'm a social worker turned waitress whose savings have been mostly burned through. I don't have Nieman Marcus money."

Raphe looked at her with concern. "Did you keep your savings under your mattress?"

Nina laughed. "No, I'm not that crazy. It's just that the last six months, with very little income, has added up. Before I left Houston, I used a lot of the savings I had for wedding planning and then on the many essentials to get by after the fire."

Raphe nodded with understanding, pulling her with him toward Nieman's. "Well, savings or no, it's my money we are spending today. I say we buy at least six dresses, since I plan on taking you to at least six swanky places this month. Though you seem to like going commando," he said wiggling his eyebrows outrageously. "I say we buy you a few lacy items to make you feel as pretty as you are."

Nina couldn't believe she was letting him do this, but he was past insisting. He was dragging her through the cosmetic section toward the escalators.

"Don't worry, we'll get some nice make-up, too. I've been shopping with Lexi many times and she always likes to match her makeup to her new clothes."

Nina smiled in the glow of his shining eyes as they ascended to the ladies' apparel. "You must be really close with your sister."

Raphe looked up in thought. "My mom and dad still have a great marriage, and they were great parents, too. Dad groomed all of us boys to look after our little sister, so that meant one of us had to tag along wherever Lexi went."

Nina stared at him with awe. "Lucky Lexi. My brother, Carlos, would have sold me to the gypsies."

Raphe laughed. "I probably would have, too, if my dad hadn't watched me like a hawk." He held her hand as they stepped off the escalator and meandered through the wide array of clothing. "I'm glad Mom and Dad raised us the way they did. We're a close-knit family and our holidays are a lot like a mushy movie." He threw her a grin.

Nina nodded. Warm currents of need skittered over her body and she chided herself for the pleasure.

Don't get carried away, Nina Salas. Just because he loves his family doesn't mean he's ready to start one with you! He may have a close-knit family, but he also has a colorful past. Remember, he dated Darcey before you. She was also a waitress at the diner — and now she's a stripper!

Nina shook off her concerns and tried to stay in the moment.

They found their way to an alcove of a designer whose name she didn't recognize. She didn't recognize any outside of the ones everyone knew. She wasn't wealthy enough to shop past TJ Maxx, and truly, she didn't see the point. The discount designer brands there were good enough for her. Why pay triple the price for Michael Kors when she could buy it for half the price?

A woman in a beautiful ivory-colored suit greeted them. "Can I help you find something nice, Mr. Nash?"

Raphe looked uncomfortable for a moment. Nina had been uncomfortable since they entered the store, but now she felt inadequate. It was obvious now that Raphe shopped in women's apparel frequently enough for the saleswoman to know his name, and Nina doubted it was because of his sister. How many women had he brought here? How many women had he slept with? She thought about their first night of unprotected sex. *Stupid! Stupid! Stupid!*

So much for staying in the moment.

Her nana, if she were alive, would spank her with a wooden spoon. She missed the grandmother who'd raised her. She'd passed away on Nina's twenty-first birthday. It was an unfortunate event, since now, all of her birthdays were saddened by the loss of her grandma.

Raphe explained to the saleswoman that he wanted Nina to have whatever she wanted and to show her anything in her size. Nina would have felt like Julia Roberts in *Pretty Woman* at that moment, except for the ice-cold water of reality washing over her elation. Who exactly was the prostitute in this scenario? Her for sleeping with him on their first date, then letting him take her to buy expensive gowns or Raphe for being a sex-addicted playboy?

Nina shook her head as the lady went to gather selections. "I can't do this, Raphe. I can't afford it and I can't let you buy me an expensive wardrobe just because we're sleeping together. Where do you get this kind of money anyway? You're a fireman, not a hedge fund manager."

Raphe caught her arm as she intended to march away. "Hey, hey, hey. Why are you so upset? Most men send flowers. I like to buy pretty dresses. What's the difference?"

Nina scoffed. "What's the difference? That's what I'm asking myself. I'm one of how many women you've brought here? It's humiliating." She broke free of his grasp and headed toward the escalators, almost barreling over the saleswoman who approached with an arm full of dresses.

Raphe followed her. "Nina, stop. Wait, will you listen to me a moment?"

She spun around at the top of the escalator. "Okay, I'm listening."

Raphe sighed. "I'm not going to apologize for being a bachelor. I'm not going to lie to you about dating other women before I met you, but I can promise you that I haven't brought anyone here since I met you, and I don't plan on it." He pushed a hand through his hair then pulled her gently toward him, allowing another shopper to descend to the first floor. "Nina, if this makes you uncomfortable, we can go somewhere else. Wherever you want. I just want to be with you and I'd really like to buy you a pretty dress. Will you let me do that?"

He hadn't let go of her arm. He wrapped his other arm around her lower back, pulling her into him. She felt the heat of his torso radiating through his crisp linen shirt. Her heart skipped a beat, then her pulse raced.

It wasn't her fight-or-flight mechanism, but a definite need to be with him, and not just in bed.

Oh God, Nina, you've got it bad.

She knew she was destined to get her heart broken if she stayed the course. Raphe was gorgeous, all male, charming and genuine. He hadn't promised her marriage, but last night he'd told her he wanted her in his life, and he made love to her like he meant it. She needed to know where they stood. She needed to hear the words.

"What is it we're doing here, Raphe?"

He grinned, "We're shopping and if I don't let go of you soon, we may be putting on a show that's at least PG-13."

It was difficult not to smile at his quick sense of humor, even harder to pull away from his embrace, but in the end, she stepped onto the escalator and descended to the lower floor.

Chapter 22

Bonnie sat across from her at the kitchen table, sipping a hot cup of herbal tea. Rosie offered up her latest batch of moonshine, but both women declined.

Bonnie shrugged. "What's the big deal? He wanted to buy you a fancy dress. Most guys buy flowers, and though it's thoughtful, the bouquets wilt within a week. At least the dress will last for a few wears."

"Because she felt like a hooker! Aren't you listening, Bonnie?" Rosie called out from the other room.

Nina chuckled. "She's right. Standing there, I felt the ghosts of all those other women he'd been with. I imagined them all lined up around him, chanting at me to run before I got a broken heart."

Bonnie shook her head. "Oh dear, it looks like it's too late."

Nina frowned. "Why?"

Bonnie stood, moving to the kettle on the stove and poured more hot water into their cups. "Because you've already fallen for him. What happens next is up to you. If you dig your heels in now and walk away, you're still going to be hurt, so why not go all the way and see where it leads?" She placed both cups down on the table and sat. "You said already, he loves his family. If you ask me, he sounds like the kind of guy who might have sewed his wild oats and is looking for the right woman to settle down with. Isn't that what you want? To have a family?"

Nina thought about what Bonnie said, knowing her friend was right. Her heart ached when she thought about Raphe dropping her off at the diner after their quarrel. He was clearly flustered with her non-acceptance of his chivalry. He said he understood and invited her to dinner, but she said she wasn't in the mood. He'd parked the truck and she jumped out without even a good-bye. She heard him call her name, but she hadn't turned back.

Nina knew she was acting immature. He was willing to talk about it. He'd said as much on the ride back from the city, but she'd shut him down. When she'd asked him to define their relationship, he'd made a joke and she couldn't handle him sliding past her question again.

Rosie sauntered in with her walker that held a Route 44 Sonic cup in the basket. "Sugar, why does it have to be forever or nothing with you ladies? Most women would be just fine with what the Nash men have to offer right now. If I were only twenty years younger…"

Bonnie snorted. "Try fifty," she murmured to Nina.

"I heard that, Missy!" The wheels of the walker squeaked as Rosie rolled over to them. She flopped down in a ladder back kitchen chair, setting her forty-four-ounce Styrofoam cup on the table. It had lost its plastic lid, and a thick straw tilted out of it precariously, covered in bright red lipstick.

"Damn, Aunt Rosie. What's in that jug?" Bonnie waved a hand at the fumes.

Rosie smiled, showing the tops of her dentures. "I told you girls this was my best batch ever."

Bonnie sighed with dismay. "Aunt Rosie, I hope you're not still takin' your painkillers with that hooch."

Rosie cackled. "Hell, that's half of what makes it so good!"

Bonnie stood up, grabbed the massive cup and took it to the sink to toss.

Rosie squealed in protest.

"I think you've had enough for one afternoon, Aunt Rose. You better ease off until dinner."

Rosie stood up again with a humph, then wordlessly marched back to the TV room.

Nina stared at the older woman in wonder. "How does she do it? At her age, I'd have keeled over by now, not to mention the hangover."

Bonnie laughed. "How do you think that woman is still here? Two hip replacements, both knees replaced, triple by-pass surgery, and a liver transplant! She's pickled, preserved I tell you."

Nina's eyes widened at the list of medical problems. "Wouldn't it be bad to drink if you already had your liver replaced once?"

Bonnie scoffed. "You'd think so, wouldn't you?" Bonnie took a sip of tea, shrugging her shoulders again. "I guess she's old enough that she plans on going out with a bang. I know I fuss and complain like a mother hen when it comes to Aunt Rosie, but truth be told. I want to be just like her when I'm her age." She paused, looking at Nina. Her demeanor grew serious. "I

116

guess you might want to look at where you want to be when you grow old. Ask yourself what's in San Francisco and why you really want to rush off and leave a man who clearly has way more than a passing interest in you."

Nina looked at her skeptically. "Enough about my issues. I know when I'm being social-worked." She smiled. "Why don't you tell me what's happening with you and Ran?"

Bonnie looked crestfallen. "He said yes to the dance, so I guess I'll find out more on Saturday night at the library fundraiser. It's out at the Cowboy Baptist Church."

Nina gave Bonnie a surprised look. "I thought Baptists didn't allow dancing or drinking."

Bonnie waved off her concern. "Oh, some Southern Baptists are still strict on that account and a lot won't let it happen on church grounds, but Reverend Haze is young and fairly modern in his beliefs. Rosie tells me he likes to drink a little himself and that the congregation has doubled since he took over and allowed wedding receptions in the church's annex building. It'll be pretty informal, so don't worry too much about the whole dress thing."

That brought Nina back to her original reason for stopping by to see Bonnie. "Hey, it seems I've ruined my shopping day with Raphe, so I was wondering if you would like to go shopping with me?"

Chapter 23

Nina didn't hear from Raphe until the day of the dance. She guessed he was upset with her exit after their upended shopping spree and she couldn't blame him. Nina had enjoyed shopping with Bonnie, but she really regretted ruining her day with Raphe. The black dress she bought was simple and pretty, with a deep cut neckline and an open back. The billowy skirt would be pretty when Raphe spun her around the dance floor.

Nina spent the morning learning how to bake. She'd been trained to prep but she hadn't learned anything more in depth than that. She'd never been much on cooking, but Maria needed help and Nina was determined to make up for her up-and-down moods since she moved to Magnolia. While she was elbow deep in flour her phone pinged. She finished kneading the biscuit dough and washed her hands to check her messages.

Raphe: *Are we still on for tonight?*

Nina thought about it. She was a little miffed that he hadn't called her, but then she knew the reason. She was really looking forward to a night out with Raphe and hanging out with the friends she'd made since moving to Magnolia. After the last two days of helping decorate the banquet hall at the Cowboy Baptist Church, with decorations donated by the high school's Glee Club, Nina was excited about the evening ahead. Old forty-five records and book covers hung on the wall and wedding streamers from past weddings hung from the ceilings and archways.

Tapping the glass screen of her phone, she sent a pic of herself in the black dress. Bonnie had snapped the image in the dressing room of the department store.

Raphe: *Nice! I'll take that as a yes. Is it okay if I pick you up at six so we can grab something to eat first?*

Nina calculated the time. It was noon now, so that should give her plenty of time at the Dipsy Doodle Hair Salon and Nail Emporium with Mona and the gals to get pretty.

Nina: *Looking forward to it. I'd like to make up for being such a pain the other day.*

Raphe: *I look forward to anything that involves making up.*

As Nina pulled into the lot, she spotted Bonnie helping Rosie with her walker. Rosie sported a tangerine turban around her snow-white hair, and she wore a bright yellow housedress with fuchsia-pink flowers. Oversized white hoop earrings with blue polka dots hung from each of her stretched earlobes. They looked heavy to Nina, and she wondered if they hurt. The bright pink tennis balls on the bottom of Rosie's walker slid across the entrance into the Dipsy Doodle. Nina held the door for them as she took in the many salon chairs filled with women in various states of color processes. Hair products and nail polish filled several shelves in the main entrance. The pedicure pods lined an entire wall and a woman delivered drinks to the guests who occupied them. Mona reclined in a salon chair, her slender legs crossed as she bobbed one pink strappy sandal. Tinfoil wrappers stuck out all over her head in a Medusa fashion.

"What color are you going for this month?" Rosie called to Mona as she scooted her way to an empty seat. Pulling her own magazine from the basket of her walker. Nina's jaw dropped as she read the cover.

"Aunt Rosie! Have you no shame?" Bonnie reached out and grabbed the old issue of Playgirl Magazine and stuffed it in her purse.

Nina couldn't help but ask, "Where in the world did she get that? I thought they didn't print those anymore."

Bonnie snorted with annoyance and they all began to laugh.

Mona leaned forward in her chair, ducking her head as the lady set up a heating lamp. "Is that the issue with Burt Reynolds? That's a collector's item."

Bonnie waved her off. "No, that was Cosmopolitan. This is just some eighties issue from Rosie's collection under her hospital bed. You should have seen the look on the service guy's face when he came to fix the motor on the bed. Let's just say that the item she keeps under her pillow rolled off her bed and into his toolbox. I think that man will be in therapy for a year."

Rosie looked at Bonnie pointedly. "That was not your story to share, Bonnie Blue Bush! Besides, I have needs and the online issue only comes out quarterly." Rosie sniffed with a look of indignation. "It's hard to turn the pages."

Nina, Mona, and the other ladies in the salon howled with laughter. Rosie waited a beat before deciding it was funny and joined in.

Bonnie shook her head as she helped Rosie up to move to a salon chair. The receptionist, with the name Grace on her name tag, came around with a tray of mimosas. Rosie took two. She downed the first one like a shot of tequila and then swigged half the other. Nina flipped through the menu selections of the salon to decide how she wanted to be pampered. She would splurge a little today. Her morning shift had been hourly wages since she was baking and not waiting tables, but she'd made enough during the week to afford a mani-pedi and highlights. Summer was coming, and it was time to brighten her look. She hoped Raphe liked it.

Mona said goodbye early, rushing out right after her new strawberry-blonde highlights were blown dry into a beautiful straight bob. It made Mona look chic. Short hair was very becoming for Mona's oval face, long neck, and too-thin lips. Her straight teeth and slender nose were her best features, but Mona often had her lashes extended and Botox injected into her forehead to smooth the lines. Nina didn't think she needed it. The woman was put together with presidential style, even if what came out of her mouth might rival Rosie's best. Maybe her chic look had to do with her position as president of the Magnolia Blossoms, or maybe it was because it was rumored that Manny Owens was running for mayor in the next election.

Bonnie opted for a trim and set. Her beautiful golden-blonde hair was put into spaceship sized rollers and she sat flipping through a magazine under an oblong orbital dryer. Rosie waddled out from the back room with fire-engine red hair and walking more bowlegged than before.

Nina stood up to help the older woman. "What's wrong, Rosie? You look pained. Do you need to sit down?"

Rosie grimaced. "That Brazilian wax took half of my hoo-ha with it. If you go back there with Deborah, don't let her too close to your lips, and if ya find a set back there, they're mine!"

Nina covered her mouth and looked at Bonnie, who just rolled her eyes.

"She always complains. I don't know why she tortures herself. It's not like Zac Efron is wandering into her bed tonight."

Rosie scooted her walker to the waiting area and eased herself into a black leather club chair. "You don't know who's visiting my bed. I told you, I have a friend!"

"Well why haven't I ever seen him?"

Rosie sat back, and set her hands on the armrests, a regal smile on her face.

"You never know Bonnie," Nina mused. "I think Rosie might have a fella. Who would go through that torture if they didn't?"

Bonnie shrugged. "I'm not into pain. I have a date with my razor, but I'm not sure why I bother," she sighed, closing her magazine.

"Aren't you excited about going to the dance with Ran tonight?"

Bonnie looked at Nina with doleful eyes. "I'm not sure why he said yes. What will we talk about? I'm going to clam up, I just know it," she complained.

Nina gave her friend an encouraging smile. "Well, maybe you don't have to. You loved dancing at the Fireman's Ball. Just use your body language. Press against him and touch his forearm when he talks to you. Look in his eyes and smile a lot. That kind of language sometimes says more than words."

"Are you crazy? He'll think I'm a loony bird," Bonnie whined as a stylist approached, unrolling Bonnie's long tresses from their roller prisons. She was going to look gorgeous. And Nina knew any man in his right mind would love to be seen with Bonnie on his arm. Now if Bonnie's male-induced catatonic state could take a rain check for the night, she just might enjoy herself.

Chapter 24

Nina and Raphe sat in a deep curved booth in Laluna's cozy Italian restaurant. It was new to Magnolia and situated across the street from Bubbles. She'd had her eye on it before but hadn't had the time to check it out. She was glad they didn't have time to drive into the city. It was a nice restaurant with warm ambiance, though rather dark for the early hour.

"I really want to take you to Braised sometime. It's Riley's restaurant, and I'm not just saying it because he's my brother—but it truly is the best food anywhere."

Nina smiled. "I'd love to." She waited until they had their wine in front of them before she broached what had been on her mind for the past two days. "I'm sorry for being so difficult the other day."

Raphe put a hand up. "You don't need to apologize. I must have seemed like a real jerk taking you someplace…" His words hung between them as he reached for his wine glass and took a drink.

Nina stayed silent. The last thing she wanted to be was another notch in his bed post. Unfortunately, she'd heard a few tidbits at the hair salon about other women he'd dated in the past besides Darcey. There was Jenna Landry, Hope Bates, Kathy Carpenter, and a long list of other nameless model types or socialites from Magnolia who frequented the salon. Her stylist, Magda, had discretely warned her that while Raphe was gorgeous and fun and generous, he was also the non-committal type. Nina's gut had twisted into knots and she opted not to share the gossip with Bonnie. She didn't need another lecture from her friend that men could change. That might be true, but in her experience they didn't. Derek never did.

Besides, who was she kidding anyway? She'd saved enough money to buy her plane ticket and was scheduled to leave Texas next week. She hadn't told anyone yet. She'd made a pact with herself to enjoy the time she had with Raphe and to let go when it was over.

She'd had a hard-enough time the past few days with the flood of friendly gossip she'd heard at the diner. Nina had innocently brought up Raphe's name to an older patron, and the woman's willingness to share gossip was almost stifling. It wasn't anything Nina hadn't suspected since the shopping incident at Nieman's, but her heart still felt like a pin cushion with each jab of dirt dug up on Raphe.

Once the flood gates opened, it seemed everyone wanted to share stories, from the time Raphe, Riley, and Ran held up the candy store on the main drag to Raphe's first date. That always led to Raphe's heroic actions that saved the woman with three kids in the high-rise, and they never forgot to mention the most recent save of the momma duck with her babies. The popular fireman was a celebrity in Magnolia.

Most of the stories made her laugh, contemplate his character, love his gallant nature, and wish he could change his bachelor ways. One thing she knew as a social worker was that you couldn't change others, they had to want to change themselves. If she stayed in this small town with all the nice, gossiping residents, she would most assuredly get hurt, because once Raphe moved on to the next waitress, her world would be crushed, and she'd just become another story for the locals to share. Better to pick up her life, move to California, and start over before her heart got broken to pieces.

Raphe already had a hold on her concentration, and she couldn't think of anything else. She couldn't ignore the attraction and what was worse, she didn't want to. Until she was on that plane, she planned to be lighthearted and enjoy the moment she was in, and right now the setting was romantic. The candlelight warmed his tan features and she longed to kiss his full bottom lip. His dark eyes stared into hers and she felt a zing of awareness.

Why do I have to make sex so complicated?

Nina squirmed in her seat with makeup-sex anticipation. Deciding to be direct, she put her hand in his lap. He grew firm instantly. The Italian restaurant boasted long white linen tablecloths and the lighting was conveniently low. She took the glass of wine with her other hand and took a deep sip, enjoying the cherry and toasted oak flavor as it permeated her senses. She'd never preferred Bordeaux before, but she loved this bottle— or maybe it was the moment she savored. Raphe leaned back against the warm brushed velvet upholstery, taking his own glass with him. He ran his hand up her thigh, taking the hem of her skirt with his warm fingers. Nina tried not to show the surprise on her features as a waiter passed their table, smiling broadly at them both. She massaged his hardness, feeling the heat radiating through his tailored slacks, then coolly slid her hand away. She'd wanted to change the subject, not cause a scene.

Raphe skimmed a finger over the sexy lace of her thong, causing her to shiver.

Who cares about dinner or the dance?

Nina's lips parted on a slight gasp. "Why don't we get the bill and go back to your place?"

Raphe shook his head no. "And miss seeing you shimmy around the dance floor in that?" He caressed her bare shoulder with one hand, while the fingers on his other hand breached the lace triangle of her small panties and slid over her pulsating clit. Nina gasped and steadied herself by holding the edge of the table. She grasped the wine glass and took an over-sized gulp of wine.

Raphe grinned as he continued to massage her.

Her lips parted as her breathing sped up. "Raphe, stop. We'll make a scene," she whispered breathlessly.

His eyes swam with desire as he held her gaze. The waiter approached and without looking away, Raphe redirected him. "Bring a bottle of your best champagne and strawberries please."

Thrilled by the growing tab, the waiter disappeared without another word.

"Are you crazy?" Nina squirmed.

Raphe smiled wickedly. "It will take him five minutes to select the best champagne, another five to find ice and a bucket, plus the glasses and strawberries. You have a solid ten minutes to luxuriate in the pleasure I want to give you."

Nina felt naughty. It was early for dinner and the tables were situated far apart, and the risk of being caught was daunting. But Raphe was right. No one would even notice as long as she could be quiet and keep a straight face.

Do I really care? I've never done anything like this…But it feels too delicious to ask him to stop.

Nina licked her lips as she grasped his wrist tight with her free hand. "What about you?"

Raphe smiled again, leaning close to nuzzle her neck. "Oh honey, I'm looking forward to all the hours of pleasure that lay ahead of us after the dance."

She brought his hand into her wetness, taking his two largest fingers into her folds. He slid them in and out of her slowly while they stared at each other over their wine glasses. To anyone in the room they looked like a nice couple on a romantic date. No one could see the thumping of Nina's heart or hear the slick, quickening motions of Raphe's hand. She took the last sip of wine, letting her head tilt back as she closed her eyes and let him push her over the edge. Her legs were spread, thighs taut beneath the table, her high heels tilted onto their strappy, laced platformed toes as her free hand stroked his girth. When she set the glass down with a small suppressed whimper, the waiter rushed forward, champagne bottle and ice-bucket in hand.

Looking at Nina with a shameless grin, Raphe pronounced, "Right on time." The waiter smiled, thinking Raphe commented on his prompt service.

If the guy only knew what level of service this table was really getting!

Nina didn't want to go to the dance, but Raphe seemed to enjoy every moment of teasing her with pleasure. In the restaurant he'd brought her to climax, and in his truck on the way to the Cowboy Baptist Church Hall, of all places, he continued to play with her—teasing her inner thighs to the point where she had to stop herself from begging him to pull over.

He grinned at her wickedly. "As tempted as I am to find a place to park and have my way with you, we both need to make an appearance for the community." He ran his hand up her thigh again before helping her down from the cab. Her dress was up around the tops of her thighs and she parted her legs, straddling his hips.

Raphe let out a low whistle. "Lord have mercy, you don't fight fair."

Looking around the full parking lot, most of the guests were already inside. The music could be heard from the banquet hall, and the deep soothing tones sounded like blues. Raphe pulled her to him. He was hard at the apex of her thighs and if it wasn't for the thin materials that separated them, they would be joined in an instant. Nina wrapped one leg around him, sliding to the ground. He pushed her against the passenger side of the cab and kissed her neck as he slid a hand up the back of her dress to her lacy thong. She moaned with pleasure then regret, as he pulled away.

"I need to think about pink elephants and baseball for a minute, then we should go in."

Nina smiled. He was right, of course. They had pushed the limits of social propriety tonight and now it was time to act like mature adults on a date instead of two horny teenagers going to prom.

Damn, but it was so sexy.

Raphe walked into the banquet hall with pride as Nina grasped his arm. He could feel almost every man in the place admiring her beauty. She was normally ravishing, but with the color in her cheeks after her orgasm in the restaurant and all the foreplay afterward, she was flushed and glowing. Raphe was struggling against another erection. It was all he could do not to think of how wet she was, or how good she tasted.

He saw Ran and Bonnie near the cash bar and tugged at Nina to follow him. Bonnie had come a long way since the day he'd met her with Lulu at the library. She might go catatonic at times or say baffling comments like her Aunt Rosie, but she also said the funniest, wittiest remarks he'd ever heard. Bonnie was a knock-out when she put a little effort into it. Standing next to Ran, she looked like a vintage version of Sandra Dee. He'd seen enough old movies with his sister and mom over the movie binge holidays. Raphe, Riley, and Ran knew all of the Sandra Dee movies because they were Lexi's favorites. Ran had half fallen in love with the young blonde movie star when he was a teen. Looking at Ran now, Raphe knew his brother was probably just as smitten with the very real vision of his dream girl.

Ran handed the ladies champagne and Raphe a beer, but he didn't care to have beer breath, so he held it without drinking. The selections were slim, and he wasn't a fan of cheap bubbles. Alcohol was a letdown at some of the events he attended. After the beautiful champagne and Bordeaux at the restaurant, it was difficult to choose a drink from the hall's bar selection. Cheap Prosecco gave him a headache, plus he was saving himself for later. Slowing his pace to enhance his performance, Raphe ordered a bottle of water.

Mona and the chief made their way over and everyone stared at Mona's harem girl costume with curiosity. The gauzy, blue dress was beautiful on Mona's sleek form, but the veil made it look like a costume and it wasn't that kind of event.

Nina was the first to give in. "Mona, you look incredible. Where did you find that coined veil?"

Mona's groan of frustration was muffled beneath the veil. "I went to Doctor Falta at the Sculpting Center in the Woodlands."

Nina frowned, obviously not comprehending what that had to do with the veil. They all waited uncomfortably until the chief finally let out a sigh and put his arm around Mona's shoulders in support.

"Ah, Mona, honey. Just take the veil off. It's not that bad and wearing the thing just draws more attention."

Mona sighed and ripped the veil off like a sticky bandage. "Oh hell, who cares what everyone thinks. I just wanted to look pretty for you, Manny." Mona looked at the chief, tears swimming in her eyes. She looked like she'd kissed a blowfish, then gotten stung in both lips by a hornet. Her usually slim smile was now bulging and deflated. It was like air trapped in a crimped inner tube. The wavy pattern was confusing and her usually pointed peaks that she drew on with lipliner were now very uneven. Raphe wondered if the chief should have encouraged Mona to remove the veil. It was odd looking at it, yet hard to look away. Mona turned the shimmering, deflated tubes of her smile on the group.

Nina and Bonnie stammered with thoughtful ways to console their friend without outright lying. "It's so different…" Bonnie started.

"I love that lipstick color, Mona. You'll have to tell me where you got it," Nina threw in.

"It'll go back to normal soon, right?" Bonnie hovered over her own question with hope.

Mona tried to make an O with her lips, and everyone reared back a little. Nina's brows scrunched up and Bonnie winced.

The chief handed her the veil back. "Here honey, maybe just for another hour until the injection settles."

Manny and Mona walked away to find a seat in the corner, and the band struck up an upbeat song. Ran pulled Bonnie toward the dance floor, and she didn't object. It was a good sign that Bonnie hadn't even finished her drink. Raphe set his beer down and grabbed Nina's hand.

"Wanna show me how high this dress twirls?"

"Not too high. I'm wearing skimpy underwear, remember?"

Raphe's wicked grin told Nina to hold onto her skirt or they would be giving everyone a show.

They danced several songs and then reconvened at the bar. Bonnie cautiously sipped her champagne as she engaged in conversation with Ran about the library fundraiser. She told the brothers how she and Nina had spent hours hanging streamers from the ceiling. Nina told them about Reverend Haze coming in to bless the bar. Apparently, he was okay with liquor being served for a good cause, but he felt the need to pray that no one got into trouble over it.

Nina thought about the trouble Raphe and she had started in the church parking lot. Energy rippled through her body as she thought of finishing what they'd started outside. The new dress made her feel sexy and the spa day had helped her put the package together nicely. The way Raphe kept staring at her sent ripples of excitement to the pit of her stomach and lower. He was downright sexy, and he knew it. He knew just how to make her all hot and bothered. She couldn't wait to get back to his place.

After an hour of lurking outside the main bustle of the party, Mona and the chief took the dance floor by storm, doing a tango that rivaled Arnold Schwarzenegger and Jamie Lee Curtis. All of Magnolia kicked up their heels and lifted their spirits. It was nice that Ran wasn't playing in the band tonight. Bonnie looked like she was finally coming out of her shell. Maybe Nina's advice to use her body language was working. The shy librarian was finally talking with Ran, saying more than one sentence answers and he looked like he was hanging on her every word. Her hands touched his forearm when she talked and somewhere throughout the night, Nina noticed Ran's arm possessively around the back of Bonnie's waist. She smiled at the blooming couple. She could tell that events of the evening were leading them somewhere.

"Hey, Nina. Would you like to dance?"

Nina was temporarily shocked to see Eli from the diner. They'd met in passing, but she didn't know him very well, other than he was the owner's brother. She looked at Raphe, who nodded and shook hands with Eli. She supposed he couldn't be upset. Eli was part of his family.

The music switched directly from fast to slow. Eli gave her a grin and held out his hand to take hers as his other hand clasped her waist. He was a good dancer and she felt light as a feather as he twirled her around the floor.

"We haven't had much time to get acquainted. How are you liking the diner?"

Nina smiled up at him. He must be well over six feet tall. "You know, I didn't think it would be something I would like, but it has surprised me." Eli twirled her out slowly and did a fancy step, sliding his arm along her back and turned her out again. She laughed. "You stay in the office most of the time. What do you do back there all day?"

Eli shook his head as he blew out a sigh. "I do everything from ordering to inventory, paying the bills and making sure all the numbers balance at the end of the month. Right now, I'm doing Melvina's paperwork too, which has me buried back in the office. It's why I haven't welcomed you properly." He gave her a nod and a winning smile.

Damn, he's really gorgeous.

"Forgive me for saying this, but you don't look much like a diner sort of guy."

He tilted his head back in a chuckle as another song started and he continued twirling her around the floor. His hard, sculpted body spelled gym addict, but his beautiful face held intelligence and his mannerisms were kind. If she hadn't met Raphe before now, she might have been interested in Eli. Melvina's brother didn't seem like a heartbreaker. He had future husband and father written all over him.

"Looks can be deceiving. I went to college to be a sports nutritionist. Melvina was the first person in our family to go to university, so I couldn't let her show me up, but the truth of it is, we grew up in the diner and it's always been home. I've thought about breaking off on my own and opening up my own fast food chain with healthy living choices, but I don't have the time to even start. I think that's part of the problem with society. We've all gotten so beat up by our schedules that we don't have time to take care of our bodies and minds."

Nina smiled at him warmly. He was going to make someone very happy one day. "You should absolutely do that! I would love a better option for lunch when I'm in a hurry."

Eli nodded as the music ended. "I came up with the idea because of my sister. She struggled with food for a long time, but half of her problem was not having enough time to make the right choices."

"Well, I haven't met Melvina yet, but I've seen her wedding photo in the breakroom. She's gorgeous and doesn't look like she's ever struggled to look good."

Eli led her off the dance floor where Raphe was waiting for them. "I thought I might need to rescue you," Raphe said to Nina but looked at Eli with a teasing grin.

"Don't worry, we were only talking shop."

Raphe made a mock expression of worry. "That's how Riley snagged Melvina. Don't underestimate the power of food. It's one of our insatiable needs."

Eli clapped Raphe on the back as he wandered over to ask Mona to dance. The chief looked momentarily relieved. Raphe arched an eyebrow, seeming to pick up on the chief's agitation as well.

Raphe took Nina's hand, leading her back to the dance floor.

"Does the chief look nervous to you?"

Raphe nodded. "Yeah, he keeps checking his pockets like he's lost his keys or his cell phone."

Nina continued to watch Mona as she began to twist and sway. The coins sewed to her veil jangled every which way as she sambaed to the Latin rhythm. The beat reminded Nina of the Fireman's Ball just a week earlier, then her mind roved to what had happened the next morning. She gave Raphe a knowing grin as she swung her own hips to the beat, rubbing playfully against him.

As Raphe twirled her around, she noticed the chief was under the dessert table. His butt was sticking out from the white tablecloth, swaying non-rhythmically. Several other men from the station hiked up the white cloth and joined him under the table. The display of sugary confections shook as they lifted the table with their broad backs.

What in the world are they up to? Nina stopped dead in her tracks, accidentally stepping on Raphe's toe with her pointy high heel. He yipped, staggered, then groaned, knocking Ran into Bonnie, who grabbed onto Mac Green, as they tumbled onto a nearby tabletop. Bonnie landed on the bottom with Mac splayed out on top of her. Ran rushed to help them both up, but Mac's wife, Katie, let out a growl and pushed Mac back down in the opposite direction before jumping on top of Bonnie and initiating a cat fight.

Grabbing a nearby dessert, Katie smashed it into Bonnie's face.

Bonnie gasped and gave Katie's hair a hearty tug that would have made a WWF wrestler proud.

"You need to cool off, lady!" Bonnie said as she grabbed hold of a nearby glass of champagne and dumped it over Katie's head.

"You want Mac, you trollop?" Katie screeched. "You can have the randy bastard."

"I don't even know your husband, you horrid woman!" Bonnie pulled up her leg and stuck her foot in Katie's belly. With a shove, she sent Mac's irate wife sailing into the next table where she landed, limbs flailing. Bonnie then hopped up on the table, pinning Katie down and grabbed hold of the screaming woman's large hoop earrings to keep her still. "Lady, you need to settle down and be taught a lesson." Bonnie scowled. "This is a community fundraiser for heaven's sake."

Katie finally stopped squirming beneath Bonnie's strategic grip.

It reminded Nina of when she went to catholic school and the nuns twisted their ears. If Nina ever found herself in prison, she'd want Bonnie to be her cell mate. In two seconds, she'd made Katie Green her bitch.

Ran helped Bonnie release the golden hoops before any real damage was done. Raphe offered his hand to Katie and the women were separated.

Bonnie huffed as Ran handed her a damp cloth so she could wipe her face.

"You get your own husband, hussy!" Katie yelled before turning and stalking toward the exit. Her husband Mac followed behind her with a garble of apologies.

Nina stood with her hand over her mouth as Bonnie noticed the crowd that gathered. Nina saw her friend's former extrovert-self sink back into the shy librarian. Her face flamed bright pink and her shoulders slumped. Katie may have been a jealous harpy but the whole fiasco had been Nina's fault. *And I still have no idea what the chief was doing under the dessert table.*

She rushed forward as Bonnie made a beeline for the ladies' room. "I'm so, so sorry, Bonnie," Nina gushed.

"Why are you sorry? I'm the one who just made a fool of myself in front of the entire town, plus Ran must think I'm a terrible klutz and off my rocker. At least I hadn't had very much to drink or taken anything from Mona's notorious Pez dispenser or who knows what he would have thought of me? By the way, what is up with that Katie Green? Talk about off her rocker!"

Nina looked at Bonnie with sympathy. The whole thing was a little over the top. "I suppose she's upset that it's the second time in two weeks that you landed in a pile with her husband."

Nina and Bonnie both broke out in giggles as Bonnie used a paper towel to wipe whipped cream out of her cleavage.

Bonnie shook her head as tears of laughter filled her eyes. "What are the odds, right?"

Nina raised her eyebrows. "Not very good odds of their marriage being saved. Raphe said that they've been in couple's therapy ever since Mac was accused of having an affair with another man's wife two or three years ago." She lifted a shoulder and gave Bonnie a shrug. "I'd chalk it up to bad luck and blow it off. No one who knows you will think it's anything else. Where did you learn those fighting moves?"

Bonnie chuckled. "Any gal who grows up near the ninth ward better know how to protect herself. In Louisiana, women fight, so we're taught early."

Nina thought about her own protected upbringing. She'd never worried about being attacked or bullied until she started her internship with CPS. She'd seen some rough places since then.

"I think I need to sign up for lessons. Are you for hire?" She was only half teasing. It was good to learn self-defense.

"Sure, you, me and Rosie can practice in the park. They have a tai chi class on Mondays." Bonnie threw another wad of whipped cream covered paper towels in the trash. "How'd it happen, anyway? That's two for two!"

Nina looked at her shoes. She felt her face screw up in discomfort.

Bonnie's voice lowered with disbelief. "Did you have something to do with it?"

Nina's head shot up and she hurried to explain. "Not at the Fireman's Ball. That was all you! But this time I was looking at Manny and about four other firemen all searching under the dessert table for who knows what... well, it was distracting, to say the least. I accidently stepped on Raphe's foot who stumbled into you guys and..."

Bonnie stopped her. "What were they looking for?"

"I'll tell you what they were looking for," said a familiar voice. Mona opened a stall door from behind them, popping out with a flare. She held one hand up tearing off her veil. The half-inflated lips were fully inflated now, giving Mona a bountiful smile that looked like it belonged on anyone but her. She slid over to the mirror and inspected the results, washing her hands, and applying more sparkly lip gloss. She carefully relined her lips like an artist at work.

Nina noticed the beautiful antique diamond sparkling from Mona's ring finger. "Mona, is that...?"

Mona smiled. "What Manny was looking for under the table? Yes, indeed." She stood up straight, readjusting the bustline of her gown before splaying her hand out before them. "And, I said yes! If that man can propose to me when I look like a troll, then he must really love me, right?"

It was a rhetorical question. Mona looked as confident as a regal queen. The ladies squealed together as each wrapped Mona in a hug.

"That's wonderful news!" Nina said. "I'm really glad they weren't look-ing for a live bomb."

Bonnie and Mona chuckled.

Mona pursed her bulbous lips. "Speaking of live bomb, loaded gun, or explosive jealous women. I missed the cat fight. Tell me all about it."

Chapter 25

Bonnie and Ran didn't stay long after the incident with Katie and Mac. Raphe and Nina left as well to make sure there wasn't another skirmish in the parking lot. Nina was relieved when Raphe started the truck. He'd forgotten to turn his high beams off, and the golden headlamps illuminated the open field next to the church, where a lone truck was parked. A pair of hot pink stiletto clad feet wiggled above the headrest, something with sparkles that danced in the light. Raphe quickly turned out onto the main road with a wide grin.

"I guess Mona and the chief are celebrating," he chuckled.

Nina moved closer toward him as he drove the short distance to his apartment. "I hope you don't mind that I asked to leave early to follow Bonnie and Ran out."

Raphe lifted an eyebrow. "Oh, is that why we left? I thought you wanted to do a little celebrating of our own."

Nina licked her upper lip. "Maybe that, too."

"Mom and Dad are watching Lulu tonight, so you won't have to share."

Nina squirmed with anticipation as Raphe pulled into his parking spot. He came around to open her door and she slid down his hard frame. He kissed her hard, running his hand up her back and nesting his fingers at the nape of her thick chocolate tresses. Tingling swept down to her loins, making her reach for his hardness. Raphe stepped back, holding her at a distance.

"Wait. Let's move this party upstairs before someone calls security. Believe it or not, I am a private kind of guy and I don't like sharing with the general public."

Nina's eyes slid sideways as she looked up at him. "Could have fooled me in the restaurant."

Raphe pulled her to him, kissing her hard on the mouth. He grasped at her like a thirsty man in the desert. Breaking the kiss to catch his breath, he pulled her by the hand to follow him up to his apartment. "Touché, I did enjoy that very much. Maybe you know me better than I know myself."

He unlocked the door and pulled her to him. Shuffling them both through the doorway, he used one leg to kick the door shut. He grabbed her up in his arms and started toward the bedroom. "Now it's my turn."

Raphe awoke with a zing of pleasure. Memories of Nina rocking against him in a heated rhythm as they found fulfillment in each other's arms, tantalized him. They'd shared a hot shower after their sheet-aerobics and then had done it all over again. He grew hard against her naked body as he thought about it now. She smelled sweet, like jasmine in summer, and tasted salty from the sweat of their lovemaking. The word passed through his thoughts and he rolled it around like a roulette ball skittering past all the numbers until it hit his favorite, thirty-six. It was Nina's age and she was a perfect fit for him.

He'd never been good at lasting relationships and he'd never cared enough to try before, but something about the way she felt against him, the way she made him hang on her every word, and the way she made him laugh or smile, told him that she was something special in his life. He was ready for the next step. The question was, was she?

He watched her stir in the morning light and he tried to calm his pulse when she stretched, pushing her backside hard against his front. He would ask her tonight to move in with him. He knew it was sudden and they had only known each other a few weeks, but she couldn't live with Maria and Jose forever. The thought of her looking for a place didn't sit well with Raphe. What would he do if she decided to move back to the city? His heart felt an intense ping at the thought. Nina was special and he didn't want to lose this chance.

His brother Riley had told him that he knew right away Melvina was the one, and now Raphe finally understood. He only hoped Nina felt the same way. She'd been upset in Nieman's the day they shopped because of his history with other women. She all but asked what his intentions were. She was hinting that she wanted more, and at the time, his fear of commitment made him falter, but not now. Their time together had shown him their connection was real.

Hell, last night was like the Fourth of July.

Nina moaned and stretched again, looking over her shoulder at him with a catlike smile. "Are you awake?" His body involuntarily flexed against her. He arched a brow. "I guess that means yes," she purred. Nina turned toward him, wrapping her leg around his hip, bringing him closer.

He moaned with desire. "I have to warn you. We're down to our last condom. If we want to have more fun, we'll have to actually make a trip out of the apartment today."

Nina's eyes glinted with mischief. "Then I guess we better take it extra slow and enjoy the scenery." She copied his words from their first time together.

A low growl rumbled in his chest as he rolled on top of her. Raphe kissed his way to the apex of her thighs, exploring the sensitive skin on the inner side of each leg. He worked his way to the center of her heat. His own need heightened by the soft moans coming from her. Nina's head tilted back, and she bucked toward the ceiling, pressing closer to his exploring tongue. He parted her lips and found the heat pouring from her center. He suckled her as his fingers delved deep inside. She pulled at his hair, imploring him to fill her with his body and after she screamed out in gasping pleasure, he slid himself into her molten hot sheath. With the first stroke he held tight to his control, tamping back the need to join her. After his pulse calmed to a normal rhythm, he built up their speed from a slow, blissfully torturous grind to a pounding rhythm that had them both gasping for air. Nina cried out as she crested a wave of pleasure that made her head fall back. Raphe let his body explode into hers as he grasped her hips tighter against his. He tightened, released, and fell against her soft curves.

Raphe was overwhelmed with more than her body. He felt a hunger to do it all again, an insatiable need to possess every part of her body and soul, sharing every part of himself with her. Joined at the hips, they lay satiated in the aftermath of their lovemaking and he thought about the word again. *Love.* Yes, he was falling in love for the first time in his life. He had no doubt, because if she said no to a relationship, after all they'd shared, he thought a part of him just might die.

Maria gave Nina a curious glance as she shuffled into the house around six in the evening. "That must have been some dance."

Nina got the feeling that Jose's wife didn't approve of her not coming home after the dance. Nina shrugged it off. She was old enough to sleep with whomever she chose.

"Yes, it was a great time. Manny Owens asked Mona Calhoun to marry him. You and Jose should have come. It was quite a party."

Maria pulled cookies out of the oven. The sweet aroma filled the small space, making Nina's stomach grumble.

"Somebody had to be at the café and since, you, Eli, and Roberta were all there and Jose had to stay with the kids…." Maria's voice trailed off as she lifted a hand to the air and shrugged a shoulder.

Nina felt defensive, "Hey, I would have worked if you'd put me on the schedule, but I was off. Are you mad at me, Maria?"

Maria turned her efforts to washing dishes, keeping her back to Nina.

"Look, I'm leaving in just a few days, so I really don't want to fight with you and I certainly don't want to wear out my welcome. I should just get a hotel. I'm sorry I've bothered you and Jose. You've been kind to me."

"What about Raphe?"

Nina's heart sank. "What about him?"

Maria slapped the dishtowel down and turned. "Does he know you're leaving?"

Nina shrugged. "I haven't told anyone except you and Jose. I can't keep living here forever. Clearly it's causing some issues."

Maria sighed. "Yes, it is. Raphe is a Nash. I work for the Nash family and they're good people. If you break Raphe's heart, how do you think Melvina or Riley will look at Jose and me?"

Nina scoffed. "Break Raphe Nash's heart? I doubt that very much. I'm leaving so I don't get *my* heart broken. Raphe has a reputation. He doesn't do commitment and that's fine with me. I knew the odds when I went all in, but the truth is I've had a crappy year and I just needed a little fun…." Nina sighed, shaking her head. "Look, there's no danger to Raphe Nash, I promise. And I won't hold anything against him either. He's been good for me."

Maria looked at Nina, shaking her head. "For thirty-six, you sure are a child when it comes to growing up."

Nina bristled, but she held her tongue out of respect. Maria was pregnant and hormonal. Her cousin and his wife had given her a roof over her head, given her the time to make other plans. Her ticket was scheduled days away, and she could make it until then, but not under her cousin's roof. She went to pack her things. There weren't many, just two small suitcases full. When Nina returned to the door, Jose had just come in. He looked at her in question. His gaze swung from Nina to Maria and back again.

"Are you leaving?"

Nina nodded. "Yes. I think it's time. Thank you both for having me. I'm going to stay with Raphe or Bonnie until my flight. I think it's time I give you your house back. Again, I appreciate all you've both done for me." Nina pulled an envelope out of her purse and put it in Jose's work worn hands. "It's just a little something...."

He looked back over his shoulder at Maria, who continued to put the dishes on the sideboard away. Nina dug in her purse and pulled out two arcade gift cards attached to the overlarge suckers she'd bought from the specialty candy shop, handing them to Maurine and Maurice. She hugged both kids goodbye and turned to hug Jose. It made her sad that she'd upset Maria. She still felt guilty that she wouldn't be around to help with the pregnancy. Nina pressed her lips together and nodded to them all before making her way to the car. She'd told Raphe she was grabbing clothes for the rest of the weekend, so she would leave one suitcase in her trunk.

Nina knew she needed to fess up about leaving, but she didn't want to spoil tonight. *I'll tell him tomorrow.*

Raphe surprised her with a beautiful bouquet of flowers and a red glossy shopping bag from Sparkle Babble. She opened the bag and pulled out a beautiful white strapless gown, simply cut with a matching pair of heels and handbag. The ivory tissue lay across the sofa as she held the dress up to herself. It was the prettiest gown she'd ever owned, and she could tell it would look fabulous on her curvy hips.

"How'd you know my size?" she exclaimed.

Raphe smiled mischievously. "I think I know every inch of you by now, and I knew when I saw that dress, it would look perfect on you."

Nina raised an eyebrow. "What's up with you buying dresses?"

She realized she was dampening the mood, but after their awkward shopping day at Nieman's, she had to ask.

Raphe cleared his throat as he left the stool by the island and sauntered over to her. He took the dress from her hand and set it aside, pulling her to him. "You lost everything you owned in the fire. I wanted you to go out with me tonight and I didn't want you to use the excuse that you didn't have anything to wear. Now, if you don't want to wear my gift, I have no issue, but I do want you to go out with me tonight. I want to show you off to the world, and then I want to come back here and make love to you."

Nina's breath caught and she swallowed hard. She'd become addicted to being with Raphe in all forms. In bed or out of bed, his hypnotizing gaze, full bottom lip and charisma radiated off him in hedonistic waves, drawing her to him like a bull to a red cape. He was her kryptonite and better looking than Clark Kent ever dared to be. His lips were close to hers now. He was holding both of her hands close to his hard chest. She could feel his heart beating with each breath.

"Say you'll come with me tonight? I have something special planned."

She gazed into his golden amber eyes and sighed. How could she say no to this man?

Chapter 26

The fancy restaurant in Houston wasn't too far from where she'd once lived. The red awning with cursive white lettering boasted Braised. She knew it was Raphe's brother's place and she didn't need to see the full parking lot to know it was booming. Its reputation preceded itself. The smell of seared steak and fresh bread assailed her senses as they breezed through the entryway and toward the beautiful mahogany bar. Raphe kept walking, calling out a quick hello to the bartender and then continued through the dining room to the kitchen. Nina dug in her heels.

"Raphe, I don't think we're supposed to be in here!"

Raphe turned to her, giving her a sly grin. "Don't worry darlin', I got a few connections."

A sleek young woman in a tight black dress approached them, holding menus to her breast like schoolbooks. "Mr. Nash. Can I take you to your table?"

Raphe nodded and Nina wondered if Raphe had ever dated the hostess. The twenty-something-year-old blonde ogled Raphe with appreciation and all but giggled at his every word. Nina wanted to roll her eyes, but Raphe didn't seem to notice the hostess. His eyes lingered on Nina.

In the center of the kitchen was a glass room with an opulent table set in the middle. A bucket of chilled champagne sat to one side and heavy gold chargers and linen napkins designated their place settings. It wasn't at all what Nina was expecting, but it delighted her to see the staff at work around them. It was like watching an artful dance. Waiters moving in and out as plates came to rest under the heat lamps. Chefs moved up and down the line, turning steaks, grilling vegetables, drizzling sauces over plates. Staff in black uniforms cleaned the floors and prep area continually. The setting wasn't so much romantic as it was spectacular.

Nina loved to people watch, but after the first few glasses of champagne and the appetizers, Raphe and she fell into the natural rhythm of conversation that took them through a plethora of memories as they tested the waters and swam out on the tides of their pasts. Sharing the waves of expectations, hopes and dreams, she opened herself up and told him about her brother, Carlos, and her desire to one day have a family of her own.

Is it my imagination or did he light up when I mentioned children?

Raphe told her more about his parents, brothers, and his high school years.

"You wanted to play professional football?" Nina couldn't believe it. Raphe looked like a quarterback. His body was sculpted muscle and his reflexes were quick. He'd caught her at the dance before she fell, but she couldn't see him playing a game for a living.

Raphe chuckled. "Not anymore. I played in college and I had a few NFL teams that were giving me a hard look, but I took a hit early on that made me think about the physical repercussions I might face, and I decided to live a simpler life. To tell you the truth, I wanted to be a fireman more than anything in the world. We used to get on my grandparents' tractor out at their farm and pretend it was a firetruck. We set the barn on fire once just to put it out." Raphe took in a deep breath, remembering. "Boy did we get our hides tanned for that."

Nina's jaw dropped in shock and then she laughed at Raphe's wayward grin. "Oh my. I guess your grandma didn't keep you at the farm much after that?"

Raphe shook his head. "We could do no wrong as far as my grandma was concerned. It was my momma who wouldn't let us out of her sight after that."

Nina raised a brow. "I guess not."

"What about you? Did you always know you wanted to help people?"

Nina pressed her lips together in thought. She took a sip of champagne and stared at the glass as if seeing the past. "My parents died when I was young. My grandma raised us, and we were okay, but I often thought of what might have happened if she hadn't been there. I missed my parents so much. It inspired me to want to help other children who weren't so lucky."

Raphe looked at her with soft brown eyes. The flecks of amber shimmered in the candlelight. The room had a solid ceiling, unlike the rest of the kitchen, keeping the interior darker than the rest of the industrial, stainless-steel laden area. It also kept the room quiet. The gold gilt chairs and white-cloth-covered table carried off simple elegance, but the way Raphe looked at her said that there was more to this evening than just upscale dining. He seemed to hang on her every word, and he was being open with her about himself.

"Not to be nosy, but don't most firemen live on a beer budget? This place definitely spells expensive." Nina stopped herself, then rushed on to apologize. "I'm sorry, That's so rude of me. Sorry I said that. It's none of my business."

Raphe laughed. "Don't worry, you're not the first to ask, and you were less blunt than most," he chuckled, reaching for his glass. "My grandparents found oil on their property back in the eighties and most of the family was given a cut. All of us grandkids got a nice chunk, not enough to never have to work, but enough that we could do what we wanted. Riley traveled all over the world learning to cook and jumped through hoops to make a name for himself. He ran out of money and had to come home. That's when he made an audition on the Food Network and became famous. I invested in his restaurant along with some of my mother and father's golf buddies. It's done well for us all. Ran hasn't touched a dime of his money." Raphe laughed. "I guess he's a simpler kind of guy."

Nina quirked her head. "Really? What does he do? I know he plays in a band, but that's just a hobby, right?"

"He's a programmer. Works from home or wherever he decides to sit down for the day. He's worked for the same company since college. Ran makes good money, so he's never had to tap into his inheritance." Raphe's brow furrowed. "You're not thinking of leaving me for him, are you?" He teased her with a glowing smile.

Nina slapped at his arm playfully, "Don't be silly. He's not my type." She winked. "Besides, it's obvious he has a thing for Bonnie."

Raphe's wide grin spelled affection for his younger brother. "Yeah, I think he's got it bad. Who would have imagined he'd get hung up on a shy librarian?" He paused. "She's quite pretty when she takes off her glasses and funny as all get out when she isn't afraid to speak. Something tells me she might take after her Aunt Rosie. I wonder if Ran suspects?" They both laughed.

"I think that may be the allure."

Raphe guffawed. "Aunt Rosie?"

Nina giggled. "A lot of men like the shy librarian type. You know, a lady in public but a freak in the bedroom."

Raphe made a mock face of shock. "Are you telling me Bonnie's into bondage?"

Nina laughed. "No! I don't know. I know she sleeps with her poodle, so probably not. I just know her aunt is a wild card. I figure there's a little bit of wild card in Bonnie as well when she lets her hair down. I think Ran sees that, and he knows he's found a diamond in the rough."

Raphe shifted. "Speaking of diamond." He motioned for the waiter to enter through the glass door. A bright robin's-egg-blue package sat on the tray with a pretty white-silk bow. Raphe reached up as the waiter tilted the tray toward him. Nina's breath caught. Raphe was full of surprises.

"I saw this leaving Nieman's the other day and Tiffany's is one place I've never shopped for anyone, so I thought it was safe to go back after I dropped you off." He grinned.

Nina flushed, remembering their awkward parting.

Raphe held her hand, "You see, I knew even then, there was something different about you. I wanted to spend more time exploring what that was." He flipped the top off the box and brought out another pretty box. Handing it to her, he nodded for her to open it. It was a beautiful necklace with a floating diamond on a thin chain. It was delicate and beautiful and exactly the type of jewelry she would have chosen for herself. She never liked gaudy costume jewelry and chose not to wear anything if she couldn't afford the simple elegance she liked.

Nina looked at him with pause. "I—I can't accept this. It's too much. The dress, the heels, the purse. Raphe, it's not right."

He took the platinum necklace from the box and moved around behind her, lifting her hair, he put his lips to the nape of her neck.

"Please let me have the pleasure of giving you something nice. There's no obligation to sleep with me afterward." His hot breath tickled her ear. She could hear the half-humor in his voice.

Feeling self-conscious as a waiter entered the small room, she lifted a hand to help hold her hair up while Raphe fixed the clasp. She could always give him the necklace back later tonight. She didn't want to ruin their evening. Everything was so perfect, and she'd never dined in such an elegant setting before.

"Nina, I have something I want to ask you." Raphe paused, waiting for the waiter to fill their champagne glasses and leave the glass room. "I know that we just met, and I also know you are looking for a place to call your own."

Nina took a nervous sip of her champagne, touching the necklace pendant at the base of her throat.

"I really like you and it may be too soon for this, but I can't take the chance of you walking in somewhere and signing a year's lease to someplace that isn't near my apartment. My lease is almost up, so I'm flexible to move if my place doesn't suit you." He took her hand and squeezed it softly. "Nina, I want us to move in together. I've never felt like this about anyone and I can't take the chance of you not being in my life."

All of the air in Nina's lungs evaporated. She wasn't sure why he'd bought her such an expensive gift. Was this why? She hadn't wanted to accept it before, but now her heart was thudding in her chest with anticipation.

Wait! He didn't say love. He said he wanted you in his life. Maybe he just wants the sex to be more convenient.

He was still gazing at her, rubbing his thumb over the sensitive part of her wrist. His eyes pleaded with her to say yes. Hell, her body was screaming at her to say yes, but her mind stamped its heel down hard. She shook her head, taking her hand away from his, grasping her flute and draining the last quarter of the golden liquid.

"Nina, don't say no. Say you'll think about it. I don't want to scare you, but I think I'm falling in love with you."

Oh my God! He said it! Well, almost.

His sexy, devilish good looks hypnotized her as he leaned toward her, brushing his lips over hers. She could taste the champagne. The waiter arrived, breaking the moment. Their order of caviar was laid out with all the accompaniments, and they enjoyed the exotic flavors of capers, sea salt, and crème fraiche. The appetizer course was followed by braised lamb with lingonberry sauce and brie, sautéed kale with golden raisins and crab tempura in ponzu sauce. When the dessert tray came, Nina declined, asking for a glass of sauterne instead.

"Excellent idea. I'm glad Mr. Wu is driving us tonight."

Nina was glad that Raphe had hired a driver as well. She had thought it was a high-end hired car from a phone app, but Raphe had chatted with Mr. Wu like they were old friends. There was still so much she didn't know about Raphe. There was so much more to the handsome fireman than most people could see on the surface.

She wondered if she'd been wrong about the love-'em-and-leave-'em part. Why go through all this trouble to woo her when she'd already fallen into bed with him? He was giving her in-depth answers about his life and sharing intimate details from his childhood. He'd asked her to move in with him, said he was falling in love, and she was seriously considering saying yes to everything. Raphe was everything she wanted in a man. He was smart, charming, funny, warm-hearted and sexy enough to melt her panties off with a single touch. If it wasn't for his reputation around town of going through women like a bag of potato chips, she would have said yes on the spot. Thank goodness the meal came to distract her from answering. She was glad Raphe was giving her the space and the time she needed to think about his proposition.

How could she get on a plane in a few days after such a declaration?

Everything had changed. The way he looked at her, everything he said, the romantic evening he'd planned to perfection were certainly not the actions of a player.

The evening had been delectable, and Nina knew she would never forget it, no matter what happened between them, but in her heart, she knew she couldn't leave without taking a chance and finding out where this thing between them was going. Nina reached for his hand and he moved closer to her.

"I think I have an answer to your question," she said softly.

Raphe looked like he was holding his breath. His eyes held her gaze and he didn't interrupt her.

"My answer is, yes."

Chapter 27

Mr. Wu politely opened the door and averted his gaze as they finished their kiss. Nina followed Raphe out of the vehicle and waited as he settled the bill with Wu.

They ascended the stairs hand in hand. Raphe jingled his keys as they turned on the landing to his apartment, soon to be *their* home. He was thinking about Nina's answer in the car, and he was already thinking of his next purchase from Tiffany. He heard laughter in the distance and his head came up, scanning the balcony. Raphe came to a dead stop as the familiar blonde and a redhead leaned across the railing in front of his apartment.

"Damn, Raphie—Gail and I almost gave up waiting for your sexy ass." The ie she added to his name shouted volumes about their relationship.

"Roxanne? What are you doing here?"

The redhead he'd found so alluring a few weeks ago now looked brash and too made up in the lamplight of the open corridor.

Roxanne started walking toward him, her arm laced through Gail's. "You turned down the beach house and Gail said you wouldn't even meet her in the city for happy hour, so we decided to bring the party to you."

It was then he noticed they each held a bottle of Perrier-Jouet in their free hands. The bottle of champagne was easy to distinguish with its painted flowers cresting the brand name. Both women seemed oblivious to Nina's presence, and that pissed him off.

"I appreciate you gals thinking of me and bringing the champagne, but now's not a good time," he said in a curt tone.

Nina had already let go of his hand, and he felt her emotional connection slipping away.

"Oh, don't be so uptight, Raphie. You know Roxanne and I don't mind sharing." Gail wrapped an arm around Roxanne and kissed her in a slow, deep French kiss. It would have been hot a few weeks ago and just the sort of night Raphe would have logged as memorable. His heart and mind had changed these past two weeks and all he could think of was the cool breeze that chilled his side where Nina had clung to him only moments before. He turned to see her retreating down the stairs. His heart lurched.

Gail put a hand over her mouth and giggled. "Oops! I guess three's a crowd. Too bad—she's a hot brunette—she would have rounded out a perfect trio."

Roxanne nodded with a heady look as she crooked a finger at Raphe. "Oh, and you know how much we like brunettes."

Raphe hoped to God that Nina hadn't heard that last bit. He held up a hand to ward them off before they could reach him. "Ladies, that's enough. You've had your fun, now go home." He didn't wait to endure more of the banter. He had to catch Nina. No telling what she was thinking now.

He ran down the stairs, taking two at a time. Raphe hit the parking lot, sliding on the soles of his hand-tooled leather boots. He saw the familiar older-model hatchback's taillights as the tires peeled out of the lot. His heart sank.

She was gone.

Stupid, stupid, stupid! How had she let herself fall for him? First, she'd almost married a man who cheated on her at worst and was indifferent to her needs at best. And now she fell for a man who collected women like baseball cards.

Nina thought about the two bimbolinas hanging off the railing in front of Raphe's apartment. They knew where he lived. They knew him intimately, and had probably slept with him in the bed he'd made love to her in. *Love.* He'd said he was falling in love and she fell for it lock, stock, and barrel. She'd fallen so hard that she was all set to cancel her plane ticket to San Francisco and was already fantasizing about redecorating his apartment for the two of them to live happily ever after.

Stupid, stupid, stupid!

Nina stopped the car in the diner lot, shoving the gearshift into park. She shouldn't have driven this far after all the drinks they'd had, but Raphe only lived a few blocks away and she had to get out of there. If he went after her, he'd go to Maria's and then Bonnie's, because she had nowhere else to go. She couldn't risk seeing him right now. She was too vulnerable, the wounds were too raw.

Nina needed to sober up. She was supposed to meet Johana at noon to drop off her car. Her friend would then drive her to the airport. Nina racked her brain for a solution. She couldn't drive to Houston right now, not in her condition. It was midnight.

A tap on the window startled Nina and she screamed with fright. Her hands flew to her heart, then she recognized Eli. She pushed the button and the window slid down.

"Eli, you almost gave me a heart attack!"

He chuckled. "Sorry about that. The way you sped into the parking lot made me worry someone was chasing you. I was just headin' home."

Nina's heart finally slowed, but the ache still throbbed. "Yeah, I probably shouldn't be driving. That's why I parked here."

"You need a ride?"

Nina thought about it. "I don't know where to go. I left Maria and Jose's to go to Raphe's and then…." Her words caught in her throat and tears filled her eyes.

Eli opened the driver's side door and helped her out. He handed her a diner napkin from his pocket and patted her shoulder. "I'm sorry, Nina. Looks like it hasn't been your night."

His voice was warm and soothing. Nina didn't know what came over her, but from the stress of losing everything, to thinking she found something really special, only to lose it all again was too much. She began to sob in earnest and Eli wrapped her in his arms. His strength was comforting. Eli could have been a quarterback for the Texans. He was all smooth muscle and super fit.

He patted her back like a newborn. "Shh. Whatever it is, it'll be okay."

Nina hugged him back. She really didn't know Eli well enough to take comfort in his arms, but he'd been kind to her, and she really needed a comforting hug right now.

"Look, I got a couch you can sleep on and a basset hound that you can cry with. Humphrey loves to wail," he chuckled.

Nina sniffed and laughed, wiping her tears on the Cupcake Diner and Dive napkin. She really didn't see any other options outside of going to a hotel. It was the middle of the night and she would be up in a few hours to get ready to leave anyway. She nodded to Eli. "Thanks. If you don't think I'll be too much of an inconvenience. I really have nowhere else to go."

Eli shook his head. "Come on." He turned to the catering van and opened the passenger door. "My car's down at the shop. Mac says it'll be done tomorrow." He beamed. "Hey, maybe I can drop you back at your car around eight and then you can drop me at the mechanic's shop."

Nina nodded and gave him a watery smile.

"See, this will help us both out." He grinned.

Nina felt awkward lounging on Eli's couch in his small condo for the night. It was almost like she'd entered a parallel universe. Eli was just as all male sexy as Raphe and he had a basset hound warming up all the soft spaces in his apartment. Humphrey was a bit older than Lulu. The white hair around his eyes, front paws and chest gave hint to his basset years. Eli stood in his condo kitchen, taking up most of the space.

"Can I get you something to drink?"

Nina gave a nervous laugh. "Like a shot of tequila or a diet soda?"

Eli raised one eyebrow, looking down at his sports watch. "I wasn't planning that kind of night, but anything to make you feel better."

Nina smiled. "I was just joking. I think I had enough earlier. It probably heightened my emotions and that's why I'm sitting on your barstool now."

Eli opened the freezer and pulled out a bottle of vodka. "I don't have tequila, but a little chilled vodka with lemon should do the trick." He poured a healthy amount into two glasses and sliced a lemon. He squeezed half in each glass and made a fancy sliver to grace the sides of their glasses. They each downed their shot and Eli held up the bottle to Nina in question. She nodded silently and he poured them another, grabbing another lemon from the basket on the island that separated them. Nina couldn't help looking at him differently now, outside the café. He wasn't all business anymore. He felt like an old friend, though she barely knew him. His warm smile and casual manner made her feel at ease. She knew if she wasn't already head-over-heels for Raphe, she would have made a play for Melvina's hot brother, but he was also Raphe's brother-in-law and she needed to focus on staying the course to get out of Magnolia.

"You wanna talk about it?"

Nina shook her head as tears welled in her eyes. Then after a brief silence, she told him everything. At the end of her story, Eli wrapped her in a warm hug again. She could smell the diner's familiar scent of coffee, cinnamon rolls, and syrup, but she also smelled a totally different scent that must be Eli. It was nice. She backed away, giving him a smile of thanks.

"I really appreciate you letting me stay. I'll try to be quiet and let you sleep."

Eli moved to the nearby living room. He lifted a large trunk that served as a coffee table and pulled out a quilt and a pillow. "You're welcome to sleep in my bed."

Nina's eyes widened. Eli quickly added. "I'll sleep on the couch. The sheets on the bed were just changed by the cleaning lady this morning."

Nina relaxed. Of course, he meant for her to be comfortable. He considered her his guest and he was a nice guy.

"Thanks, but I'll take the couch. I won't sleep if I think I'm stealing your bed."

Eli placed the items on the couch and called for Humphrey to follow him. He turned at the small hallway and pointed toward a door. "Bathroom's there. Sorry, I don't have an extra toothbrush. It's just me and Humphrey, but please make yourself at home. I'll wake you in the morning."

The old basset yawned and jumped up on the couch as if waiting for Nina. She smiled at Humphrey and joined him, petting his long basset ears and giving him a kiss on the forehead. Eli looked at her with something she didn't want to define. For all his brotherly politeness, maybe he did have an interest in her.

"Well, I can't compete with that. I guess he'll be sleeping with you if you'll allow it. I'll leave my door open a crack in case he changes his mind."

Nina nodded and Humphrey did a little moonwalk on the quilt before laying on top of it.

"There are more blankets in the trunk. Help yourself." He turned toward his room, hesitated, then turned back. "Nina, Raphe's a good guy. He may have a past, but it doesn't mean he's incapable of sharing a future with you." He tapped twice on the door frame to the hallway. "Don't sell yourself short. He'd be a lucky guy if you give him half a chance."

Raphe drove by Maria and Jose's first, but didn't see Nina's little Ford. Her car wasn't at Bonnie's either. Maybe she went to some other friend's he didn't know about. He didn't think she would go by Mona's, but he drove by just in case. No luck.

As he drove past the diner, he spotted a car in the empty lot. His heart raced as he realized it was Nina's, but it was empty. *Where could she have gone?* For a moment he thought of terrible scenarios of thugs dragging her off into a beat-up van or the police arresting her for drinking and driving. *Should I go by the police station?*

He tried to think straight and calm his beating heart. Surely, nothing so drastic had happened in such a short time. She probably just called Bonnie to pick her up. He'd check with his friend, Roland Karr, down at the station, just to make sure. He scrubbed his fingers through his hair. The night had been perfect, aside from Roxanne and Gail showing up unannounced and on the prowl. He was happy and falling in love with Nina and then his past came back to bite him in the ass. *Who am I kidding? I've already fallen. Hard. I should have worked harder convincing her that my past is my past.* Everything changed when Nina walked into his life. Or rather when he walked into the diner and she was there. Damn, it just wasn't his night.

Raphe called the station first thing in the morning. He needed to take the day off and make things right with Nina. The chief didn't ask why, and Raphe didn't tell. He liked that the chief treated his men as responsible adults and respected their privacy. He still needed to collect his thoughts and work through what he wanted to say.

Raphe called his mother to make sure Lulu was still okay and told her he'd be by later to pick her up. He hoped Nina would be okay with their canine guest for the night. Melvina and Riley were coming home tomorrow and it wouldn't look good if Raphe had pawned Lulu off on his parents for days. Besides, he missed Lulu and wanted to see if she'd fattened up any. He was actually excited about the prospect of puppies. Would they look like Jake or Humphrey or both? He'd read somewhere that there could be multiple fathers for the same litter. *Imagine that?* He tried, but he couldn't get past Jake's head on Lulu's body. It wasn't exactly cute. Somehow, he knew whatever Lulu's puppies looked like, he'd be smitten.

"Of course," his mom said on the phone. "I haven't minded keeping Lulu. If you want, I'll bring her over to Riley's when they get back tomorrow." Raphe's mother loved dogs, and they'd lost their Great Dane just a month before. They hadn't recovered from the heartbreak yet to get another family dog.

"Naw, it's all right, Mom. Two nights is enough. I'll come get her later this afternoon. I got something to do first."

"Well, don't be too late, and I'll save you some of my homemade lasagna."

Raphe moaned with anticipation and regret. "I don't know if I can stay for dinner. I'm sort of up in the air right now with plans."

Raphe's mother scoffed. "Raphe Rudolph Nash! Don't tell me you don't have time for dinner when you don't even have plans yet."

It sounded bad to his own ears, but it was too much to explain and the last person he wanted to tell that he'd fallen in love was his mother. She would scream with excitement, dance around in the living room, and start planning his wedding before he'd even proposed. "Mom, I hate it when you use my middle name."

"Rudolph Valentino was a handsome man! You should be honored to be named after such an iconic actor."

"Yeah, Mom. Every time Ran and I sit around and talk about our names, we agree that our mother naming us after an iconic sex symbol is just the thing we would have asked to be printed on our birth certificates. Where was dad when you named us anyway?" They'd had this conversation a hundred times. He smiled, looking out the window of his apartment as he talked to his mother.

She harrumphed, then chuckled. "Your father would have agreed to Moonbeam or Sunshine if I had wanted it. Besides, that was the deal. He chose your first name and I chose your middle."

Raphe nodded to himself. "Yep, good old Dad."

His mother chuckled. "I hope you'll be lucky enough to love someone that much one day."

Raphe saw where the conversation was heading and curtailed the direction with, "I appreciate that, Mom. Anyway, I gotta go. See you around five to pick up Lulu. Set two extra place settings. I'll be bringing someone for you and Dad to meet."

Chapter 28

If anyone could set Nina straight on who Raphe really was, it was his mom and dad. They had been married forty-seven years and were still in love to this day. He loved seeing his mom's posts on social media with his father's protective arm around her shoulders or his mother's laughing smile. They were a storybook pair and he very much wanted that type of relationship for himself. Nina had lit an inferno inside him, and it wasn't only lust fueling the fire. He loved her quick wit, warm heart, even her hot temper. He liked watching Lulu cuddle up next to her on his couch, as she spent an hour or more stroking the sweet basset hound. She spoke lovingly of Maria and Jose's kids and the children she'd worked with through her job at CPS. His parents would love that about her. Nina loved children and hopefully, they would have several.

He dialed her number again with no answer. It was already eight o'clock and he began to worry again. His cop friend, Roland, hadn't filed any reports on Nina or anyone fitting her description last night. Bonnie hadn't seen her. Maria hadn't answered the phone, but it was probably because she was at the café. Raphe took a shower and headed to the Cupcake Diner and Dive. He'd probably catch Maria working and possibly Nina, too, though she hadn't said anything about having to work today.

Raphe noticed Nina's car was gone when he parked at the diner. He would have to appeal to Maria to tell him where he could find her. Stepping through the diner door, he found it was standing room only. The chief and Mona were waiting for a booth to be cleaned and about ten other patrons were waiting to be seated. Pop was seating guests as Roberta called out orders through the cook's window to Maria. Eli rang up checks at the register, and Raphe was shocked to see Darcey plowing through the kitchen doors into the area behind the counter. Her eyes caught his and she scowled, sticking out her tongue.

Mona poked him in the chest with a broad smile. "Hey there, Raphe. I thought you were sick." Thank goodness her lips were thin again. He liked her natural smile.

Raphe looked at the chief, "I, uh… took a personal day. In fact, I'm looking for Nina. Have you seen her?"

Mona's eyes took on a look of pity. The chief cleared his throat and pulled at his collar.

Raphe began to panic. "Where is she?"

Pop grabbed two menus and motioned for Mona and the chief to follow. Mona looked at Manny, who looked at Raphe with a sigh. "She took Eli to the shop this morning and then told him she was flying to California. She's at the airport by now."

Raphe felt like his legs would collapse. He gripped onto the hostess stand.

Mona squeezed Manny's arm, looking at the chief with an imploring gaze. The chief took in a deep breath. "You want to join us? You look like you could use a seat."

Raphe gathered up his wits. He'd been sucker punched before, but this was all new to him. He'd built up this dream of finally trusting someone and now that he'd given his heart, she was flying across the country with it.

He turned, walking toward Eli at the register. "Did Nina say when she was coming back?"

Eli looked uncomfortable. "She told me she was quitting—said she was moving to California to stay with her brother."

A lady held her check in front of Eli's nose. "I only had one cinnamon roll. There are two on the bill. That waitress charged me for two!" She complained.

Eli gave her a flat smile and took the lady's check. "Sorry, ma'am. It's Darcey's first day back. How about I comp both rolls and send you home with a hot coffee to go?"

The lady preened. "Alrighty then, that'd be nice."

"Which airport? Which airline?" Raphe barked at Eli.

Again, Eli shrugged his shoulder. "I just dropped her off here to get her car this morning, and then she took me to get my car from Mac. Outside of that, I don't know anything." He gave Raphe a look of pity. Eli looked like he had more to tell but was holding on to it for now. "Sorry, Raphe."

Raphe went behind the counter and passed Darcey, who blanched as she almost lost the grip on her tray. He made his way to the kitchen and looked at Maria, who was placing a fluffy omelet on an oval plate with home fries.

"What airport? Which airline?" He repeated.

Maria shook her head. "I'm sorry Raphe. I don't know. Her brother Carlos lives in San Francisco. Jose probably knows where. I didn't ask Nina about her trip. She said she would tell you last night."

Raphe leaned against the kitchen door as Darcey slid through and dumped a tray by the dishwasher's station. "Serve's you right, you jerk. How does it feel to get dumped?"

Raphe shook his head, holding his tongue. Darcey had the right to be hurt, but he'd never lied to her about the relationship. He'd said they were just having fun and she'd agreed. He'd broken it off when she kept showing up at his place in Houston unannounced. She'd taken it badly and apparently went in an entirely different direction. Seeing her at the café was a sign that she was trying to turn her life back around. He didn't want to be the reason she left again. He bit his tongue and walked away. As he was leaving, Mona called out his name. The chief murmured something to Mona, but Raphe kept walking.

He couldn't fly off to California to chase Nina down—not today anyway. He only hoped she would call him when she got there, and they could talk. Then he would fly there to tell her in person how much she meant to him and how he wanted to change things between them. He wanted a life with her, and Raphe was pretty sure she wanted one with him, too, if she could accept his past.

Nina boarded the plane, gripping a bunch of tissues she'd grabbed in the airport ladies' room. She'd started crying last night and it kept catching her in waves. She couldn't be crying all these tears over Raphe. He'd asked her to move in with him. She'd been upset by the two women who showed up at his apartment unannounced, but when she calmed down to think about it, he hadn't invited them.

Nina knew Raphe had a past when she met him. She knew his reputation preceded him and she'd still gone out with him. She'd still slept with him. He'd told her he was falling in love with her. She was sure he wouldn't have said that to either Roxanne or Gail. People changed, so why wasn't she giving Raphe the chance to prove what he said was true? Why was she on this plane running away to her brother?

Nina honestly didn't know. So much had happened since breaking up with Derek, then losing him along with everything she owned in the fire. Her leave from CPS had expired and she hadn't wanted to go back. She couldn't live with Maria and Jose forever and after seeing those women waiting for Raphe, it terrified her to think she could lose the last thing she really cared about. *What if it doesn't work out between us? What if Raphe thinks he's in love but doesn't have it in him to settle down?*

Images of the blonde and redhead kissing each other while holding magnums of champagne made her think of Raphe's previous carousing. He'd said he'd given up a trip to Vegas to watch Lulu. *How many other wild flings had he been involved in?*

Nina buckled her seatbelt and glanced at her cellphone before turning it off. He'd called multiple times, but she hadn't listened to the messages, nor had she read the many texts. She didn't want to see or hear what he had to say because she knew she would cave. She knew she would stay, and she knew he would break her heart. She'd be safer in San Francisco.

Chapter 29

Melvina and Riley waved from the porch as Raphe drove down the long gravel road to the ranch. He would avoid telling them about Nina. He knew Eli, Maria, or Mona would convey the news of his heartbreak within hours, minutes, or seconds of their arrival back in Magnolia. Nothing stayed secret for long in a small town, and Raphe didn't feel like hashing through it all over again.

He was actually happy to distract them with the recount of Lulu's wild romp with Jake at the fire station and then with Humphrey in Mona's car. Surprisingly, Mona hadn't called Melvina to tattle on him, so his sister-in-law was about to be shocked.

Lulu bounced out of the truck bare bottomed and tail wagging. Raphe held up a gift bag to Melvina as he approached the porch. "We might have lost the blue and white pair. Hope hot pink is ok, though I don't think you'll be needing them anymore."

Melvina laughed, stooping down to greet her eager basset pup. "Yeah, you can return those. Lulu's appointment to get snipped is next week. We won't have to worry about doggy diapers anymore."

"I'm real sorry to tell you this, guys, but Lulu's pregnant." Raphe glanced between Riley and Melvina, then down to sweet Lulu with her innocent basset brown eyes as she danced at Melvina's feet. Neither seemed to hear what he'd said, so he continued. "Vet Tarleton said she was strong and able to have healthy pups in about seven weeks. And, before you get mad, I want a puppy and I promise to find homes for all of the others, however many she has. Mom and Dad said they'd take one or two. Mom watched Lulu a couple nights for me and they're ready for another dog."

"One or two? Are you serious, Raphe?" Riley's mouth dropped in surprise. He put his arm around Melvina's shoulders and chuckled. Melvina still hadn't said anything. "I told you Raphe knew nothing about taking care of women."

Raphe winced. His older brother had no idea how his comment had struck home. Riley seemed to sense that his joke was ill received. He clapped Raphe on the shoulder. "It's not that big of a deal. It's my fault for missing that last vet appointment to have Lulu spayed."

Melvina glared at them both. "It is very much a big deal. There are too many unwanted pups in the world. How are we going to find good homes for all of Lulu and Humphrey's babies?"

Raphe cleared his throat. "Um, they may not all be Humphrey's." He winced as Melvina went through a second compilation of facial expressions that didn't express joy. "I'll find good homes for all of them. I promise. Please don't be mad at me, Melvina. I've had a really bad few days." He paused. "I never intended for this to happen. It was a sequence of events that no one could have prevented."

Riley looked at Raphe with concern, then to Melvina. "It'll be all right." He patted his wife's shoulder then squeezed her to him. To Raphe, he said, "Things like this happen and they have a way of working themselves out." His chin rested on Melvina's head. "Let's all head down to Bubbles and have a drink. We'll laugh about it together."

Riley had always been his champion for getting Raphe out of trouble when it counted and for that he was grateful, but he politely declined.

At least he had the excuse of going to work. "My shift starts tonight at six." He promised he'd see them at the weekly family dinner, then scratched Lulu behind the ears and left. He didn't know what he'd be doing when the puppies were born, but he'd better start looking for reliable homes that could pass the Melvina test.

Lexi kneeled in the garden in front of Raphe with Damien by her side. The youngest of her three boys had a dimple in his left cheek and a smattering of freckles across his pert nose. His hair was the color of Ran's, Riley's, and Raphe's. They shared a common coloring that told others they were brothers. People often mistook Damien as Raphe's own son when they were seen out together. Lexi's blonde coloring was so different than the boys and their father Jack.

"You still pining over Nina?"

Raphe sighed. "I don't want to talk about it, Lexi."

She smiled gently at him, tilting her head as she planted another row of peppers. "I know you don't want to, but sometimes it helps."

"Yeah, Mom's been harping that same advice, but I don't feel like it yet." It had been three weeks since Nina had left. He'd left about a gazillion phone messages and texts on her phone.

"It's been a while now, Raphe. She hasn't called you, or texted you, and she hasn't come back. I think it's time to move on. Melissa is back in town. You had your eye on her back in high school."

"Melissa Thompson?"

Lexi chuckled and nodded.

Damien made a car noise as he drove his play car through the mound of dirt he'd excavated. "Yes, she always had a thing for you too, but then you moved off after high school and she married Frank Ernst and moved to Dallas. She's been divorced over a year now."

Raphe shook his head. "No way. Divorced women have a ton of baggage."

"No way!" Damien repeated.

Lexi scowled at Raphe and he muttered a curse under his breath. "I'm sorry. That wasn't a nice thing to say."

"Don't listen to your Uncle Raphe, Damien. He's just a bitter old Neanderthal."

Raphe's mouth dropped. "That's not true. I'm thirty-eight. Barely into my prime."

Lexi scoffed. "Yeah and you aren't getting any younger. There are a ton of women out there, some that might even put up with you. What's so special about Nina?"

Raphe used the small shovel to dig a deep hole before putting the seeds in and patting the dirt back over it. He was working on a row of peas. "I don't know." He paused. Nina's smiling face came back to him with crystal clarity. How she laughed when he dipped her in his arms while dancing, how she moaned underneath him when they made love, how she had confided in him about her family and the children she'd tried to protect through her job. "It's everything about her. She loves children and gets so upset when she see's wrong in the world. She's passionate and I don't just mean in the S-E-X way."

"Sex!" Damien repeated, staring awestruck at Raphe.

"He's seven and in the second grade, Raphe. He can spell three-letter words." Raphe's look of shock turned to a chuckle and Lexi joined him

161

laughing. "And he can say the four-letter ones too, so watch your mouth." She shook her trowel at her brother.

Raphe nodded, reaching across Lexi to Damien and giving him a noogie on top of his head.

"You'd like her, Lexi. She's beautiful, smart, warm and has a fiery temper like you." He winked.

"Well right now I'm not real fond of the woman who's breakin' my big brother's heart, but if she comes back and apologizes real nice, I might give her a chance."

Raphe could only hope.

Chapter 30

"How's the pregnant bitch?"

Rosie and Bonnie were sitting on either side of Ran at the long mahogany table that graced his parents', Ronald and Regina Nash's home. At least once or twice a month, all the siblings and their significant others, if they had one, gathered for brunch in the formal dining room to catch up and spend time together.

Raphe hefted his fork, topped with crispy home fries, midway to his mouth as he began to choke and cough. He grabbed his mimosa and drained it as Riley clapped him on the back, smiling.

Raphe noticed his mother and father continued to smile politely at Rosie's outrageous comment as Melvina answered. "She's doing really good, thanks. The vet says he counted six pups in the ultrasound. Raphe says they've all been spoken for."

That was news to Raphe.

Rosie's brows knitted together. "I was hoping you'd let me take one. I'll be a bit lonely when Bonnie here ties the knot with Randolph."

Now his mother's face lit up in surprise. "Ran, you didn't tell us!"

A cacophony of coughing and choking made its way around the table. Bonnie turned pink and Ran looked like he was searching for something on his plate and a ghost had eaten it.

"Aunt Rosie, we are not engaged!" Bonnie fussed, then made a general apology to the table for the confusion.

"Well, like that famous gal singer says, if he likes the sex, he better put a ring around you." Rosie punctuated her comment with a firm nod at Ran and Bonnie. "You need to tell 'em, no huggy, no lissy until I get a wedding ring." Rosie wiggled her long, wrinkled fingers with red painted fingernail polish. Each long appendage had its own sparkly bobble of a ring glinting in the sunlight.

"Lissy?" Bonnie repeated in confusion.

Rosie's face sobered. "Yeah, like listen. Lissy. I won't listen to your sorry butt anymore if you don't buy me a damn ring. You have to tell men what-cha want, little lady. They don't know how to read your mind. I mean, hey, why buy the cow if you can get the milk for free?"

Bonnie's cheeks were flaming red now, but Raphe doubted it was only embarrassment coloring her cheeks.

He couldn't help but chuckle as Melvina sprayed a bit of her mimosa onto her plate as she choked with laughter. Raphe's parents didn't know what to do. They'd been properly warned that no one could be held accountable for what came out of Rosie's mouth, but she was Bonnie's family, and Ran wanted to include her. Rosie made Ran burst with laughter on all occasions, but she'd caught him off guard with the engagement comment. Raphe wondered how Bonnie would react to Ran's sudden catatonic state.

Raphe thought of Nina and how well she would fit in at the table, sitting next to him. Nina loved Rosie's antics and Raphe knew his parents would love her.

Rosie didn't pause to get the joke but continued. "Looks like you better man up, Ran. I hear there's a sale going on at Desmond's Diamonds." She gave them all a wink before asking, "What's for dessert?"

Maria set a cup of steaming hot coffee down in front of Raphe. He sat at a booth, avoiding the counter today and almost every day he'd come in now for two reasons. He didn't want to talk to anyone he knew about Nina and he wanted to avoid Darcey. The saucy waitress seemed to have put the axe away over their parting long ago, and she had talked to him briefly a few times at the cafe. She'd called him several times, but he hadn't answered. There was a palatable indifference between them now that didn't need to be warmed up or cooled down.

He was glad Darcey had left the strip joint and was using the money she'd saved to attend classes at the local community college. That's what a lot of dancers claimed they were doing with their hard-earned money, but Darcey was really doing it. She was getting a degree in hospitality so she could one day run the diner or someplace else that would let her take charge.

"How are you doing today?" Maria's warm affection was appreciated but not desired. He knew she felt partly responsible for his heartbreak and he was mad at himself for letting people see how Nina's leaving affected him. Raphe would have avoided the diner altogether, but he needed to eat, and The Cupcake Diner and Dive had become his home away from home. The men who cooked at the fire house fed everyone on shift and his mother cooked on Sundays for the family, but he couldn't handle her pity right now.

"I'm just fine, Maria. Don't fret over me. You got lots of customers this morning. I'll have the usual, then I need to get to work. My shift starts in an hour."

Maria nodded, then left with his order. Riley came up to the booth shortly after Maria, sliding into the opposite side. "Hey little brother. Mind if I join ya?"

Raphe smiled and nodded. He guessed if he had wanted solitude, he should have nuked a biscuit from the freezer.

"Any word yet?"

Raphe supposed Riley was asking about Nina. The way gossip ran around Magnolia, he was surprised Mac Green hadn't pulled up a chair and asked. Raphe shook his head. "I just don't get it. I know her ex-fiancé cheated on her and she felt guilty when she broke up with him the night before he died. She knew of my reputation before we even dated, but Gail and Roxanne didn't do me any favors the night they showed up." He shook his head, remembering the sexy duo sauntering toward him and Nina on the balcony. "I shouldn't be mad at them. It's my own fault for being who I was before. That guy would have said yes to it all. I guess she had a right to run. Nina was different than those gals. I suppose she thought I would end up hurting her."

Riley nodded. "You did have quite a reputation."

Raphe scoffed. "It was never a problem before."

Riley smiled like he was halfway enjoying himself. "You weren't in love before. It hurts, doesn't it?"

Raphe blew out a sigh. "I don't know what to do. I'd go after her, prove to her I'm a good guy and that I can see this through if she'd just give me half a chance, but what am I supposed to do? I can't just fly to San Fran and start hollerin' out her name in the airport. My hands are tied."

Riley nodded again. Maria dropped off another cup of coffee for Riley and set down the stack of pancakes with eggs, rancher's bacon, and warm syrup in front of Raphe.

"Well, I see your depression hasn't hurt your appetite," Riley teased.

Raphe pulled the plate closer. "No, if anything it's made me a workout maniac and that just makes me eat more calories."

"The single ladies are gonna love that. Have you thought about getting back on the horse?" Riley nudged.

Raphe shook his head. "Naw, I'm not ready. Last thing I need to do is get tangled up with someone I don't care about. When Nina comes back…"

Riley stared at him and Raphe looked away. "I'm just not ready yet."

Riley ordered his breakfast and then changed the subject. "Casino Nights has just been announced by the Blossoms. Melvina's helping Mona with all the details. You gonna go?"

Raphe nodded. "Sounds like fun."

"It's weeks away, so you got plenty of time to get it together and find a date."

Raphe scowled. He knew Riley was trying to nudge him along, but he wasn't ready to see himself with someone else. "Maybe I'll ask Lexi. I'm not the only one who needs to start living again."

Riley smiled with genuine pleasure. "That'd be nice. I bet she could use an adult night out. Maybe Mom and Dad can babysit?"

Melvina joined their table, sliding in beside Riley. The couple was still as lovesick about one another today as they had been when they got engaged two years ago. It made Raphe's heart swell to see Riley so happy. He tried to put aside his own broken heart.

"How are the cakes?"

"I think someone is looking for compliments." Riley raised his eyebrows.

Melvina gave Riley a playful slap. "No really, yesterday Maria made the pancake batter and today I did, so I need to know which recipe is better."

Riley chuckled. "See, she hasn't changed. She's still just as competitive in the kitchen as she was the night of the Best Buns Bakeoff."

Melvina snorted. "It was said that my rolls actually won that contest," she teased.

Riley's mouth opened wide as he gave Raphe a mocking stare. "Did you hear that? Now, Melvina Nash, everyone in town knows you made up that rumor so you didn't have to take second place to me."

Melvina laughed. "Well, you can't argue that I beat you fair and square in the five-alarm chili competition."

Riley's wide grin said it all. "You used my brisket from Braised."

"My recipe called for the best and everyone knows where the best can be found."

Riley patted Melvina on her leg. "It's sitting right here next to me."

His brother was looking at his wife with more emotion than Raphe had the stomach for. "All right you two, get outta here before I lose my breakfast."

Melvina stood up, kissing Riley before she left. "Did you ask him?"

Raphe lifted his brow in curiosity. "Ask me what?"

"There's a new blossom, and she doesn't have a date for the Casino party. I was hoping you might come by Bubbles tonight and meet her."

Riley clasped Melvina's hand in his. "It's not a good time, sweetheart. I got a guy at Braised who might want to join us instead."

Melvina leaned over and gave Raphe one of those sisterly hugs she was always giving Eli. He wouldn't mind, except he saw sympathy in her eyes. Raphe stood up and threw a few bills on the table for Maria. "Thanks, you guys, but I gotta get to work."

Maurice sat on the steps of the diner skipping rocks across the pavement. Raphe stopped and looked down at Maria's son. He was a good-looking teen and Raphe was sure he probably had lots of girls chasing him at school. The kid looked like he'd lost his best friend.

"Aren't you and the boys supposed to be washing trucks today?" Raphe pulled a stick of chewing gum out of his pocket and offered one to Maurice.

The teen didn't look up but nodded, ignoring the gum. "Did someone kick your dog?" Raphe asked, joking.

Maurice shook his head, no. "I haven't got a dog."

Raphe looked back into the diner where Melvina was talking to Maria. Maybe she would let Maurice have a puppy. He'd ask his sister-in-law to ask Maria and Jose before getting the kid's hopes up.

"Wanna tell me what's got you down?"

Maurice's dark hair fell across his forehead in long locks, making him look like a young version of Elvis. His jeans and white t-shirt were reminiscent of the era too. "Women." His complaint sounded matter of fact.

Raphe wanted to laugh, but stifled his chuckle, trying to look serious. The kid was obviously heartbroken. Raphe wanted to tell him it wouldn't be the last time and give him some advice about the difference between a crush and true love. Young hearts actually healed quicker than older ones, but hell, what did Raphe know about it all? Nina was the first woman he'd fallen in love with and he was almost forty.

"I hear you, Maurice. You wanna ride to the station with me? Then you can tell me all about her."

Maurice stood up, nodding. He made a loud sniff, then walked alongside Raphe.

They drove the few short blocks to the station in silence before Maurice finally said. "I love her so much."

"Who?"

Maurice looked at him with sad brown eyes. "Heather Casey. She's in the grade ahead of me. She's dating this jock dude and he doesn't deserve her."

Maurice had a crush on Melvina a few years before, but now had moved on to women just a year older than himself. It was progress.

Raphe put the truck in park. "Have you told her how you feel?"

Maurice shook his head again. "She doesn't even know I exist. She only likes football players."

Raphe wasn't sure if it was good advice, but the kid could use some direction and he was a great runner. "Have you thought about going out for the team to impress her?"

"Tryouts for next year start in two weeks. She'll be on summer vacation before we even start practice."

"If you want to get her attention, Maurice, you gotta earn it. Sometimes it's a long road." Raphe wished he had taken his own advice and told Nina he loved her when he had the chance. He clapped Maurice on the shoulder. "Let's go clean some trucks and think of a strategy to win."

Chapter 31

Six weeks had passed since Nina had left, and Raphe was still not himself. He'd worked every shift he'd been given and took any extra shifts that were offered. He'd avoided calls from Roxanne and Gail and even one from Darcey inviting him to come to her new apartment. He'd shaken his head with worry. Melvina wasn't too mad at him when she heard about the drama between him and Jose's cousin, but lately he'd avoided the diner. He paid one of the young recruits to bring him takeout. His life had become dull and tiring and he wondered what he could do to get out of his funk.

Ran pulled up to the station and got out of a new car with a long box of what was undoubtedly Melvina's cupcakes. Several cheers went up as Ran moseyed into the station. Raphe stirred his coffee, wondering why his brother was visiting.

Ran chatted with a few of the men before approaching Raphe.

"I thought you could use some diner treats, seeing how you've been exiled from the café." Ran smiled.

Raphe scoffed. "I haven't been exiled. I just haven't had time to be hanging out at the diner." He decided to change the subject before it could even begin. The last thing he needed was a heart-to-heart at work. "Trade in your motorcycle for a respectable car?"

Ran snorted. "Never. I picked it up last week. Bonnie's tired of getting her hair messed up every time I take her out, and her aunt kept groping me on the bike when I took her to therapy. Plus, I got tired of bugging dad to use his truck when it rained."

"You drove Rosie to therapy on your motorcycle?" Raphe couldn't help smiling at the image of Rosie gripping Ran as they made the short trip down the main drag.

Ran nodded and they both broke into a hearty laugh.

"How's it going between you and Bonnie?"

Ran looked like he was thinking about how to word his response. "It's going good. Rosie has a nurse coming in to stay with her now and I'm going to ask Bonnie to marry me." Ran paused for a minute, making himself a coffee, then biting into one of the cakes. "I'm going to do it, Raphe, and I want you to be my best man."

Raphe was caught off guard. He knew that Ran and Bonnie had become inseparable, but he had no idea that things were getting so serious. "It's only been a couple of months since you met."

Ran nodded. "I know, but when the right woman walked into my life, I knew I didn't need to wait a year to make up my mind. I want to start forever with her now."

Raphe was speechless. He knew what Ran was saying. Hadn't he said the exact same thing to Nina? No, he'd said he thought he *might* be falling in love. He'd said he wanted her to move in with him. He'd never mentioned marriage, and then his past had chased her away like a bat out of hell and the rest was history.

"So, what do you say? Will you be my best man?" Ran's grin clearly indicated that Raphe would say yes.

Happiness for his brother washed over him and he finally found the right words. "I'd be honored. I'm really happy for you, man." Raphe clapped his brother on the shoulder, then clasped Ran to him in a bear hug.

The chief interrupted them to pour a cup of coffee and grab a cupcake. "What are we celebrating?"

Raphe glanced at Ran, waiting for him to share the news. Ran smiled. "No celebrating just yet. I've still got to pop the question first." He winked at the chief and then said good-bye to Raphe.

The chief smiled broadly and clapped Raphe on the shoulder. "Congratulations are in order, I think."

Raphe nodded. "Yep, it looks like our summer months will be booked. First, you and Mona, and now Ran and Bonnie."

The chief smiled knowingly. "Oh yeah, but you know these things always come in threes. I wonder who will be Magnolia's third lucky couple?"

Nina sat on the toilet staring at the bright blue line of the home pregnancy kit. She looked down at the waste can where two other kits with similar blue lines had been tossed. *They can't all be wrong, Nina. You've really gone and done it now.*

Since moving to San Francisco, she'd jumped into things full speed ahead. She didn't give herself time to dwell on Raphe or what could have been. Nina finished a continuing education class to fulfill the credits she needed to apply for her social worker's license in California, took the state exam and then accepted the first job that was offered.

She applied for a job at the private school down the street from her brother's Victorian home, and now she could walk to work. The area was beautiful, and the neighborhood was convenient to everything she needed. The pay was better than what she'd made with her state job, but then the cost of living was higher. The weather was beautiful, but the people weren't as warm as they were in Magnolia. Nina remembered that first day in the café and how that man in the overalls had talked down to her, thinking she didn't understand English. *Ok, so not everyone in Magnolia was perfect.*

People were people wherever you went, but she'd liked the friendly smiles of the diner customers and she really missed laughing with Bonnie, Mona, and Rosie. California wasn't the same. Here, people were wary of strangers and no one really smiled unless they knew you. She didn't know many people, but Carlos had introduced her to a few of his programming friends from his company. They were nice enough, but she hadn't made any real connections yet.

Sighing, she tossed the white stick in the trash. It was official, she was pregnant. Now the question washed over her with dread. What would she do? Her brother was a devout Catholic like their grandmother had been. Nina had quit going to church long ago, but her upbringing triggered a wave of guilt. She was unwed, she couldn't have an abortion, and adoption was out of the question. She knew without asking herself that she was having this baby. The question was, how to tell her brother and could she tell Raphe?

"Hello, Rosie. Is Bonnie there?"

"Nina! Where have you been? The town hasn't been the same without you. I made a special batch of moonshine just the other day and I was thinking about all the fun we had. Why'd you have to run off and break that young man's heart? He's too gorgeous to be moping around much longer.

You better get that Latina booty of yours back to Magnolia before I have to give that man a pity-fuck."

Nina blanched, then she giggled, and let out a breath she'd been holding for way too long.

"You mean, he's still single?" Nina asked hopefully.

Rosie harrumphed. "I honestly don't know what that man sees in you or why he's waited so long. Hell, there's a line out to the county-line waitin' for that hunk to quit pining over you, and let me tell ya, I haven't seen this many young available women in Magnolia in three decades. I think they are coming from as far as Dallas!"

Nina laughed. She knew Bonnie's aunt was trying to make a point, but a part of her heart palpitated with the thought of truly losing him. She'd never called Raphe back. She'd never told anyone the address of where she'd gone. Maria obviously hadn't shared her location with Raphe, or maybe he never asked. Fear skittered down her spine. She'd tried her best to forget him, but she hadn't. Nina knew that even without the pregnancy, she would still be making this call to Bonnie. She might have been running herself ragged trying not to think about what could have been, but Raphe was imprinted in her brain and her body pined for his touch. As soon as her head hit the pillow each night, she found herself blissful in his arms or tossing and turning from him being just out of reach. Her lack of sleep was impacting her ability to concentrate, and she felt empty inside.

She would now have a part of Raphe no matter what he decided about the baby, but she knew she had to tell him first before telling anyone else.

"Thanks, Rosie. I appreciate the kick in the ass."

Rosie cackled. "So, when should I tell Bonnie you're coming?"

Chapter 32

Raphe put on his tux and looked down at the puppy bed in his bathroom. He'd picked out the runt of the litter and named him Rudy, after his mother's favorite actor. He was tri-colored like Humphrey and had big soulful brown eyes like Lulu. All the puppies looked like purebred bassets. He supposed old Jake's attempt at procreation hadn't taken. There were six pups in the litter, two lemon and four tri-colored.

His mom and dad adopted two lemon-colored pups. Mona and Manny took a tri-colored one. Ran and Bonnie agreed on a pup and Manny's sister kept another. There was only one puppy left and it was being heavily bid on between Rosie and her caregiver and Maria and Jose. Raphe wanted Rosie to be happy but wasn't sure she would live long enough to take care of the dog for its whole life. This dog pregnancy fiasco had taught him there were lots of things to consider when taking on responsibilities.

He looked down at Rudy. "Don't worry little buddy. I'm ready for the commitment. I'm going to be the best dog papa ever and there will be lots of rides in the firetruck and in my souped-up ride." He smiled thinking about his brother Ran and Bonnie with their new puppy, Marquis, riding in a kit car he'd bought for his motorcycle. Raphe supposed it was the first of many steps that Ran would take before settling down and buying a minivan. Tonight was the night he would pop the question.

Mona's casino night fundraiser promised to be fun and everyone with money to donate from Dallas, Houston, and San Antonio would be at the gala. It was being held in a swank hotel in The Woodlands. There would be a cash bar and Mr. Wu would be driving them all. Rosie was watching Rudy, so Mr. Wu would pick up Raphe and the pup first, then Ran, and finally, Bonnie. His mom and dad were watching the boys, so Mr. Wu would swing by and pick up Lexi on the way to the hotel. It was nice to have so much family around. Raphe had to admit, he didn't miss living in the city.

Riley and Melvina were getting picked up from Braised by one of Riley's drivers, and they would meet them at the gala. Riley had been prepping the appetizers all month and wanted to check to see everything was loaded properly into the catering van before they left the restaurant. It was going to be a fun-filled event with great food to raise more money for the new library.

Mona was a real dynamo when it came to throwing a party and getting people to open their wallets. The hotel donated the ballroom and the Blossoms arranged the rest. It was a good distraction for the evening, and it was nice to get dressed up in something other than his fireman's uniform. At least there would be something else for him to do besides dance. Most of the fundraisers were bake sales or dances but after twirling Nina around the dance floor at the past two fundraisers, he couldn't stomach the thought of dancing with someone else.

When they got there, they made their way to the bar to get drinks. Melvina looked beautiful in her red-sequined gown standing next to Raphe's celebrity chef brother. Together, they were the perfect couple. *Just like Mom and Dad.* And now, Ran would follow in their footsteps. Bonnie hadn't a clue. His soon to be sister-in-law ordered a glass of champagne and Ran paid the bartender. He was beaming with pride at Bonnie's petite beauty. Her blonde hair was done up in an elegant style with a long strand falling strategically along the side of her cheek. It highlighted her one dimple. The white evening gown's iridescence caught the chandeliers and glimmered like a beacon for all to see. This was not the same shy librarian Raphe had met several months ago.

Raphe tried to ignore the hole in the pit of his stomach as he watched the couples disappear to the dance floor. He took a fluted glass of champagne along with his rocks glass and headed to the roulette table. He had Wu to drive him home. It was time to be charitable and let go. Cocktails flowed, dice tumbled, and the roulette wheel kept spinning. He was feeling pretty good and Mona would be happy when the numbers came in from the fundraiser. Raphe wasn't the only one spending a bundle.

"How's my favorite brother?"

Raphe glanced sideways at his younger sister and thought it was appropriate that she be the one to check in with him. Lexi had lost the love of her life, too, and had never moved on. She'd married her high school sweetheart and had three beautiful boys before Jack departed this world in the line of duty. Raphe felt a pang in his heart for Lexi. She'd been through a lot. It made his heartbreak seem petty, but he felt the loss of Nina now, just as fresh as he had the day she flew to California. Nina still hadn't called him back, and he had no idea how to find her. Raphe knew it was time to get over it, and he supposed that Lexi was probably about to give him that very talk. He motioned for the cocktail waitress and waved his glass of Glenlivet.

"Favorite brother?" He raised an eyebrow. "Should I be worried?"

Lexi laughed. "What makes you say that?"

Raphe grinned. "Oh, I don't know. That lizard I put in your bed. The hamsters I let loose at your slumber party. The mud pie I put in your Easy-Bake Oven…"

Lexi laughed. "You think I still hold all that against you? Believe me, those stunts have nothing on my boys. Damien put a nest of baby moles in his teacher's desk on the first day of school. Gus took Chef to school with him on the bus and I had to drive over to pick him up yesterday. Bert kissed three girls in his class on the same day, and had them all fighting over him, oh, and just the other night the three boys used my best bed sheets to make a tent in the backyard. Not to mention, I found my underwear on Shrek and Donkey. When I asked them why, they said, 'Because they didn't have any that would fit!'"

Raphe tried to stifle his guffaw. It wasn't ever nice to laugh at a joke pertaining to a woman's size. Lexi was a normal size and looked fabulous in her silky, strapless green gown. Her straight blonde hair was a pretty contrast. She deserved to have an adult night out more than anyone.

"I think you could use a drink." Raphe accepted his glass from the waitress and ordered Lexi a champagne.

His sister rewarded him with a smile. "Thanks. It's been so long since I've been out, that I almost forgot I could drink."

Raphe gave her a wan smile as he placed his bet. "Lucky number?"

Lexi smiled. "Mine or yours?"

"Yours of course. Mine hasn't been hitting tonight."

"Seventeen."

Raphe knew it was the age she was when she met Jack in high school. He took a five-hundred-dollar chip from his pocket and put it on seventeen, straight.

Lexi put her hand on his arm. "Raphe, don't bet that much. It's just a silly number."

Raphe looked down at Lexi with a knowing smile. "It's not silly and this is for charity. Your boys love going to that library and the money I spend will help that dusty old institution survive. Let's bet it all on Jack tonight. Maybe his spirit will give us the luck we need."

The wheel was already spinning, and the white ball skittered through the numbers, slowing and bouncing across seven, twenty and thirty-two before skimming the five and finally falling onto seventeen black. Raphe pumped his fist in the air and turned to hug Lexi, who automatically threw her arms around him squealing. "We did it!" They rocked back and forth hugging each other with more than happiness for their win. Raphe was holding Lexi, silently telling her he'd always be there for her. He loved that her number won and somehow it really did feel like a sign from Jack in some way. Riley, Ran and others gathered round. A massive amount of chips was being counted out.

"How much is that?" Lexi asked, excitement vibrating through her voice.

"Seventeen thousand-five-hundred going out." The dealer announced as he pushed the pile forward to Raphe.

"Wow! I'm taking you to Vegas with me little brother," Riley teased.

Raphe pointed to Lexi. "And I'm taking her. It was Lexi's number that won."

Melvina hugged Lexi, then Bonnie hugged them both. "What a wonderful way to help the library."

Raphe laughed, "And fun too. Now where do I cash in my loot?" He teased.

Mona approached them, rolling her eyes. "You don't cash it in, it's for charity!"

Melvina laughed. "You can shop in the donations room and pick out a cruise, a necklace or something that was donated for the event… or you could donate your winning chips to the house in honor of the new library and they will resell the leftover prizes at the next silent auction." Her eyes were shiny with pleasure at the success of the event. Riley's arm around her waist looked as if it anchored her from floating away on a cloud.

Raphe chuckled, "No guilt trip there." He walked the short distance to the donation box in the center of the room and placed all of the thousand-dollar chips in the sealed container. A loud cheer went up. Several people walked over to Raphe, clapping him on the back.

"Nice win, Five-Alarm."

Raphe turned to see whose silky voice whispered in his ear.

Chapter 33

Nina called Bonnie as she boarded the plane. "Are you sure it's okay if I crash with you and Rosie? I haven't gotten paid yet and it's everything I had in my account to get this last-minute ticket."

"Are you crazy? What a silly question. We miss you! Besides, it's casino night tonight, remember, and you don't want to miss it. There's supposed to be a real roulette wheel and everything."

"Yes, I remember Mona mentioning it at the library. Sounds fun, though I'm kinda watching my pennies."

"Don't worry, the drinks are on me."

"Okay. Johana's picking me up at the airport with my car and I'll have to take her back. Maybe she can loan me the lucky peacock again. It worked last time. Oh Bonnie, do you think Raphe will be upset if I just show up out of the blue like this? It's been three months."

"Oh, well, that reminds me. Wu will be bringing Ran and Raphe here to pick me up, so don't rush over to the house until after seven. You should still have time to get ready and meet us there."

"Perfect. It's a date."

The plane ride was smooth, but Nina's anxiety level was high. She wasn't showing yet, but she wondered if she would still fit into the peacock-colored gown. That should be the last of her worries, but she wanted to look perfect for Raphe. She needed to make amends, even if he didn't want to give their relationship another chance. He was the father of her child, and she hoped he would want to play a part in its life, regardless of their relationship status.

Johana was waiting with her car and it was good for Nina the lucky peacock still fit, though it was definitely more form fitting than before. Her breasts were double the size, making the evening gown pop.

Nina drove the forty minutes to Bonnie's to get ready. Rosie opened the door with a basset puppy hanging out of the basket attached to her walker.

"Oh, my goodness! How adorable," Nina gasped, reaching down to pet the tri-colored pup.

"This is Rudy. I'm babysitting tonight."

"Is it Lulu's?" Nina calculated that it must be about six weeks old.

"Yeah, Raphe dropped him off before the shindig and he'll pick him up on the way home." Rosie led the way into the kitchen and let the puppy down on the piddle pad. Rudy squatted to do his business and Rosie cooed and praised the tiny puppy.

Nina was impressed. "Smart guy." Her eyes went to the pan of brownies on the table. Rosie followed her gaze. "You want one? They're regular. I gotta stay sober tonight on account of Rudy."

Nina's stomach growled, but she declined. She couldn't take a chance that they weren't *regular,* and she didn't want to tell anyone about the pregnancy before telling Raphe. "I'll pass, thanks. It's seven-thirty. I better change if I'm going to join the others."

Rosie led her back to the spare room and pointed out the guest bathroom. "Use whatcha need to look pretty. I'll be on the couch with Rudy watching Animal Planet. I think my soaps are too adult for his young eyes. If we doze off before you go. Have a great night." She smiled at Nina with a playful wink. "And this time, don't fuck it all up, okay?"

"Sheila, hello. Haven't seen you since…" He barely remembered breaking up two years ago just before the calendar contest. He wondered how she knew about his nickname that originated from the event. Raphe remembered that she'd left him for some producer, and he also remembered he'd been relieved to be single again. They hadn't remained friends, but there hadn't been any hard feelings either. Sheila put her arms around him, purring in his ear. "My, how I've missed you. Do you want to get a drink?"

Raphe's body stiffened. He'd been alone for a long while now. The spell without female company had been enlightening to his life, not because he had to find other things to fill up his free time, but because he'd started to build real relationships with the people surrounding him, including his family. He enjoyed gardening with Lexi and the boys, dinners at his parents' house on Sundays, helping the chief with things around the station, mentoring the Firecrackers and watching his brother with the woman of his dreams. He couldn't wait to see Bonnie's face when Ran popped the question. He'd grown since Nina had left Magnolia, and he supposed he should be thankful for the crash course in adulthood, but his heart still ached, and it wasn't in need of company for the night. Raphe untangled Sheila's arms from around him.

"Sorry, not tonight." It was at that moment he saw Nina standing on the stairs of the grand ballroom in the blue peacock gown she'd worn for the Fireman's Ball. She looked as beautiful as the first night he'd seen her in it, even more so. Spotting him with Sheila, her face crumpled, and she turned to leave. Raphe climbed the stairs two at a time to the top, catching her in the chandelier lit foyer, just outside the ballroom.

"Nina," he touched her arm, turning her toward him.

She was shaking. "I'm sorry. I don't know why I came here. I don't know why I thought you could change. It was all a mistake." She tried to pull away, but Raphe didn't let go.

"Nina, that's not fair. You left me after I asked you to move in with me. I told you I was falling in love with you and you ran."

Tears streamed down her cheeks. "How can you say you're falling for me when you're always in the arms of someone else?" She motioned back to the ballroom.

Raphe looked back over his shoulder, thinking about what she'd just seen. "You left months ago, Nina, without a word. You got on a plane and flew away. You didn't return my calls, and I had nowhere to look for you. Was I supposed to wait around forever?"

Tears slid down her cheeks and Raphe wanted to take her into his arms and tell her that he still loved her, that he felt more for her now than he ever had and that he couldn't stand the idea of losing her again, but he held his tongue. He needed to hear her say why she'd come.

Nina shook her head. Her voice was calm. "No, I knew you wouldn't wait for me, but Bonnie said she didn't think you were seeing anyone since I left. I thought…just maybe…."

He pulled her into his arms, holding her tight, then kissed her as if she were the last drop of water in the burning desert of his heart. She didn't resist. Instead, she kissed him back, holding onto him tightly as her body curved into his. Applause resounded around them and Raphe turned to see Lexi, Ran, Bonnie, Riley, Melvina, Maria, Jose, Mona, Manny and a few other friends standing at the entrance to the ball room.

Raphe smiled down at Nina. "Does this mean you're back?"

"Are you still single?" She arched a brow in question.

Damn, he loved her sassy beauty.

"Not anymore." He kissed her again, sending up another cheer from their friends and family.

"Then yes, I'm back, but we need to talk." Nina bit her lip. She looked worried and that's the last thing he felt right now.

"Come meet the rest of my family and I have another secret that I hope Ran will get around to sharing before the night is over. Can we enjoy the evening first? I'll have a conversation with that lucky dress of yours later." He grinned wickedly.

The clock struck midnight and the band paused to introduce Ran Nash of the Tomball Cats for a solo. Bonnie stood at the bottom of the stage with Nina and the rest of the Nash family.

Lexi looked at Raphe with a quizzical gaze. "Is this what I think it is?" Raphe shushed his beautiful sister and gripped Nina tight to his side. He hadn't let her out of his sight since she'd found him. He had told her that he wanted to leave, but they had to wait for Ran first. She guessed this was the big secret. A love song for Bonnie, maybe?

Ran called Bonnie up to the stage where he grabbed his guitar and played a beautiful ballad. The guests cheered and then he went down on one knee. Nina felt the tears of joy cover her own cheeks as she watched Bonnie tear up and say yes. There wasn't anything shy about the way she threw her arms around Ran and kissed him full throttle in front of everyone. The ballroom was again filled with celebratory music and a waiter arrived with several glasses of champagne for them to toast the newly engaged couple.

A few songs later, Raphe grabbed her hand and pulled her toward the hotel elevators. "I called Rosie and she'll watch Rudy the rest of the night. The chief has cleared me of duty tomorrow, and I won't make it back to my apartment before making love to you. So, you have a choice. It's you, me, and the lucky peacock here in a room, or in the car with Mr. Wu driving, and I gotta tell you, I think Wu is too old and frail to see what will happen in that back seat."

The elevator doors slid open and Nina stepped in. "Okay then. I guess you already have the room."

Raphe smiled, waving the key. "Yeah, I kinda figured you'd say yes to the presidential suite." He pressed the button to the top floor.

She gave him a concerned look. "I thought you had a thing against high buildings."

Raphe blew out a breath, "Consider it good therapy for me. Besides, you're worth the risk." Nina didn't need to be prompted. He'd been saying all the right things. She leaned in, kissing him full on the mouth as she ran her hands over his sculpted chest.

Bonnie told her the redhead was an old flame of Raphe's but that he hadn't shown any interest, and the stunning blonde was his little sister. Nina didn't get a chance to have much conversation with Lexi because of the large group welcoming her back and celebrating Ran and Bonnie's engagement, but she liked what she'd seen among the members of Raphe's family as they bantered and teased each other. It was something she truly longed to be a part of.

Raphe led her to the spacious suite that overlooked a manufactured lake. The water sparkled beneath the lights of the hotel and the spray of the fountain. Raphe disappeared into the minibar area. When he returned, he'd removed his jacket, bowtie and undid the first two buttons on his shirt. He moved toward her with two glasses and a bottle of chilled champagne.

"As much as I would like to devour you in one bite. I think we should take it slow and enjoy the scenery." He winked. "I really want to savor this night together."

Nina's heart leapt. She couldn't wait to make love with Raphe again. It had been months now, and she wasn't sure if it was the abstinence or the hormones that made her want to pour the champagne over Raphe's naked body and lick it off.

Should she tell him about the baby now or after they made love? Would the news be more special if they were cuddling and sated from a night of hot sex? But what if he didn't want a child? Then there wouldn't be any hanky-panky and damn, she needed to get laid. Her brain rambled over possible outcomes, but in the end, if he didn't want to take responsibility for their very irresponsible sex, how could she want to sleep with him? Nina watched Raphe as he popped the champagne cork and poured two glasses.

What would she say? If she told him she was pregnant it might overwhelm the moment, but she couldn't drink the champagne. She loved Raphe, and she wanted him to love her back. She wanted him to want this baby as much as she did. A kaleidoscope of emotions tossed around inside her, making her feel confused and vulnerable.

Rosie's voice filled her head. *Don't fuck it all up.*

"I'm pregnant." Nina blurted out.

One of the champagne glasses Raphe had set down wobbled off the edge of the end table and crashed to the floor. "What?"

Nina pushed her shoulders back and sat up straight on the couch. She had more confidence now. If he balked, she was out of there. She wanted this baby and she didn't need a man to tell her whether or not she could have it.

"I'm pregnant with your child, our child," she corrected herself.

Raphe sunk down on the sofa next to her, ignoring the broken glass.

"Is this why you came tonight, to find me?"

Nina nodded. "I had to tell you."

His eyebrows knitted together as Nina stood. "It's okay. You don't have to be a father. I just thought you should know."

She started toward the door, but his hand shot out, grabbing hers. "Nina, stop running away. If we're going to work through things, you have to stop and face the issue."

"I don't need your pity or your help, Raphe." Heat ran through her body and she felt like her heart would leap from her chest. She'd flown all the way to Texas to tell him. What had she expected him to say, yippee? She wasn't ready for this kind of rejection. She felt uncertain, vulnerable, and yes—hopeful all at the same time.

Please, God. Make him want this baby.

Raphe stood up, grasping both of her shoulders. "I need to hear how you feel about me, Nina. I'll be that responsible father. I won't shirk my responsibilities and I will love my child, but I need to hear how you feel about us."

Nina's heart tilted, but she was scared. She'd thought about Raphe every day since leaving Magnolia, even before she knew she was carrying his child. She thought she could get past the heartbreak and move on, but she longed for him at night when she lay alone in her bed, when she ate lunch in the school yard watching the children play, and in the morning when she brushed her hair, thinking about him running his fingers through it. She missed him with every fiber of her being.

I have to tell him. But what if he says no?

She was trembling and damn it the tears were starting again. "I love you, Raphe. I'm scared to say it. I've been scared all along of losing my heart to you. I didn't think I could survive it after everything I've been through, so I left before you could hurt me."

Raphe wrapped her in his arms, kissing the top of her head. "Did you know you were pregnant when you left?"

"No."

"Is it the only reason you came back?" he whispered.

Nina looked up at his worried gaze. "No, but it gave me the courage to take a chance."

Raphe nodded. "Did it ever occur to you that I might be taking a chance as well? These feelings I have for you are like nothing I've ever felt and if you think you're the only one worried about a broken heart..." he said, his eyes bearing intense feelings. "...you're wrong. These past few months without you have been torture.

"When Ran came to the station to tell me he was getting engaged, it near about killed me. I wanted it to be us getting engaged. I know I asked you to move in and I didn't have the guts to tell you I was already in love with you. I'm not making that mistake again. Nina Salas, I love you and I want you to be my wife, mother of my child and a part of my family." Raphe dropped to one knee. "I don't have the ring, but I'll buy you the prettiest one I can find. Just say yes, you'll be mine forever."

It was more than she could have hoped and yet she knew it was what she wanted from the start. She pulled back the blue folds of the gown and kneeled in front of Raphe. "Yes, Raphe, I want that more than anything in the world."

Raphe kissed her hard and they clung to each other as they slid down to the plush carpet. He unzipped her gown and freed her breasts, teasing both nipples with his tongue. Growling his delight in her larger size. He rose above her, shedding his shirt and pushing his dress slacks down to reveal his hardened shaft. Pulling her gown up, he glided his hands to the elastic of her lace underwear. He pulled them off in one quick sweep, again shoving the billowing folds of her blue gown out of his way. Delving lower, he kissed her quickly at the juncture of her thighs, making her moan in ecstasy. He laved at her slick folds until she thought she would explode

183

from the pleasure. Without warning, he tore his kiss from her and joined himself to her.

"I'm sorry, I couldn't wait to be inside you."

Nina moaned with pleasure as he rocked back and forth with her, his heart beating hard against her chest, his breath heavy and the look of smoldering desire etched lines of pleasureful pain on his face. "I need you with me now and forever. I don't think I can ever get enough of you, this, us," he groaned, his breath catching as she tightened herself around his shaft, flexing her inner muscles over and over.

Nina shuddered, gasped, then moaned as he rocked them both over the edge and into a simultaneous climax.

"I guess we're not stopping to enjoy the scenery," she breathed against his ear, still caught up in the rapture they'd shared.

Raphe flexed inside of her showing her there was still more to come. "Oh, there's plenty more to see, I promise."

Nina stood at the foot of the bed, staring at Raphe. She didn't want to wake him, but she couldn't leave a note and run away. After last night, she wanted to do things right, so she sat on the edge of the bed and ran a hand through his silky brown hair. She loved the devilish good looks and his after five shadow. The golden-brown facial hair gleamed in the early morning light. Dawn's rays streaked through the curtain they'd left open last night when she looked at the fountain below.

Raphe stirred, smiling at her when his eyes fluttered open, then his face cleared from its dreamy state with concern. "Hey, where are you and the Lucky Peacock going?"

Nina smiled. Yes, indeed, this had become her lucky dress. She was going to have to make a deal with Johana to keep it if her friend would be willing to part with the beautiful gown. "I have a flight to catch."

Raphe sat up now, pulling back the sheets and coming toward her. "Why? You just got here. What about last night?"

Nina smiled at him, putting her hand on his naked chest. Her fingers drew small circles in the crisp brown hair that dusted his pecs. "I need to tell my brother, Carlos. I've stayed with him all this time and he deserves to hear it from me in person." She felt sad, knowing how disappointed her brother would be that she'd conceived out of wedlock, but this was a modern era and she was thirty-six. If she was going to have a family, this was the time. Convention and Catholicism be damned. She couldn't worry about the order in which the child was conceived. It was a precious gift, and Nina wanted to celebrate her good fortune. She was going to be a mother. "I'm afraid my brother won't be pleased."

Raphe's eyebrows furrowed. "You're his sister. Why would he be upset if you're happy?"

"He's pretty traditional, and I was engaged less than a year ago. We're Catholic. You and I aren't married."

"Not at this moment, but we're going to be. You said *yes*." He pulled her to him and kissed her. The kiss deepened and he pushed her back onto the bed.

Nina put her hands against his shoulders. "I'm going to miss my flight, Raphe."

He made a low growl and nibbled at her neck. "Miss your flight and I'll buy us tickets to go together. We can be married there, with your brother as a witness to our joining."

Derek hadn't even wanted to meet her brother and now Raphe was willing to drop everything and fly to San Francisco to meet her brother and marry her.

"What about your family, Raphe?"

"They'll be okay. There're enough weddings going on in Magnolia this year to satisfy the masses, and I don't want to wait. It sounds like your brother will want to see you married as quickly as I want to make you my wife." He smiled, leaning down to nip at her bottom lip. "Besides, the best thing about getting married is the honeymoon. We'll be halfway to Hawaii, so we can just go on from there."

Excitement pulsed through her as she considered his offer. "Are you sure?"

Raphe laughed. "I'm a man, Nina. If you're worried I'll be crushed by missing out on a big wedding with the cake and all the hoopla, don't be." He paused, looking at her with a more serious expression. "But darlin', if you want all that, I understand, and we can plan the biggest wedding ever."

Nina's heart melted. She had wanted the big wedding when she was engaged to Derek. She'd made all the arrangements and even bought the dress, but all those plans seemed empty when the time grew near. She didn't want to go through all that stress and hassle again. She didn't want to wait. "All I need is you in my life. I want to marry you today and I want to be with you for the rest of my life."

Raphe kissed her tenderly, sliding his lips over Nina's. Tilting his forehead to rest against hers, he breathed in and out steadily, closing his eyes. "I can't tell you how long I have waited to hear that, Nina Salas." His eyes met hers and he kissed her softly this time.

"Soon to be Nash," she smiled. It felt good to say it. With Derek, she'd planned on keeping her own name, but with Raphe she wanted to share every part of her life with his. She wanted their children to be a family, all raised under one home, with love and a strong bond.

Raphe rolled Nina on top of him, skimming his fingers up the fabric of her dress again, lifting it away from her body. He smiled when he realized she hadn't put her underwear back on. Straddling him, she glided herself against him, showing Raphe how eager she was to join with him in every way. He lifted as she came down on him hard, both of them gasping with desire and pleasure. Her head fell forward. The dark tendrils of her hair covered his face and chest. "I love you," they both said at the same time. She fell against him, as he gripped her to him, thrusting hard. They crested the wave of desire and sailed into an ocean of ecstasy.

Nina hugged him tight, their bodies slick with sweat. "I'm so glad Lulu ate your condoms."

Raphe laughed. "Don't worry, Rudy will take over where Lulu left off. I've already lost a deck of playing cards, a new pair of trainers and the TV remote. It's a good thing you don't care much for panties. I bet he likes them too."

Epilogue

Nina sifted through the boxes the movers had brought in. She didn't have many things to move, but Raphe had a bachelor's apartment worth of things. They'd bought a new home just off the main road in Magnolia near the diner and Bonnie and Rosie's place, although Bonnie and Ran had bought a new home not too far from town. They weren't moving in together until after their wedding in a few months.

Raphe and Nina had shopped for new furniture, including the things they would need for the baby's room. They'd traded her old car in for a sleek new minivan. She thought she'd somehow feel uncool with something that screamed soccer mom, but instead, she felt elated. She wanted to fill the van with their children and have the big family she'd always craved to be a part of.

Lexi and the boys were great training for her. Nina loved seeing them all at Sunday dinners and gardening on Saturday afternoons with Melvina and Riley when they had the time.

Nina called Bonnie to see if they were still meeting Melvina at the café to design Ran's groom's cake. It was going to be some sort of cupcake motorcycle with a basset hound and poodle hanging out of the kit car. Nina had laughed when Bonnie told her what she was planning. Nina worried she might feel left out with all the wedding plans under way, but her new family had embraced her, keeping her busy at every turn. They included her in everything, and she was amazed at how she felt so much a part of their lives in such a short time.

"Hi Bonnie! Are we still on for later?"

"You bet your sweet ass we are," Rosie cackled. "I'm bringing one of my Playgirl Magazines so Melvina has a likeness to recreating the naked bachelor for the cake."

Nina stifled a giggle. "Rosie, the cake isn't for the bachelorette party, and I don't think Melvina does nude cakes, especially of her brother-in-law."

Bonnie called out from the background. "Aunt Rosie, put those magazines back under the bed before I let Marquis use them for potty papers!"

Nina heard the rumble of Raphe's truck in the drive. The man installing the blinds was just finishing up the last window treatment. She peeked through their new Roman shades to see Raphe's handsome backside as he was reaching into his truck. She touched her stomach as the baby fluttered. She jumped, then smiled. It was the first time she'd felt the baby kick and she couldn't wait to go for their sonogram. Raphe was driving them to the appointment.

Lifting Rudy out of the truck, Raphe saw her through the window, smiled and waved. When Rudy finished marking her new rose bush, Raphe brought him inside. He grabbed her up in a deep kiss, ignoring the window treatment installer, who cleared his throat as he held out papers for them to sign. Nina laughed. "We're going to be late for our appointment."

Raphe grabbed the ledger and scrolled his name across it. The man nodded and gathered his tools. Seeing the couple was busy, he let himself out. Nina had seen the older man's smile and knew he didn't mind their ignoring him while they kissed.

"With you in my arms, I want to be late for everything. People better get used to it."

Nina laughed, lacing her arms around his neck. "What about tonight?" She was speaking of their post-wedding reception that his mother and sister had insisted on. Everyone they knew would be there and they would celebrate their official union, even though it happened almost two months ago. Their trip to Hawaii, lying on the beach, and making love for hours in the oceanfront hotel, was amazing and sexy.

So much had happened in such a short time. Carlos had surprised her with his excitement of becoming an uncle. He liked Raphe right away, and they'd made plans to go deep-sea fishing in a few months. She knew it would be impossible for her to go by then, but she was really happy Carlos was flying in to meet the rest of her new family. Raphe's father would captain the family boat they kept at a boat slip in Galveston. She couldn't wait to go out on it later with Raphe. She'd never fished before, but the idea of it sounded fun, and if nothing else, she would enjoy the boat ride and the sun.

Raphe picked her up and started toward the bedroom. She tried half-heartedly to protest as he eased them onto their new king-sized bed.

He chuckled at her question about them being late. "Oh, they'll wait." He kissed her deeply then stared into her eyes. "Our love will always come first. I promise you that."

Double Trouble Kisses

Hot in Magnolia Book 3

SNEAK PEEK

Tabitha Graham swiped her newly cropped dark hair from her face, reminding herself of the prize. An airline ticket to Greece would be hers if she could actually pull off the scheme that her identical twin sister had put her up to.

She blew out a long sigh, fanning herself with a tourist bureau pamphlet. *It must be a hundred degrees in Magnolia!* Assessing her surroundings, she decided the small town wasn't as cute and cozy as she'd thought it'd be.

A few of the store fronts were empty and some of the wood siding had seen better days. The new signs and buildings dotting the highway said progress, but it looked slow coming to this sleepy little town.

She looked across the street at the Cupcake Diner and Dive with longing. What she needed right now was a big glass of iced tea to cool her nerves. She fumbled in her purse for her cell phone to check the weather app. It had to be triple digits. She could feel the sweat dripping down her back and beading between her breasts. *Ick!*

Tabby rifled through her shoulder bag as the light turned green. She crossed the intersection, still rummaging for her phone. The heel of her designer shoes clip-clacked against the pavement for several sure steps, before one dipped and wobbled, bringing her to a sudden stop. She could feel the scrape of concrete against the Italian leather wrapped heel. *Oh crap! I knew I should have worn respectable flats.*

Tabby licked her lips as she stared at the bakery cafe, so close, yet so far away. She'd seen the well-known *Cup Cake Diner and Dive* on one of the Food Network series and had always wanted to order one of those three-tiered chocolate cupcakes with ice-cream in the center and Bavarian cream on top.

`She could blame the heat for her distraction, but the truth was, she was nervous. Pretending to be Taylor had been easy-peasy back in high school when it was just for kicks, but now, they were adults, and her twin was a big-time reporter on the five o'clock Houston News. This twin-switch was a whole different bag of tricks.

Scanning the intersection for any immediate danger, Tabby relaxed. No cars were barreling in her direction. She looked down at the pavement, feeling another wave of heat assault her. She couldn't see her foot clearly because of the full yellow skirt of the sundress she wore.

This was all Taylor's fault! Regretting saying yes to this risky idea, Tabby admonished herself once more. This was ludicrous. If she'd just said no, she wouldn't be sweating through her new sundress and ruining her pricey new pair of Ferragamos…Of course then she wouldn't be going to Greece, either.

Her heel was good and stuck, and she felt like a fool standing there without a clue how to get it out. Maybe a driver would take pity on Tabby and help her before mowing her down. Her strappy Roman sandals had three buckles up each side. She sighed, kneeling down to start unfastening the straps.

Keeping her eye on the main road, she yelped as she saw a truck careen from a cross-street and pick up speed in her direction. Tabby waved her hands furiously, though she was sure the driver must see her in the bright canary-yellow sundress. A random breeze blew at the folds of her skirt, sending the hem skyward. Thinking about the lacey pink thong she wore, she brought her hands down quickly to catch the Marilyn-skirt-tease. *Geeze, the diner is packed, and I just mooned every customer sitting along the windows.*

The truck wasn't slowing down, and Tabby began to panic. The vehicle was close now, and to her dismay, it looked like no one was inside. Giving up on the last buckle, she pulled furiously at her calf, trying to release her wedged heel. Just when she thought all was lost, someone grasped her by the waist from behind, dragging her out of the truck's way.

Her foot was free, but the Ferragamo sandal bounced around in the street like a kernel of popcorn. Tabby cursed, "Damn it! My shoe."

It was then that a dark head popped up in the cab of the truck. A young teen who had probably just gotten his license gleefully held his phone in one hand and grasped the wheel with the other, swerving across the solid yellow line.

"Damn it, Maurice! Put that phone away before you kill someone!" She felt the rumble of the man's angry outcry. He still held her firmly to his hard chest. She couldn't see him, but she could smell his shower-fresh scent.

Tabby cleared her throat. "Um — Thank you very much. Can you put me down now?"

The man set her down and his massive form shadowed her petite frame as he towered over her. He must have been at least six-feet-four, but the breadth of his chest and shoulders made him look anything but spindly. He was nicely built and all muscle.

"Are you lost?" His rich voice made her glance up at his face with interest.

Tabby gaped. Her rescuer resembled a celebrity heart throb. Perfect teeth, golden tan, sandy-blond hair, and salted caramel eyes — yum. He even sounded like an actor who played in one of those action movies that Taylor loved so much.

Tabby was a rom-com gal herself, but she also liked historical series on BBC. This guy could be her Mr. Darcy or Poldark anytime.

Wait, should she be alarmed? No one in Houston would look twice at a woman digging in her purse or tackle her in front of a moving truck to save her life— especially someone as perfect looking as this man. Was he some sort of scam artist preying on unsuspecting women? He was way too good-looking to be a nice guy. A gigolo maybe? She clutched her bag tight to her side. "I'm fine. I was just looking for my cell phone and my shoe got caught." She pointed to the road where she could see the leather heel covering was nicked beyond repair.

Tabby turned back to the tall stranger. His face was like a work of art. It was hard to hold eye contact. His Adonis features made her look down with self-consciousness. He probably thought she was an idiot.

Uh-oh, looking down was a big mistake! He was wearing a tight T-shirt and loose running shorts. She tried unsuccessfully to pry her eyes away from his perfect runner's thighs.

Damn, she'd never seen legs like that on a man before.

A tail wagged furiously by his sculped calves, distracting Tabby's appreciative gaze. A lemon colored basset hound stood at the man's feet with its tongue lolling out to one side. Tabby figured they probably looked a lot alike at the moment, both drooling over the man in the equation.

Tabby lit up as the dog did a tap dance of excitement to greet her. Forgetting about her brush with death and her wariness of the gorgeous, half-naked stranger, she bent down to scratch the basset's ears.

A man with a super cute dog buddy who rescues damsels in distress must be okay, right?

"Oh, how adorable!" she squeaked. Tabby was a sucker for dogs, especially long-bodied ones with short legs. Her dachshund, Dino, was a black and tan firecracker. He was all teeth and tail, but she loved him to pieces. It was a shame the mailman didn't feel the same.

Forgetting she wore only one shoe, she lost her balance, falling forward into the brawny man. With an unladylike squawk, Tabby flailed her arms around until they landed around the guy's waist. Her head rested awkwardly against his hip.

With a small grunt of surprise, the stranger lifted her back to a standing position with ease. Amusement glinted in his eyes. "Are you okay?"

Tabby felt as stupid as she must look. Reaching down, she unlatched the straps around her other ankle and stepped out of her remaining shoe. "I should thank you for saving my life. I'd been stuck to the darn pavement for what felt like a lifetime in this heat, and I didn't want to ruin my new shoes. I guess I'll be interviewing the mayor barefoot and doing the backstroke in a pool of my own sweat."

The man grinned, walked into the street and bent to retrieve the lost sandal. Like Prince Charming, he returned and kneeled in front of her. He wiggled both shoes back onto her feet, clasping each strap with care. His gentle touch was uncharacteristic of such a large, muscular guy. She wanted to protest. How could she let a perfect stranger put his hands on her feet? But she couldn't stop staring at him. His back muscles rippled under his T-shirt and his biceps danced about until he finished clasping her sandals and stood.

He held his hand out to her, "Hi, I'm Eli, Eli Banks."

Tabby stared dumbly at his hand. Strangers never stopped to introduce themselves to her in Houston, especially not strangers who looked like sexy, beach-body movie stars.

Finally finding her tongue, Tabby cleared her throat and pushed her shoulders back, clasping his hand in a too eager shake. "I — I'm Tab-Taylor Graham." She pushed her bangs back from her forehead. "I guess you're my knight in shining armor. Thank you for saving my life." Her French manicured nails touched the cross pendant her grandmother had given her for her confirmation. She still wore it for luck.

Geez, could she sound anymore besotted and desperate. Eyes up, Tabby, and quit drooling!

Like what you've read so far? You can buy Double Trouble Kisses on Amazon. Or visit minettelauren.com to find out more.

About the Author

As soon as Minette was old enough to write, she composed a play in one act called *The Love of Seth and Beth* inspired by the movie, *Gone with the Wind*. Undeterred by the play's questionable success, she's been in love with writing ever since. Growing up in a small town outside of New Orleans, Louisiana, has fueled a lot of Minette's creative endeavors. She travels often and takes advantage of anyplace with a view that inspires her to write. Minette now resides in Texas, where she loves to write outdoors by her pool, with her five furry writing muses. Besides her menagerie of tail-wagging pooches, she also has a loving husband, three turtles and four parrots to keep her company. Together, they make all of her dreams come true.

Sign up for Minette Lauren's newsletter on her website: minettelauren. com. Follow Minette on Amazon, BookBub, and Goodreads. You can email Minette at info@minettelauren.com